WILLOW FOX

ONE
EMERSON

RAIN PELTS THE CEMENT, pouring overhead as it splashes down on the broken umbrella. I've managed to hold the latch open, but if I move my hand just slightly, it slams shut on me.

That's about how my week's been going.

~~Shitty.~~

I have a new job lined up, well, new as in it's for the Eagle Tactical crew. A contract assignment they've given me. They need a full-time bodyguard, and none of their crew can handle the workload on the east coast. They're based out of Breckenridge, Montana, and I'm standing in the deluge in New York City.

It's not exactly my dream job, but that is no longer an option.

Plus, I need the money.

And by the looks of it, the guy I'll be protecting has plenty of it.

I took the subway and walked the last mile and a half in the rain up to his front gate. The house is nestled behind the iron décor, offering a false sense of security.

I'm not just taking in the whole of the property but also the details. There's a surveillance camera at the front entrance and additional cameras aimed at the iron fence along the side. Should anyone choose to climb it, the pointed arrows at the top should deter them.

Assuming there are no blind spots as well. I'll need to examine the footage, the cameras, and the entire house to make sure everything is working as it should be. The team prepped me on the client, Mr. Kylor Greyson, and his daughter, Bristol.

The Eagle Tactical guys set up the security system years ago when Kyler moved into the property.

He's well known, practically famous if you're into sports.

He's a hockey player.

Me?

I've never been to a hockey game and haven't spent more than a few seconds channel-surfing past one. That's my idea of a sport.

I press the buzzer as lightning illuminates the sky. Thunder pounds overhead, and the gate unlocks before I have time to speak.

He doesn't ask me to show my identification or prove who I am over the surveillance system. And while he's expecting me, given the fact I'm here to protect his family, I'm not happy with how the security within the house is being run.

Quickly, I step in through the gate and hurry across the cobblestone driveway to the front of the house. It hardly should be classified as a house, considering its grandiose size. It makes a mansion look like a shack.

I shut my umbrella while under the front porch and leave it outside, not wanting to make a mess upon entering.

The front door swings open, and a gentleman in dark jeans and a white t-shirt stares back at me. He's got a thick head of dark hair that I refrain from running my fingers through.

One glance, and I recognize him.

How could I not after doing my own bit of

research before meeting him? I needed to know what kind of person would want to stalk him or his kid.

It's strange, but I guess being in the limelight does that. People think they know you because they've been to your game or watched you on television.

He probably has dozens of women lining up to be the next Mrs. Greyson, begging for his affection and attention.

"Hi," I say. It's not the most proper and professional introduction, but the cold rain seems to have stolen the words right out of my mouth. I wipe my feet, my heels not the least bit saved from the rain or mud puddles I splashed through on my way here.

"You're wet." His dark gaze stares right through me.

I shiver.

He isn't wrong.

But it's not the fact I'm soaked from the rain that sends a tingle through my core.

He stares at me as though I were naked, seeing right through me, pinning me with those dark eyes and long thick lashes. He's every girl's wet dream.

"I hadn't noticed," I say with a smirk.

"Can I help you?" he asks, glancing me up and down. He folds his arms across his chest, allowing me inside but blocking me from entering beyond the front entrance.

"I'm the new bodyguard," I say. I suck in a sharp breath. "Did no one inform you that I was coming? I'm Emerson Ryan." I hold out my hand to introduce myself. "I've been hired by Eagle Tactical to protect Mr. Greyson's daughter, Bristol."

He scoffs and steps back as if I've burned him. "The hell you are. There's no way you're capable of protecting *my* daughter. I was told that Mr. Ryan would be here to protect Bristol."

"Ms. Ryan," I correct him. "And I'm plenty capable of protecting your daughter."

His gaze moves over my body, lingering a little too long on my breasts.

I sweep my foot out and knock him onto his ass, staring down at him on the wooden floorboards. "See, plenty capable. You don't have to worry. I trained at Quantico."

I offer him my hand to stand, but he doesn't take it. He dusts his jeans off, although he seems fine, except for his ego getting a bit bruised.

I remove my wet coat and find myself an empty space to hang it by the door, making myself at home.

"Why don't you work for the FBI anymore?" He turns and walks away from the front entrance. "Are you coming?" he asks flippantly, waiting for me to fall in line with him.

I hurry to catch up to him. He's nearly a foot taller than I am, and his strides are huge. It's no wonder he's an athlete. The man is built for it.

"I resigned from the FBI," I say. I don't want to delve any further into that topic.

"Resigned or were fired?" He spins around to face me as we stand in the hallway a little too close.

I feel that sizzle between us and do everything I can to push that feeling away. Bury it. He doesn't get to hold my heart.

"I'm waiting," he snaps.

I refuse to cower to him, even if he stands a foot above me. I stare up at him, unwavering. "I quit after my boss was sexually harassing me." There's more to the story, but it's not a path down memory lane that I want to travel.

"You didn't take it up the chain of command?" His brow tightens, and his bottom lip frowns. There's a softness to his features, a warmth that he exudes when he shows concern. Although, I'm not sure if it's for me or the fact he's disappointed.

"I did, and it was his word against mine," I say, shifting uncomfortably. "Since I'll be spending time with your daughter, I don't imagine that will be an issue."

"You have nothing to worry about," Kyler says.

"Of course." I force a smile. The tension between us makes the room feel several degrees warmer. Or maybe it's the fact that his gaze hasn't left mine, and I'm not used to having such attention cast on me.

It won't last. He's one-hundred percent off-limits.

And I swore I wouldn't get involved with a married man.

I glance down at Kyler's left hand. There's no wedding ring.

Not that it should matter. He's still the client. My boss. And nothing can happen between us, nor should it. As far as I'm concerned, I'd be happy never dating again. Men, sex. It's all highly overrated.

And if that isn't reason enough, he has to be a playboy. The man is a star athlete on an NHL team. He can have any girl he wants. What makes me think he'd even look twice at me?

"Good," I say, and clear my throat when he's standing a little too close and staring too long at me.

"I'm still not convinced you're the best person for the job," he says, leaning against the wall.

Is he waiting for me to convince him?

"Give me two weeks," I say.

"I'll give you one."

TWO
KYLER

IT'S HARD NOT to stare at the new bodyguard the Eagle Tactical team sent me. They assured me that Ryan Emerson is the best they have and great with kids.

What I didn't expect was that Ryan was her last name and to come face-to-face with a tiny young brunette who doesn't seem capable of looking after herself, let alone my daughter.

But she knocked my ass to the floor. I give her props for that, but I still have my doubts. Sure, she worked for the FBI, but she could have been a paper pusher all day where it was safe, and she never needed to use her skills.

By week's end, she'll be gone. There's no way

she'll survive Bristol, my daughter, and the threats against my family.

And they're not idle threats, either.

If I don't do exactly as instructed, they've promised to come after my daughter and kill her.

The only problem, I don't know who *they* are.

I could quit the league, leave hockey, and become a stay-at-home father. But that wouldn't exactly solve the problem.

Whoever these men are who are threatening my family, they won't stop if I walk away from the NHL. And I'm not about to quit my job. I live and breathe hockey. It would be like stealing away the last bit of oxygen that I need for survival.

And if that's not bad enough, the Italian Mafia is inches from my doorstep. But I've kept that from the security team I contacted. All they know is that there is a credible threat against my family and my daughter.

That's all they need to know right now.

Keeping them in the dark is protecting Bristol. I'm following their demands, doing what they require of me. And no one, not even my younger brother, knows about the real threat.

"Can I meet Bristol?" Emerson asks, already familiar with the assignment: my daughter.

"She's asleep in bed." It's well after nine o'clock, and if she doesn't get enough sleep, she's incredibly moody, just like her mother used to be. "You'll meet her tomorrow. In the meantime, I'll take you upstairs and show you to your room. If you're not tired, you're welcome to come back downstairs, and we can continue our conversation."

The brunette sucks in a sharp breath. "I think I'll retire to bed," she says.

It's probably best, although I do well to hide my disappointment.

Beside the front entrance is her small suitcase. I can't imagine that it holds a week's worth of clothes. "Is that everything you brought?" I ask, lifting the handle. It's heavier than it looks. It's no match for me, but I imagine Emerson would struggle with it up the stairs.

"I can carry my luggage," Emerson says.

"You can, but I've got it," I say. I lead her up the stairwell and offer her the guestroom next door to my daughter. I'm just across the hallway, although I keep that little tidbit to myself.

The house may be enormous, but I don't need her sleeping on the opposite wing when she's hired to look after and protect Bristol.

I open the door and flip on the light, letting her

look around while I place the suitcase on the floor beside the bed. "There's a private bath through that door and a walk-in closet attached."

Unlike most women who fawn over the size of the estate and the sleeping arrangements, she hasn't said much of anything. Although most of those women share my bed, they're not given a room to themselves.

"Is it not to your liking?" I ask. It's not as though I'm expecting a compliment, but she doesn't look impressed.

"Everything seems fine. Would you mind if I looked at the security footage and cameras? I'd like to have a look around so that I become familiar with the property before going to bed."

Her question strikes me off-guard.

She's all business. And while she should be, it's also late, not business hours. However, a live-in bodyguard doesn't necessarily work a nine-to-five job. Technically, she doesn't start until tomorrow, but I insisted when I spoke with Declan that there was no need for her to get a hotel for the night.

Did she just fly in from Montana, or is she a local?

I rub the back of my head, glancing her over. It's hard not to watch her and focus on the way her hips sway as she walks. It's been too long since I've bedded a woman. Having a six-year-old daughter makes it difficult. Oh, and there's the celebrity status too.

That's not to say I haven't had my share of women when my daughter has a sleepover at my cousin's place or my brother's for the night.

But it's never more than a one-night stand.

Women tend to want my bank account. They throw themselves at me, but it's never real. And it doesn't help that I became a billionaire before I could legally buy alcohol. It's not a happy story, but it's mine, whether I like it or not.

It weighs me down when I think about the investment, where the money came from, and what has happened since.

Most billionaires would walk away from sports and retire. Kick their feet up and lounge on a beach somewhere in the South Pacific or wherever suits them.

I'm not like most billionaires.

I enjoy the sport, the thrill of the ice under my skates, and the fans shouting in unison. There's a rush of adrenaline I get in the arena that I don't get anywhere else.

And I've tried.

Parachuting out of an airplane was fun and exciting, but it didn't give me the same satisfactory rush. And having a kid also takes precedence. I can't throw myself out of an airplane. The same could be said about me being a father and my away games, but Bristol stays with my cousin on those days and loves it.

"Sir?"

When I haven't answered Ms. Ryan quickly enough, she steps toward me. "We don't have time to waste, Mr. Greyson. If the threat is viable, we need to secure the house, and I want to make sure everything is working properly."

"It's viable, all right," I mutter, brushing past her.

I feel the heat of her gaze on my back as she follows me down the stairs and to the security office. I open the door, gesturing for her to step in first.

The far wall is covered floor-to-ceiling with surveillance screens. They're high-end and can merge into one giant screen or twenty individual screens which each focus on a camera around the property. There aren't too many cameras inside the home. One leads up from the basement stairs, and there are cameras at each entrance of the house and garage.

I tower over her petite frame as she stands with

her arms folded across her chest, glancing over the equipment. "Show me the controls," she says.

There's a long wooden desk with a control board and computer linked to all the cameras. I lead her to the panel and provide her with the password to access the system.

Within seconds, she's tapping away at the keyboard, zooming in and out with the cameras, glancing at the screens. I'm not sure what she's looking for or doing, but this isn't her first time.

I shuffle on my feet, shifting the weight slightly, not wanting to feel like a complete ass for what I said earlier and worse for thinking that she was incapable based solely on her size.

She is small.

She is petite and quite adorable, I realize, the longer I stare at her.

But this is all business. I didn't bring her into my home to have lurid thoughts about the bodyguard. I grimace.

Just thinking of her as the bodyguard seems comical. I run my hand over the back of my neck and exhale a heavy sigh.

"Something wrong?" Emerson asks. She glances at me over her shoulder.

I shake my head. She already knows I'm not

impressed by her size. But if she can protect Bristol, that's all that matters.

"You seem to have a pretty good idea of how to use the surveillance system," I say, and clear my throat, trying to distract myself from the fact she's leaning forward, head slightly tilted to the side, her cheeks red, likely from the chill outside and the rain.

She's still in her damp clothes, although with her shoes off and the jacket discarded, she's less soaked. The hem of her pants is wet, and her hair is damp and messy, but it makes her even more irresistible.

Fuck.

My cock twitches in my trousers.

I clear my throat and head out of the security office, leaving her alone. If Declan trusts her, then I should as well. Besides, she's here to help, not make my life more complicated.

The heat dissipates the farther I am from Emerson. I stalk to the kitchen, open the fridge, and grab a bottle of water. I twist the cap off and turn around, glancing at the entrance of the kitchen. Emerson seems to have followed behind me.

I didn't hear her leave the security office.

I didn't even hear her footsteps against the wooden floorboards. I blame it on being distracted. Not that I need to listen for where Emerson goes, but

I thought she'd be playing with the surveillance equipment a little while longer.

And I really don't want her to see the tent I'm pitching. Thankfully, the counter is in the way to combat my embarrassment.

Hockey.

Pucks.

Anything to make me think about something other than what's under Emerson's damp clothes. And her nipples have made a grand appearance through her shirt.

But I open my mouth, and I can't stop myself. My filter tonight seems to be broken. "You're still wet," I say.

Her brow furrows, and there's that sexy little head tilt again.

"It's just from the rain. I won't melt."

"You should dry off. You're no good to me if you get pneumonia," I say.

She bites down on her bottom lip, and I can't tell if she's holding back or if something else is going on inside her head.

Did Declan send me Emerson as a joke? We go way back and have a history together. He's well aware of my situation with my daughter. I don't date anyone because Bristol is my entire universe. I don't want to bring someone into my life who is going to fuck things up with my kid.

And just being in Emerson's vicinity lights a fire inside me that I hadn't realized had been extinguished.

Hockey.

Mouthguards.

Penalty boxes.

Sports references aren't helping in the slightest. The thought of Emerson at a game, wearing nothing but a jersey, flitters through my mind as she bends over in the penalty box, teasing me.

For fuck's sake, I need an ice bath. Not even a cold shower will help me come down from this high I have around her.

And we just met.

"Daddy!" Bristol tears down the stairs, her footfalls not the least bit silent.

I glance at the clock. She should be in bed asleep.

There's little chance that Emerson or I woke her. We've been quiet enough that sound isn't traveling into my daughter's bedroom upstairs.

She runs into the kitchen, breezing past Emerson, and throws her arms up in the air for me to catch her.

"What are you doing awake?" I ask, lifting her into my arms.

"I had a bad dream," Bristol says, wrapping her arms around my neck as I cuddle her.

I rub her back, and her head falls against the crook of my neck.

She sniffles. Her cheeks are red, her eyes matching with dried tears that have recently streaked across her face. "Are you my new nanny?" Bristol asks, turning her head just enough to meet Emerson's gaze.

Emerson opens her mouth, and I stop her before she can explain anything to my six-year-old daughter.

"Yes, she's here as your nanny," I say, hoping that Emerson will go along with it. The last thing I want is to scare Bristol. The nightmares have been more frequent over the past few weeks. If I explain to my daughter that there's a credible threat against our family, she may never sleep again.

I don't want to put that burden on Bristol. She doesn't deserve it.

"Oh," Bristol says and sniffles. She rubs her wet nose against my t-shirt. Thanks, kid. I'm pretty sure my shirt is smeared in boogers.

"Hi, Bristol. I'm Emerson."

I practically hold my breath, waiting to see if she goes along with it, lying to my kid. It's for Bristol's sake. Scaring her isn't going to do the slightest amount of good. She has enough fears as it is. I don't want her to be afraid of the dark and never want to be alone.

At least believing Emerson is her nanny might help her acclimate to having someone constantly around to protect her.

Bristol doesn't say anything, just stares at Emerson for a few seconds before she sniffles again. "Daddy, can I sleep in your bed?"

HIS DAUGHTER IS ABSOLUTELY ADORABLE.
I've discovered she's six, in the first grade, and
enrolled at a private school. Not that I'd expect
anything less for a man who is wealthy as sin.

I'm not sure of his exact net worth, but Forbes
puts him somewhere between millionaire and
billionaire.

I did a Google search.we

I'm not proud of it.

Call it research.

There are plenty of photographs of him. Not too
many of his daughter. He's done well to shield her
from the spotlight.

Not that I haven't done my fair share of
investigating his background to determine how

credible the threat on his family is and why I'm tasked with watching Bristol.

Shouldn't I also be protecting Kyler Greyson?

And sure, I can protect Kyler when he's at home, but I can't protect him while he's on the ice. But at least the arena has guards and security, a full staff trained to protect the players.

I sip my mug of coffee, the caramel macchiato creamer making it taste not the least bit bitter. Dessert in a cup for breakfast. Plus, it helps keep my ass alert in the morning, a necessity when taking Bristol to school.

The kid is in the first grade of an eclectic private school. It's top-notch, super chic, and will probably help her carve the path to get into Harvard or some other Ivy League college one day.

I'm sure that's why he's sending his daughter there, for the best education and the brightest future. Rich parents tend to dote on their kids, giving them everything they can to encourage them that they can be anything they want.

It's not my place to break it to her that the world is cruel and unjust.

"Emmie," Bristol says as I sit beside her in the backseat of the sedan. Kyler has a private driver, Mitchell, who takes us everywhere. I'm not sure if it's because he doesn't trust my driving, which he's never seen, or he's just so rich he has money to throw away for a chauffeur.

She's given me the nickname *Emmie*, and I haven't corrected her. She likes Emmie better than Emerson. Some adults might find it off-putting or disrespectful, but I take it as a win.

I need Bristol to trust me so that I can adequately do my job and protect her. Although, I'm not keen on the fact Kyler chose to lie to his daughter about why I was hired.

When the driver pulls up to Bristol's school, I step out with her, waiting for her to grab her backpack from the backseat. "You're coming in with me?" She stares up at me with wide, unsuspecting eyes.

An ordinary nanny would drop her off and pick her up.

"I need to speak with the headmaster," I say, patting her shoulder as she slings her backpack on. It's practically bigger than she is, but it doesn't appear too heavy or bulky.

She gives me a wave goodbye and races off to be with her friends as they hurry inside the school. The kids are all dressed in blue and gray school uniforms. She blends in, which is both good and bad.

From the outside, everything appears normal. Mundane. Did Kyler inform the headmaster that I would be coming? How much does he know about the threat to the Greyson family?

The chauffeur waits for me outside the front entrance and shuts the vehicle door as I head inside the school. Immediately, I'm greeted by one of the teachers or staff members of some sort.

"Can I help you?" the woman asks. She's wearing a lanyard around her neck with an identification tag. I should be relieved that they're quite on top of security, but there are no metal detectors or any other type of surveillance system that I can see. No cameras. No high-tech equipment.

"Yes, I'm Emerson Ryan. I'd like to speak with the headmaster."

"Do you have an appointment?" the woman asks, glancing me up and down. Her brow tightens, and she looks at her watch.

She probably has to be in class soon with her students. A bell chimes and the kids start to hurry inside their respective classrooms.

"I don't," I say. "Mr. Kyler Greyson assured me I wouldn't need an appointment."

Her eyes widen, and the woman nods. "Oh, I see. This is about Bristol and Liam."

"Yes," I say, although I'm not sure what transpired between the two students. Kyler has kept me in the dark, but it is only my first week on the job. The background that we dug up when trying to focus on potential threats was on Kyler. No one looked into Bristol directly. After all, she's six.

"Come with me," the woman says as she ushers me down the hall, through the hustle and bustle as the students head into class and the second bell rings. She's quick and light on her feet, and her strides make me have to jog to keep up.

The main office door is wide open, and she leads me inside to the front desk. "They'll be able to help you here," she says before hurrying to her classroom.

I can only imagine the chaos of leaving a roomful of elementary-aged children alone, more specifically, first graders. I'm assuming that woman was one of Bristol's teachers. Why else would she have known who Bristol was and about some type of skirmish between Bristol and Liam?

Maybe I'm jumping to conclusions. For all I know, the two could have been caught kissing on the playground.

Although, I doubt it.

I introduce myself to the woman behind the desk, and she has me take a seat and wait for the headmaster to be available.

A few minutes pass, and I shift uncomfortably, not liking the idea of Bristol being on her own. Although if it's a kid she has to deal with, that's far less concerning to me than a real threat—the kind that involves violence and men with guns.

Eventually, I'm brought into the headmaster's office, and I introduce myself.

"Hi, I'm Emerson Ryan," I begin, and the gentleman cuts me off before I can continue.

"I know who you are," he says, gesturing for me to have a seat. "You're here on behalf of Kyler Greyson. He couldn't be bothered to show up or return our calls regarding his daughter."

I exhale a heavy breath. "He is incredibly busy, as I'm sure you can understand. Given his public image, status, and wealth, I've been brought in to protect his daughter."

"Protect her?" He laughs sourly and rubs his forehead. He removes his spectacles and leans back at his desk. He's an older man with a protruding belly that sticks out from his desk as he does so.

"Is that what he told you? That his daughter needs protecting from Liam Moretti?"

"Moretti," I repeat, the name clicking on my tongue, "as in the Moretti crime family?" Any sane person would have probably not asked that question aloud, but I've been known to push when it's not always appropriate.

Having worked for the FBI for even a short time, I have plenty of knowledge of the crime families in and around New York City. We had a team tasked with taking down the Russian Bratva. They weren't successful at the time I left the bureau, but it wasn't my unit. And I haven't followed up to find out if they ever did take down Mikhail Barinov or his men.

The headmaster clears his throat, pushes his chair back, and stands. He briskly walks to the door and shuts it before turning around to face me.

"The walls have ears, Ms. Ryan," he says. "It would be wise for you to remember that."

I bite down on my tongue, opting not to divulge that I previously worked for the FBI. The hairs on my arms stand on end around the headmaster. There's something about him that's not quite right.

Maybe it's the fact that he's well aware he has students enrolled in his school who have parents who are involved in organized crime. I try not to overanalyze the situation like I typically would as a federal agent. The fact that the guy is taking money, whether it be from a donation or school fees, the money is dirty.

But that's not my job to worry about or uncover.

I'm here solely to protect Bristol.

"I've been hired by Mr. Greyson to protect his daughter, Bristol," I say. "Mr. Greyson has reason to believe his daughter may be in danger."

He exhales a nervous laugh.

Sweat glistens on his forehead.

"Is that really necessary?" He reaches into his pocket for his handkerchief and dabs his forehead.

What is he hiding?

"You tell me," I say, refusing to let my gaze waver. "Break it down for me. What happened between Bristol and Liam on school grounds?"

He nods and shuffles back to his desk. Finding the leather chair, he sits, his stare constantly moving around the room. He's anxious, but I can't tell if it's out of guilt or fear. What do the Morettis have on him?

"The two children are in the same class together. Liam sits behind Bristol and thought it would be fun to lift her chair with his feet. It was just a little harmless flirting." The headmaster waves his hand dismissively. "She took things too far."

"What did Bristol do?"

"She punched him."

I bite down on my bottom lip to keep from saying something I shouldn't. I have a plethora of questions, but I have the sneaking suspicion that there is more to the story that the headmaster is leaving out.

"I will speak with Bristol," I say, "and with Mr. Greyson when I bring her home this evening. When did this incident occur?"

"Friday."

I'd already had the job with Kyler Greyson lined up well before last Friday, which means the incident with the Moretti family either goes further back or something else is the threat to Bristol and Kyler.

———

After I finish discussing the situation regarding the children, I make it clear I need to see the security measures that are put in place. It was obvious that I was able to easily walk up and into the school.

Whether the Moretti family is the threat or not, I need to know that Bristol is safe in her classroom.

Convinced that Bristol isn't in any immediate danger, I return to the town car, and the gentleman opens the back door for me. "Mr. Greyson has asked you to meet him at the ice hockey arena."

The stadium hires its own private security, so I'm a bit taken aback by his request for me to meet him at the venue.

"Did he say what it was about?" I ask, hoping to gather at least some information before arriving.

Mitchell isn't particularly forthcoming. He merely shakes his head and shuts my car door before he steps around to the front of the vehicle.

I glance at my phone. There are no messages from Kyler or any of the Eagle Tactical team. Declan assigned me the job, but he hasn't called or texted. Not that I expect him to check in and see how things are going. I'm plenty capable of handling the assignment.

I shove my phone into my purse. My stomach tenses, and I'm not sure if it's because I'm leaving Bristol behind at school, where I know she's as safe as she can be, or the fact that something just doesn't feel right.

What is Kyler hiding? It has to be something. There's no reason that his life would otherwise be in danger, or rather, his daughter's.

I need to know what the actual threat is and whether it's credible. How can I be expected to do my job in the dark?

The ice hockey arena is on the opposite side of town. We're ushered in through a side entrance, and Kyler stalks out of the building on our approach.

He yanks open the back door for me just as the town car comes to a halt.

"You're late," Kyler says, like it's my fault for driving too slow.

There was traffic, and I had to make sure Bristol was safe before leaving her at school. "You neglected to mention we had an appointment," I say, stepping out of the vehicle.

He slams the door shut behind me. His dark gaze rakes over my body for a little too long. His jaw is tight. He's tense. I imagine he never gets any time off between work and being a single father.

"Did you bother checking your phone?" he asks and holds out his hand, palm up.

I just stare at him blankly.

"Your phone," he states, shaking his head, waiting for me to get on the same page as him.

We're on two different planets at this point.

I grab the cell phone that he provided me with and show it to him.

Meanwhile, the driver pulls the vehicle away from the curb, leaving me alone with Kyler. Well, not completely alone. We are standing outside the arena, which towers above us.

Kyler snatches the phone from my fingers and shoves it in my face to unlock it. "Real classy," I mutter under my breath.

He doesn't comment on it and flips through until he finds the calendar app that he clearly felt it necessary to show me, right now, outside, by the curb. Apparently, it couldn't wait.

He's *that* type. The one who has to have things done immediately and won't put his feet up for two minutes to relax. He's probably the type A, where if it isn't done his way, he'll go back over and do it again.

This should be fun.

I bite down on my bottom lip as he shows me the appointment for meeting him at the arena. I glance at my watch. "I'm three minutes late," I say. "And you failed to mention the scuffle between Bristol and Liam at school. I got to hear about it from the headmaster." I don't mention the brief introduction with the teacher, who happened to know about it as well. I have the sneaking suspicion he wants me to get right to the point.

"Kids," he says and gives a mere shrug. "Bristol was defending herself. I don't see the problem."

"Violence isn't a problem?"

"She told him to stop. He didn't. So she did the next best thing."

"And you don't think that would be telling a teacher?" I ask.

"I didn't raise a tattletale." His gaze is locked on mine, unwavering.

The heat between us sizzles, and I exhale sharply and take a step back. It's too hot. Too much and too fast.

Kyler is intense.

His intensity bleeds off him and seeps into my veins.

I'm not sure whether I love it or hate it.

I clear my throat. "Were you aware that Liam's father runs the mafia?" I ask.

"Antonio Moretti? Yeah, I've heard."

He doesn't look shaken by the news as I expected, which I find mildly troubling. It's not a secret that the Moretti family is involved with organized crime. Still, I wouldn't expect the average person to have the same knowledge as myself, a former federal agent.

I let his comment go. Questioning him about his

knowledge may seem a bit off-putting, and I need to win his trust.

"I didn't invite you here to talk about *him*," Kyler says, and his gaze burns right through me. He's hot, but he's the kind of hot where he knows how good-looking he is, and it makes him arrogant.

A woman breezes past us in a short, black pencil skirt and a dark-red blouse with one too many buttons opened. "Morning, Kyler." She flashes him with a smile, and I can't tell if it's genuine or if there's interest in him beyond the superficial. He is a top dog on the ice. And incredibly handsome.

I don't blame her for wanting to get his attention, except my stomach pangs with dread, and I can't quite fathom why.

"Morning, Brittney," he says.

I shuffle my feet as his gaze follows the woman waltzing toward the main entrance. He's checking out her ass, and her hips sway, giving him quite the show.

"Seriously?" I mutter a little too loudly.

"Jealous?"

I clear my throat. "Of you and Barbie? No. She's just interested in getting in your pants," I say. I don't know if that's true, but it comes out a little too hastily before I can snap my mouth shut.

"You're definitely jealous." He smirks, his gaze eating me alive.

It's hot under his stare. I want to remove my suitcoat and strip down, let the cool wind caress my skin, but I can't do that in the stadium lot. I'm pretty sure if I started stripping, someone would have me arrested.

Not the best plan to keep Kyler close and protect him and his little girl.

Yes, he hired me to protect Bristol, but she's not my only responsibility. He needs someone watching his back, and with women like Brittney vying for his attention, it's going to be hard to keep him under a tight leash if he likes to flirt with other girls and even date them.

"Are you going to invite me inside?" I ask, gesturing to the stadium behind him.

"Walk with me." He stalks toward the door, grabs the handle, and yanks it open. There's security at the entrance, but they know him and let him inside. I'm handed a visitor's pass as he leads me through a maze of hallways.

"The stadium has private security. Why do you need me here? Wouldn't it be best for me to stay with your daughter?" I ask as I practically jog to match his strides.

"Bristol is at school, and you're still on the clock." A smirk grazes that face, but it's not warm and genuine. It's almost like he has something planned, and I'm going to regret accepting this job from Eagle Tactical.

Thanks, boys, for throwing me to the wolves—or rather, just one wolf, Kyler Greyson.

Don't get me wrong. The eye candy helps make up for his annoying habits already. I've only been in his home a few days over a long weekend, but he likes to blast his music when he cooks breakfast and tends to leave the dishes in the sink until mid-afternoon when he cleans them.

"Keep up, M&M," he quips.

"M&M? You aren't seriously giving me that as a nickname." I have half a mind to pummel his ass to the ground, but that tiny voice in the back of my head reminds me that he's my boss.

"You're tiny. Seems fitting."

"You're an ass, but you don't hear me calling you puckhole."

He chuckles under his breath. "That's cute. It's nice to see you have a sense of humor, M&M."

I scoff at his nickname and jab him with my elbow.

"Did you seriously just assault me?"

I stop walking. My mouth hangs agape. "No," I say, and I'm not even sure what to make of his comment. He's the one making up nicknames. I just retaliated. It wasn't that bad.

He stops walking and glances back when he realizes I haven't chased after him. He's used to all the girls chasing him, probably since grade school.

"Relax," he grunts and gestures for me to join him. "I don't bite. Well, not unless you're into that sort of thing." And he winks at me.

Fuck.

"Are you flirting with me, Mr. Greyson?" I ask and suck in a nervous breath. My voice quivers, but I hope he doesn't notice.

Kyler smiles as I catch up with him, and he keeps walking, turning the corner, and I'm right at his side. I swear we've walked in circles, but maybe I'm just not paying enough attention to my surroundings while flirting and ogling Kyler Greyson.

I bite down on my bottom lip, the pain slightly piercing, enough to jar me back to reality. I need to focus.

"I wouldn't dream of it," he says. "Come on. I'll give you the tour."

We reach the locker room entrance, and I'm

about to ask if it's appropriate for me to follow. He tugs on me to keep up, grabbing my arm.

The warmth and sudden contact feel natural as his eyes stare right into my soul. The man could tell me to walk off a bridge, and at that moment, I'd do anything for him.

A man comes barreling around the corner and rips Kyler from my grasp, pointing a gun at his head.

Instinctively, my fingers reach for my belt, where I secure my weapon, but I don't have a gun on me.

FOUR
EMERSON

THE GUN in the assailant's hand glistens under the harsh fluorescent overhead lights. Adrenaline surges through my veins. My heart pounds in my chest, and I act on instinct.

I'm trained for this type of scenario, and while I haven't had to endure it aside from practice at Quantico, physically, I'm here now, faced with the grave situation at hand.

I'm the only one capable of calming the man down and keeping him from pulling the trigger.

"You don't want to do this," I say, my gaze locked on the perpetrator as he keeps one arm secure around Kyler and the other with the barrel of the gun poised at his forehead.

Having my weapon right now would be helpful,

but I intentionally left it behind, locked in the safe at Kyler's home, because I couldn't bring a gun onto school property, certainly not before meeting with the headmaster and getting the appropriate approval. And seeing as how Kyler neglected to secure that authorization and Eagle Tactical couldn't have done so without Kyler's express permission, I'm currently screwed.

I don't even have a Taser on me.

Just my wits and charm. Plus, my training and instincts.

"I don't see another choice," the man growls at me and glances behind him briefly as he keeps Kyler as a hostage, walking him backward.

I'm not familiar with the arena. There's another door, but where does it lead? To the shower? The ice arena?

The armed man is distracted. Just enough that I can make my move, and I lunge at him, yanking the gun upwards into the air while wrestling him down to the floor, tackling him and forcing the assailant onto his stomach, yanking his arms behind his back. I manage to kick the gun away from him.

"Oww!" he scowls.

"Grab me some zip ties," I say, glancing over my shoulder at Kyler.

He's got a huge grin on his face as he folds his arms across his chest, watching me.

"Help me, would you?" I shout at him.

"For fuck's sake, man, let me go," the assailant whines and tries to break free from my grip. "Someone tell her!"

"Tell me what?"

Several men in jerseys slowly emerge from around the corner, their cell phones capturing the whole exchange, and I realize this was all an elaborate setup.

"You can let Jasper go," Kyler says. He takes a few steps, bending down and grabbing the gun from the ground. "He's my brother. And this isn't a real Glock."

Fuck me.

"You're an asshole." I should probably watch my words, considering he's my boss, but I don't care. "I could have shot your brother."

He glances me over thoroughly. "You don't have your gun on you." It's not a question, it's as though he made sure of it, and I'm a bit flustered by the accusation, even if it's not intended as one.

"I couldn't bring my gun onto school property."

"Precisely," he says with a smirk.

"You planned all of it," I say, and I have half a

mind to pummel his ass to the ground and embarrass him in front of his buddies. "You don't think I can protect your daughter." I take a step back, the air around me hot and suffocating. Maybe it's also a bit of the testosterone permeating my nostrils. The room is filled with men twice my size.

Meanwhile, Kyler Greyson is composed. Calm. Collected.

I'm a mess, thanks to him.

"I needed to see what you're capable of and how you would react. You surprised me," Kyler says. And that smirk is back, the one that makes me want to wipe the grin off his face. Like he proved his point, and I didn't just make an ass out of myself in front of him or his teammates.

"You're still an asshole," I say and storm out of the locker room.

I attempt to head in the same direction that we came from. It's a maze of hallways, and Kyler is right behind me.

He grumbles something unintelligible under his breath. I'm not sure if he's cursing me or what, but I hurry my pace to get away from him.

Seconds later, he's strolling alongside me.

Damn his long legs, making it effortless to catch up. "If you want to play games, you can find someone else. I wasn't hired to entertain you and your brother."

"Hey, wait a second." Kyler grabs my arm, and I shrug out of his hold, but I stop walking, turning to face him. I don't know why I give him the opportunity. Nothing he says is going to make me forgive him for his inexcusable childish behavior.

I stare up at him, waiting for his grand apology.

Boy, am I severely mistaken.

"You can't quit," Kyler says. "I signed a contract."

"You can take up your complaints with Jaxson Monroe, the owner of Eagle Tactical," I say. "I quit." I turn on my heel and hurry down the hallway for the exit. Grabbing a ride from his chauffeur seems a bad idea, given the fact I just quit. So, I grab my cell phone and request a ride-share service.

I have to walk around the outside of the stadium to catch my ride. It's not ideal, but at least it's still light out.

I eye my phone. My ride is ten minutes out. In the distance, I catch a glimpse of Kyler in his jersey, stalking toward me.

There's no avoiding him. He's not out here for a nice leisurely stroll.

"Just great," I mutter under my breath. "Come to grovel?"

"Hardly." His jaw is tight, and his eyes are piercing and sharp. His gaze sends butterflies into my stomach as he studies me. "I thought you'd make it a week, M&M. It's a shame you can't even realize I was trying to help you."

"You're delusional if you think your little antics back there were helpful."

"They were helpful to me. I needed to see that you were capable of subduing a man twice your size. You proved me wrong. You are plenty qualified to protect my daughter."

"You should have thought about that before you humiliated me. You know what? It's not even that. I don't care that you embarrassed me in front of your teammates. It's the fact that you blatantly lied to me. How am I supposed to protect someone who can't be honest with me?"

"You're supposed to protect *my daughter*," he says.

"Why does your daughter need protecting?" I ask, staring up at him. He's tall and brooding. I hate the fact that he's handsome, and I bite down forcefully on my bottom lip, dispelling any such thoughts from my mind.

"Bristol's mother, Ashleigh, she has ties to the Italian mafia."

FIVE
KYLER

I HADN'T INTENDED to share Ashleigh's secret with anyone. I swore to Ashleigh that I would keep our daughter safe, give her a good home, and protect our daughter from her uncle, Antonio Moretti.

But enrolling Bristol at a private academy had proven more challenging than I originally anticipated. Antonio happens to send his children to the same school. I'm sure it's a coincidence. The institution is known for being elite and highly sought out.

But the fact that his son and my daughter are in the same class, it's unsettling. I tried to shake it off as a mere coincidence. Antonio doesn't know about Ashleigh, Bristol's biological mother. From what Ashleigh told me, Antonio went missing before she was born. He was kidnapped, but one of those at-home DNA tests had confirmed her suspicions long before she was pregnant with Bristol.

He shouldn't know about Ashleigh. But it wouldn't be hard for him to find her. And so, when she became pregnant with Bristol, she wanted to protect our daughter by any means necessary.

I didn't expect Ashleigh to walk away as a mother or leave me as a single parent. But that's all in the past.

Ashleigh granted me full custody before disappearing.

"What do you mean Bristol's mother has ties to the Italian mafia?" Emerson asks. She's fidgety with the news. Her eyes are wide and bright as she folds her arms, tapping her fingers against her forearm.

"It doesn't matter. She's out of the picture. But if the Italians find out Bristol is their blood, I don't know what they might do."

"How closely related are we talking?" She taps her foot, and I can sense the cogs rotating in her head, trying to piece it together with the bits I've given her.

Given that she's former FBI, I expect her to be relatively familiar with the Moretti family. They're the only Italian mafia organization in the New York area. Of course, there's also the Russian mafia run by the Barniovs, but I should consider myself lucky my daughter doesn't have ties to them.

"Does it matter?" I'm trying my damndest to keep Ashleigh's secret while still protecting Bristol.

"And Antonio Moretti has his children, Liam and Sophia, enrolled in Briarwood," Emerson says, reiterating what I've already told her.

"Yes." I nod, waiting for further instructions from her.

She curses under her breath just as the vehicle she's hired pulls up to the curb. She opens the back door, tells him she's canceling the ride, and then spins around to face me. "If you pull any more of that crap you did earlier, I'll shoot you myself. With my real gun."

"Got it, M&M."

"And no more stupid nicknames." She jabs her finger into my chest.

Emerson is cute when she's pissed. Her cheeks are flushed, and her eyes pin me, making my cock harden. The things I could do to her if given a night together. One wild, abandoned night. Don't they say good things come in small packages?

She's definitely a small package that I'd love to unwrap slowly and methodically. I'd take my time undressing her, savoring every inch of her naked skin.

"We'll see," I say, silently relieved that she's sticking around. I'm not sure why, considering the fact that an hour earlier, I was questioning her ability to keep my daughter safe.

Did I want her here for me?

That was a thought I needed to squash before it became outright dangerous. My little firecracker is off-limits.

Mine?

I clear my throat and usher her back inside the stadium, doing my best to dispel any lingering thoughts of Emerson. I did manage to cast a glance at her pert little ass.

What I'd give to see her naked, writhing beneath me, begging for my cock, giving up all control as she lets me take her and possess her.

Down, boy.

Those are wicked thoughts bound to land my ass in boiling water and without a bodyguard for Bristol.

"You can have the rest of the afternoon off until Bristol is released from school," I say. Expecting Emerson to work twenty-four hours a day, seven days a week, isn't fair to her. Besides, she's no good to me if she's burned out or distracted.

———

The minute Emerson is away from the arena, Jasper comes barreling down the hallway, heading right for me. "Where's the cute bodyguard?" He wiggles his eyebrows suggestively.

He's the only one who knows about Bristol's mother. It was on his suggestion that I hire someone to watch over my daughter when I can't be around. He's been on my case for years, and with the recent threats, I finally took the plunge.

And the team, they all think I hired Emerson after a stalker incident with an overzealous fan.

"I sent her home to rest or whatever," I say, waving my hand in the air. "I don't need to worry about any threats here, and if she's burned out before Bristol gets home from school, I'm screwed."

"You'd like to be screwed by her," Jasper says with a wicked grin.

He's right, but that isn't the point. "She's my daughter's bodyguard. I'm not fucking her."

"Well, not yet, anyway. Are we still on for this weekend?"

I'm grateful Jasper manages to steer the conversation away from Emerson, but I had completely forgotten the gathering I planned with my buddies.

"Fuck."

"You forgot." Jasper folds his arms across his chest, glancing me over. "That's uncharacteristic of you. I thought by now you'd be hiring caterers and a full staff to entertain—"

"Shut up," I growl at my younger brother. "Don't give me a reason to kick your ass."

"Like you've ever needed a reason before?" Jasper quips. "And please tell me you're inviting the bodyguard."

I don't have time to plan a gathering, although it's usually nothing extravagant. A few of my buddies get together, have drinks and dinner, and bring their spouses or dates if they're so inclined. We tend to sit around the fire pit in the backyard when the weather cooperates and just chill the fuck out.

It would be good to see the guys and unwind for a couple of hours.

"I'm sure Emerson has better things to do than attend a barbeque," I say.

"If you don't invite her, she's going to feel left out."

"If I do, it'll be awkward as hell. I mean, what if she starts gossiping with Levi's wife about me?"

"Oh, you can count on it," Jasper says and smacks me on the back. "If she's not doing it, I sure as hell will. It'll be fun to—uh, what do the kids call it these days, spill the tea."

"You're an asshole. You know that?"

"I know you keep me around because you love me," Jasper quips. "And I love to give you hell."

SIX

EMERSON

"EMMIE!" Bristol squeals as she runs out of the school building and across the lawn where I stand, waiting for her. I'm still within the school grounds, and the teacher is grumbling under her breath, as the kids don't seem to listen and wait until their parents check them off the list for pickup.

I step toward Bristol's teacher, the young woman with whom I had conversed earlier when I had first arrived before the school day began.

"I'll need to see your I.D.," the woman says, smiling politely.

At least she knows I'm picking Bristol up. I have a sneaking suspicion that Kyler called the school office to confirm my arrival.

I initial the sheet as requested, and the teacher hands me back my driver's license.

I inhale a sharp breath as Antonio Moretti stalks toward us. He has one little girl clutching his hand and a gorgeous woman on his arm. She seems to be trying to wrangle the little boy over to her.

Apparently, the mafia don is married or at least involved with the woman. I hadn't done my due diligence on the family. I only discovered earlier today Bristol's relation to the Morettis.

His gaze is hard, his jaw sharp as he stares at Bristol, shooting daggers at the six-year-old. If looks could kill, he'd have murdered her by now.

I refrain from causing a scene. The last thing I want is to put Bristol in further danger than she already is. Perhaps I should discuss transferring Bristol out of Briarwood Academy and suggest she attend someplace less problematic. A private school where the mafia doesn't have their children enrolled.

"Mr. Moretti and Ms. Ryan," the teacher says, gesturing for us to hold on a moment. "I'd like us all to schedule a meeting together with both families so that we can discuss the in-classroom issues we've been having."

"I don't see why we need to attend," Antonio says. "My son isn't the problem."

"And you're saying that Bristol is?" I'm appalled that he thinks his son bears no responsibility for the issues at hand.

"Please, if we may," the teacher says and forces a smile. "This would be best left to the parents. Could you pass the message along to Mr. Greyson for us and let us know when he will be able to attend on behalf of his daughter."

"Right." My jaw ticks. There is no chance I'm allowing Mr. Moretti and Mr. Greyson alone together, even if Bristol isn't in attendance. "I will pass the message along."

Bristol and I hurry across the lawn, my hand gripping hers as I practically tug her toward the driver.

"It's not my fault," Bristol whines as I hurry her to the awaiting vehicle. Mitchell opens the back door, and Bristol climbs in first. I scoot in beside her and glance back to see Antonio Moretti getting into the vehicle behind us. He, too, has a driver chauffeuring him and his family around.

I'll need Declan or Jaxson to do a little reconnaissance work on the Moretti family. If they're the main threat to Bristol, then sitting down with them to discuss the children's behavior at school isn't going to make the problem disappear.

We should be getting her as far from Antonio and his men as possible.

"You look mad," Bristol says as she stares at me.

"Put your seatbelt on."

Mitchell waits for her to buckle herself into the booster seat before he pulls out into traffic.

"Is Daddy going to be mad at me?" Bristol asks. She snaps her seatbelt and shifts in her booster seat to face me.

I don't know Kyler well enough to determine if he's going to be upset, disappointed, or just overly concerned. Perhaps it could be a bit of all three.

———

Kyler isn't home when we arrive after school. I have a key to the front door, so I let Bristol inside and do a quick sweep of the place to make sure it's just the two of us.

I'm not his daughter's nanny. I'm her bodyguard.

Why isn't he home?

"I'm hungry," Bristol whines. She drops her backpack by the front door, along with her coat and shoes.

"What time does your dad normally get home?" I ask.

Bristol shrugs. "He picks me up from school."

"Jackass," I mutter under my breath.

Bristol's eyes widen. "You have to put a dollar in the swear jar." She grabs my hand and drags me into the kitchen. On the marble countertop, there is a glass gallon-sized jar stuffed with one-dollar bills.

"How about we don't tell your dad what I said?" I try to bargain with the kid. It's not the dollar that's the issue. I don't need her tattling to Kyler about the situation. He's already questioning my ability as his daughter's bodyguard. I don't need to give him any more ammunition.

"Make it two dollars." Bristol holds up two fingers.

The kid knows how to negotiate. I nod and grab two one-dollar bills from my wallet, stuffing them inside the clear jar.

"Who gets all this money anyhow?" I ask.

"Daddy says it's for my college fund, but I'm saving up for a unicorn!" she squeals excitedly.

I'm not going to be the one to burst that bubble. At least she's not saving for a horse or some other expensive creature that she could actually buy.

My phone pings and I grab it from my pocket, glancing at the screen.

Kyler: I'm running late. I'll be home to make dinner.

Damn right, he will. My job isn't to cook and clean for the Greyson family. I'm supposed to be protecting Bristol, and if I'm distracted with entertaining her, I can't do my job.

"Is that Daddy?" Bristol asks, trying to peer at my phone.

I show it to her, and her eyes narrow, trying to read the text. It takes her a minute before she seems to comprehend what it says.

"Can you make me a snack?"

"Didn't you have lunch at school?" I lean back against the counter, folding my arms across my chest, giving her the most pointed look imaginable.

"Yes, but that was hours ago. I'm starving," she whines like she hasn't eaten for weeks. "I'm going to die if I don't eat."

"That isn't going to happen over a couple of hours." I head toward the fridge and yank it open, having a glance inside. "See anything you want?" I ask.

She shrugs and then points at the fruit bin.

I open up the plastic bin and grab a pint of raspberries, rinsing them off before handing her the dripping-wet container.

"It's wet!" she squeals and shucks water at me from her little fingers.

Thanks, kid.

"Grab a paper towel." I gesture to the counter, trying to make her self-sufficient.

"It's too tall. I can't reach, and Daddy puts the fruit into a plastic bowl for me." Bristol points at the cabinet and waggles her finger, waiting for it to open.

"Do you know magic or something?" I chide, glancing at her. "Because last I checked, wiggling a finger doesn't open cabinet doors. Unless you go to Hogwarts, but I'm pretty sure there isn't a magic curriculum at Briarwood."

"You need a wand, silly, but there could be!" Bristol giggles. "Abracadabra, open the cabra—net."

Shaking my head, I give in, using just one finger to pull the cabinet open. I retrieve a pink plastic bowl and hold out my hand for the raspberry container. I dump the contents into the bowl and wait for her to use the magic words I'm looking for. Either a *please* or *thank you* would suffice.

"Thank you," she says with a wide-eyed, eager grin, and I hand the fruit back to her in the bowl.

She's a cute kid. Spoiled beyond compare, but that isn't her fault. Her father is a billionaire.

For the next couple of hours, I have her seated at the kitchen table going over her homework assignments, which are far more than I remember doing in the first grade.

The sound of a car door slamming sets my adrenaline pumping. "Stay here," I say as I waltz out of the kitchen and head toward the front of the house, glancing conspicuously out the window.

Kyler stands outside, his cell phone pressed against his ear as he talks animatedly to whomever he's on the phone with. He doesn't look particularly pleased with the caller.

"Emmie!" Bristol calls for me, and I exhale a heavy breath and make my way back into the kitchen. "Is this right?" she asks, wanting me to check her work.

Thankfully, she's only in the first grade and not the eleventh or twelfth. I can easily handle glancing over her work, except for her math, where she's shown her work is a bit of a nightmare. I can't even fathom how she came up with the answer that she did, but it is right.

"Yeah, that looks good," I say, cringing.

"Then why are you making that face?" Bristol asks, staring up at me.

Saved by the sound of the front door. Kyler heads inside the house, and Bristol jumps up from the kitchen table and tears out to the hallway, sliding on the wood floor in her socks to greet her father.

"Daddy!" Bristol squeals excitedly, and he holds out his arms for her as she runs right for him. He lifts her, spinning her around and giving her a hug.

The girl is six. She's not a toddler, but neither seems to care. She's having fun, and he can still practically toss her around without hurting his back.

"You're late," I say a little more tersely than I intend.

His gaze moves from Bristol to me. "I can't exactly leave practice because you want me home."

"Give us a minute, sweetie," I say to Bristol, yanking Kyler out of the hallway and away from Bristol's little ears.

"Sweetie? I didn't know we were starting on pet names," Kyler jokes to me. He's trying to disarm the situation. At least, I think that's his intent, because the anger sizzling seems to dissipate when his eyes shine down, almost as if he were smiling.

"This," I say, gesturing between us, "is a business arrangement. I'm not your daughter's nanny. I'm the bodyguard. You shouldn't be expecting me to babysit your daughter."

"Got it. I'll hire a nanny," he says a little too quickly.

"And what do you plan on telling Bristol? Since she thinks I'm her nanny." I fold my arms across my chest, waiting for him to think up a brilliant excuse to fix the predicament he's found us both in.

"Obviously, not the truth," he says, his gaze sending a shiver down my spine. My insides are toasty the longer his gaze lingers, and I feel the heat of his breath against my cheeks. He takes a step closer, pinning me back against the wall.

He doesn't touch me.

The man doesn't have to, and I'm still practically a puddle of goo. The wall holds me up as I exhale a nervous breath.

There's zero chance that he's going to kiss me.

But his gaze lingers on my lips a little too long before he drags his eyes back to my stare. "We could tell her the truth, that we've been secretly dating, and you're my girlfriend."

I laugh at his words.

He can't be serious.

"You said it. I can't have two nannies. How would that look? And I need someone capable of protecting my daughter. That's your job. You can help me hire the perfect nanny."

"You want me to be your fake girlfriend?" I still can't get his words out of my head. "It's insane!" I squeak a little too loudly, and he brings his hand up to my lips, his finger grazing my mouth, silencing me.

"Bristol likes to eavesdrop. She wants to be a spy, and I can't have her spilling our secrets unless we want the world to know about us. Hiring you as my fake girlfriend would be good PR for me."

His eyes light up, and I'm pretty sure he's talking before he's thinking.

I shake my head. "I did not agree to this." I shove my hand between us, gently pushing him backward. "I'm your daughter's bodyguard. That's it, Kyler." I glance around the room. "Are there hidden cameras? Is this some type of reality show where you tell me you had me fooled?"

I slip quickly from his grasp, and he runs a hand through his unkempt hair.

I don't dare admit that he looks boyish and suave with his messy bedhead look. He's recently showered and still smells of soap from after his game.

His tongue darts out to the corner of his lips, staring at me. "I'd pay you for your services."

"You couldn't pay me enough to fake date you," I say a little too quickly.

"Is that so?" he asks.

Did I just challenge him?

That was not the plan. Neither is faking dating my boss. He is my boss, technically. We have a contract that we both must abide by, but it seems that he wants to change the terms.

Typical of a billionaire. Always out to get what they want.

What about what I want?

Having his strong arms wrapped around me doesn't sound that bad. I could handle a few pictures in public. How bad could it be, pretending to date a star hockey player?

My stomach flutters at all the possibilities, but my brain is screaming at me that this is a terrible idea. This morning, he had me believing he was being held at gunpoint.

"What will your teammates think?" I ask. "They saw me in the locker room. They're not going to believe I'm your girlfriend." He's crazy if he thinks either one of us can pull it off.

And worse, we'd have to lie to Bristol. It's not bad enough that we've already been doing that, but I don't want to break her heart when she finds out the truth.

"And the headmaster at the school?" I ask. "He

already knows I'm your daughter's bodyguard. You can't keep it a secret forever."

The smile on Kyler's face grows even wider. "Right. You know I called him and explained everything after you met with him this morning."

"Explained what?" I don't like where this is going.

"I told him that you concocted the bodyguard story so it wouldn't put pressure on our newly formed relationship, especially with the media looking for a bite of the dirtiest details of our lives. He already thinks we're an item."

"And what about your brother? Can he keep it a secret?"

"He already thinks we're fucking. It won't take him long to buy whatever story I sell to him."

I smack his arm, and he grabs my wrist, refusing to let me go. "Did you just hit me?"

"What do you think, Einstein?" I shoot back.

He drags both of my arms above my head, pushing me up against the wall, this time trapping me. I have nowhere to go, and while I could outmaneuver him with my legs, the truth is that I don't want to.

It's a dangerous game, and I want to see where this leads.

Will he kiss me? Touch me? Taste me?

My breathing deepens, the longer he holds me against the wall, my chest rising and falling. I'm not the only one feeling the heat sizzle between us.

I swear his cock is poking me, and I want to glance down, but if I do, I'm worried he'll pull away from me. I want that even less.

"Cat got your tongue?" I ask, staring up at him.

His eyes have darkened, and he leans down. I swear his lips will graze mine, but he doesn't kiss me. His breath lingers over my lips, the heat melting together, mixing like an aphrodisiac, and I'm under his spell.

"Are you in?" he asks, and his voice is thicker, heavier. I swear the scent he evokes is a heavy musk that permeates all of my senses. He smells amazing, and I want to reach in and lick his neck, tease him, drive him over the edge. I want him to beg me to let me fuck him.

But I would guess he'd make me be the one to do all the begging.

"What are the terms?" I force the words past my lips. My jaw feels heavy, the words like a lead balloon, while my legs grow wobbly under his spell.

"We would have to kiss, make public displays of

affection, have people believe that we're a real item in public."

I thought this little game was to convince his daughter that we're together because having two nannies seems outrageous. "Why does the public care what you do?" I whisper, staring into his piercing blue eyes.

My insides flutter, but this time it's not my stomach doing the dance. I want him more than I've wanted anything or anyone.

I blame it on his proximity. The fact he has me nestled against the wall, and he doesn't seem intent on letting me go anytime soon.

His breath tickles my neck as he leans in beside my ear. "It's not only my daughter who needs convincing this is real. We'll have a nanny who has to believe we're together. And the team," he says, grazing my ear.

"The team you outed me to that I'm a bodyguard?"

Did he miraculously forget what happened with Jasper?

"They'll believe any story that I sell them," Kyler says, a little too confident.

My eyes involuntarily slip closed, and I feel a silent shudder ripple through my body. The man knows how to turn me on, even when I'm fighting it. And for the record, I am fighting it. Just maybe not hard enough. I press my lips together, mulling over his words. "But they're not the public," I say. "What's your endgame?"

There has to be more, something he expects out of all of this. "It would keep the spotlight off my daughter," Kyler says.

And that's reason enough for me to agree.

I'd be doing my job. Protecting Bristol.

"You're not convinced," he says and pulls back slightly.

I whimper in protest from the lack of warmth, and the electricity humming through my body has since vanished. He releases his tight grip on me. "I'll pay you six figures on top of the initial contract."

"Seven. I want seven figures," I say. "If I have to put up with your ass and pretend to like you, I won't do it for a penny less."

He smirks and holds out his hand. "Deal."

SEVEN
KYLER

I PUT it into writing that I'll pay Emerson a minimum of 1.2 million dollars to put up with my shenanigans. Well, it wasn't in those exact words. And yes, she weaseled another two hundred grand from me when she realized the arrangement is ongoing until the threat with the Moretti family is extinguished.

That's the only threat I've told her about. But it's not the worst one out for blood.

I agreed to pay her one hundred thousand dollars per month during the ordeal and with the remainder paid in a lump sum if completed sooner.

It'll give her an incentive to play my games. And if we go over the course of a year—which I don't think is even a realistic possibility with us pretending to be an item—then we'll renegotiate a new contract.

I won't let that happen.

She's not getting any more of my money. She may be good with Bristol, but paying her seven figures as a glorified babysitter is insane. Yes, she's a bodyguard, but she's being adequately compensated by her employer.

And I'm letting her double dip. She gets paid by both Eagle Tactical and me. And yes, the Eagle Tactical team will be made aware of the arrangement because I don't want them firing her ass or kicking me to the curb as a client.

"This better be good," I say, answering my phone. I'm showered and dressed before the sun comes up. It's a practice day, and I've got to assemble for training. Which at least means I'll get out early today.

"Why? Did I interrupt you banging the hot bodyguard?" Jasper asks with a laugh. "There's no way you hired her for her skillset. Tell me, how many times a week are you putting it to her?"

I growl at his insinuation. "Do you want to lose a few teeth?"

"I didn't call to talk hockey," Jasper says, and I swear he's probably wearing the biggest smile on his face. He knows how to get under my skin. "Do you need me to bring anything to the party?"

"That's tonight?" I repeat, already having forgotten about the backyard barbeque and get-together I had planned. Which was really my younger brother suggesting we all get together at my place to hang out for drinks and to chill out because his place was too small and embarrassing to host a party.

I've been playing in the league for four years. It might be Jasper's first year, but he's known the guys since my first year of playing. I've made sure to include him whenever I host any gatherings with the team.

He was a bit starstruck in the beginning, but now they're like family to him, and he's ecstatic that he's part of the team. We're lucky he didn't get drafted to a different city.

"Yes, the party you're hosting is tonight," he says. "Do you need me to bring anything?"

"You're not old enough for beer," I mock, and I swear I hear him growl back at me. He's two weeks shy of his twenty-first birthday.

"I can bring it if you're so desperate to get laid by the bodyguard."

"She's the nanny," I say, correcting him,

reminding him that's what he's supposed to be referring to her as—until I make it public that she's not the nanny and she's my girlfriend. The last thing I need is him tripping up in front of his niece.

"Right." Jasper laughs. "I can't keep your fake shit straight. Are you sure you're not banging it out with her? Because if you're not, I'd love my shot at the cute little—"

"You're an asshole." He's lucky that he's not within my vicinity, or I'd be taking a swing at him.

"An asshole that you love, other than your own." Jasper chuckles. "I'll see you at practice. I'll bring chips and dip tonight."

Why the hell couldn't he have waited until we got to practice to mention the party? Probably because he knew, with the stick up my ass that I've had all week, that I'd blocked out the invitation to the guys.

Mostly, that stick was caused by the one and only Emerson Ryan.

She'd managed to turn me into more of an asshole than I'm used to being lately, which was another reason to convince her to be my pretend girlfriend. She no doubt could play the part and put up with my shit better than anyone else. She isn't starstruck like most of the girls I run into.

I shove my phone into my pocket and head out of my bedroom. Bristol is still sound asleep, but Emerson opens her bedroom door as I head into the hallway.

"You're up early," I say, glancing her over.

I don't usually see her before practice.

"I was going to go for a run on your treadmill. I hope that's all right."

I have a decent-sized home gym that I've created, not that I use it all that much. Most of my work is done with the team, but it's nice in the evening, if I want to clear my head, to do some weights, or go for a run indoors.

That's not to say that I don't love running outside. I prefer it, but Bristol can't keep up with my pace, and I can't ask my cousin or my brother to come and help with my daughter every time I want to leave the house. Which meant a home gym made the most sense. It was practical, even if I don't take advantage of it as much as I should.

"Sure."

"Have you had a chance to pull out some resumes for nannies?" Emerson asks.

"I have a list on my desk, but I haven't narrowed it down. I still need to do background on them."

"I'll do that," she says a little too quickly.

"Good. Oh, also, tonight I'm having a few of the guys from the team over—"

"You want me to get lost. I get it." She nods. "What time should I plan on coming back?"

I'm surprised that she thinks I want her gone when my teammates come over for drinks. "Actually, I'd like you to be here when they arrive."

"To watch Bristol?" she guesses. "You remember that I'm not really your daughter's nanny and—"

"I know," I say with a heavy sigh and head down the stairs. She's right on my heels, even though she has to hurry to keep up with me. She's got little legs compared to mine. It's cute how tiny she is. "Maybe tonight, we tell the guys the truth—that you're my girlfriend."

She's silent, and I glance at her over my shoulder as I reach the landing in the hallway.

"Is that a problem?" I ask.

Is she having second thoughts about our arrangement? I haven't deposited the first payment into her bank account. Not until we're publicly acknowledged will she receive a transfer to her account. I need to know that she's not backing out.

She smiles, but it's forced. Anyone can see right through it, which means she's going to have to work on our fake relationship. "Of course not."

Her hand grips the banister of the second to last stair, white-knuckled.

She's having doubts, but I'm not sure if it's because we're lying to my daughter or if there's something else she's not telling me.

I'm sure this won't be easy for her, being the center of attention for a while, but that's why I'm paying her adequately to compensate her for the headaches that go with being in a relationship with me. Not that I'd have to pay someone to really be in a relationship, but this is fake.

She takes one step down, and we're the same height. My hand grazes her hip, pulling her tight against me, my lips crushing hers, proving to her that we can do this. It's as much an attempt to prove to myself that I'm not making an even bigger mistake.

Emerson is rigid, and everything with her feels forced. No doubt even Bristol will see through the farce.

Emerson's lips are sealed. She doesn't grant me entrance past her mouth. It's a chaste kiss.

If this is going to work, I need more from her. It's obvious there's an attraction. I won't deny the fact that she's gorgeous and sexy, and I'm certain she feels something for me. Most women throw themselves at my feet.

But Emerson is different.

What makes her tick?

She does like men, right?

Maybe she's not into sweet. Some girls like the bad boys. The rough, unrefined ones who they know are bad news. Is that her type? Or something in between?

It shouldn't matter. This is nothing more than an arrangement. But I want to know what drives Emerson wild. She's too buttoned up and stuffy.

How the hell was she ever an FBI agent? I certainly don't see her playing undercover if she can't even pretend to kiss me like she means it.

Unless it's me.

She's just not attracted to me. I don't rev her engine like other guys.

My heart pounds in my chest. Imagining her with another man makes my blood boil. Who is this other man? Why would she let him kiss her? I tug my fingers into her hair, fisting her long locks, and tilt her neck back, guiding her mouth farther up toward me, taking control.

She gasps, slightly taken aback by my forcefulness, and her lips part.

I take it as an opportunity to explore her mouth, her lips, and her tongue.

This time, she's not as cold and rigid as the first graze of our lips. She melts into my touch, her fingers fisting my shirt, tightening her hold against me as she succumbs to her desires.

Well, that, or she's a fantastic actress, but I doubt it's the latter, given the first few seconds of our lips locked together.

The pads of her fingers move down to the hem of my shirt, teasing my hips and stomach, her fingernails dragging over my skin, causing my insides to warm.

I pull her tighter, my cock throbbing from just a simple kiss.

I break apart and swear I hear her whimper. Her eyelids flutter open, and her cheeks are red. She's slightly breathless. "What was that for? No one is around," she says. Her demeanor is soft and sweet, unlike what I'm used to being faced with when she's throwing questions at me. It's usually an interrogation.

"I needed to make sure that you could play the part of my girlfriend. And I didn't want our first kiss to be in front of everyone."

"That means there will be a second," she whispers.

I don't answer. I leave her standing there while I head out the door, where my driver is already waiting for me. "Morning, Mitchell," I say as he opens the back door for me, and I slide into the backseat.

———

The day goes without a hitch, and by evening, I'm hosting a gathering with the guys. Mostly, it's the team, but there are a few friends I've made over the years whom I invite, including Levi Luxenberg, who happens to own the Luxenberg hotel chain.

We met a few years back when we shared a private jet after a scheduling mix-up, and the rest is history.

We're gathered in the backyard, a bonfire roaring to life as the guys sit around. Levi brought Clare, his wife, but they left the kids at home with a sitter. She's nestled on his lap as they share one of the Adirondack chairs.

His arms are wrapped around her waist possessively. He doesn't need to worry; none of the guys would steal her away, but if she were single, he would have quite the competition.

"So, where's the hot new nanny?" Jasper quips, giving me a wink.

"What's that look for?" Noah asks. He's one of three goaltenders on our team. His job is to communicate, and I swear it goes well beyond the ice when he's reading body language. Not that it's much of a secret, either, with my younger brother mocking me.

"She's busy in the house," I say, trying my best not to turn around and glance over my shoulder at the open window shades. I want to look for her, find her, drag her outside, and show everyone that she's mine.

Even if it's pretend, it doesn't feel that way.

"So, I hear this new '*nanny*' is hot." Owen grins and uses air quotes. "Wait, is this the chick we met at practice when she tackled Jasper to the ground? Is she single?"

"She is recently off the market," I say and clear my throat. The flames of the fire flicker upwards toward the sky. I shift uncomfortably from the heat and pull my chair back a step.

"What was she doing at your hockey practice?" Clare asks. "Have you met the elusive boyfriend?"

She's watching me and curious. Her eyes tighten, and she glances at the house. "She's coming outside. I'll ask her about him—"

I open my mouth to stop her, but it's too late.

"Join us!" Clare shouts with a friendly wave and beckons her over.

I glance over my shoulder, and Emerson has a beer bottle in hand. She stalks methodically toward us, and I stand, heading over toward her.

"What—" Before she can finish her question, I scoop her up into my arms, carrying her back to my seat, showing everyone that she's *mine.*

"You're the boyfriend?" Clare says, dumbfounded as she stares at me, her mouth agape. "I'm such an idiot."

Emerson takes a swig of her beer. One arm is gingerly wrapped around my neck from carrying her. "Telling everyone about us?" Emerson asks with a sly smile. "I thought we were going to do it together."

She stares straight into my soul, her gaze never leaving my face, and I'm sure I have the stupidest grin known to man covering my lips.

Playing the role of her boyfriend makes me way too happy. I shouldn't be playing with fire, but what's the worst that could happen? I've already been burned.

"How does this work?" Owen asked, leaning forward, a little too curious about our situation. "Does he pay you for '*nanny*' services and girlfriend services?"

"Give me your beer," I growl at Emerson, prepared to chuck it at him.

She raises an eyebrow. I don't know how she does it, but the gesture is sexy. "Why?" she asks, holding it away from me, just out of arm's reach, teasing me.

"He deserves something thrown at him."

"And waste a perfectly good beer?" She scoffs at my suggestion and brings the bottle to her lips, tilting her head back and downing the contents.

God, she makes everything look sexy.

With her cute little mouth wrapped around the neck of the bottle, my cock twitches.

She shifts her hips on my lap, and she's only making me harder. Is that on purpose? Is she toying with me because she wants me, or is this a game to her, and she's really good at her little act?

"I'm happy for the two of you," Noah says. "It's good to see my man happy for a change. Maybe some of that luck will finally rub off on the ice. I'm tired of our losing streak. Have any sisters?"

"I do, but she likes pussy," Emerson says, and Noah's mouth drops.

I have no idea whether she's making shit up or just trying to get a bigger rise out of me, which is working. Pussy? Those words coming from her lips are tantalizing.

"God, woman," I grumble under my breath and grab her beer when she's not paying close attention.

"If you throw that—"

"It's empty." I scowl. I was planning on drinking it. Tossing it at Owen is no longer a priority.

She smirks all too knowingly, and I can't just sit there and take the sass without doing something. I lean in, stealing her breath away with a heated kiss.

Levi, Clare's husband, whistles as the world around us melts away. My fingers tangle in Emerson's hair, pulling her lips upward, her mouth opening as I get lost in the moment with her.

I keep reminding myself this is all an act. I need to convince my teammates that Emerson is *mine*.

She shifts her weight, grinding against me as she pushes me back against the chair. I swear I'm seeing stars, and it's not the night sky that I'm looking at because my eyes are shut, and she's lighting up the heavens as I feel things buried deep within me.

The kiss we shared the other day on the stairs was pale compared to the heat sizzling and emanating between us now.

My heart pounds loud enough that I'm confident everyone within a five-mile radius can hear it.

"Gosh, you two, get a room before you make another spawn out here for everyone to see."

"Spawn?" That captures my attention, and I turn my head, glaring at Jasper. I could kill him right now.

"Yeah, you know, the little thing that runs around here and recites the alphabet in song version."

He's referring to my kid, obviously. But Bristol hasn't done that in years. "My daughter is a lot more grown-up than you are," I snap back at my brother.

Emerson pats my chest reassuringly. "Settle down there. I'm sure he's just playing with you."

"I'm not," I mutter under my breath, annoyed that he managed to interrupt a perfectly good moment between Emerson and me. Even if it isn't real and we're just pretending to date, I'm sure as hell enjoying it.

Probably because I haven't stuck my dick in anyone in months.

Not that I intend on doing that with Emerson. That's a line we won't cross, given that this is a business transaction.

And it's Emerson.

She'd probably chop off my dick if given the opportunity. The girl is a real firecracker. And while I'm comfortable pretending she's my girlfriend, there's no chance it can come to fruition.

We'd undoubtedly kill each other first.

But she's a good actress, making me believe she wants me. Even my body believes her. But my heart should know better.

Owen stands up and stretches his legs, approaching the fire. "How long did it take for the two of you to hook up? She's been '*nanning*' for your kid for what, a week? Really stuck it to the '*nanny*,' didn't you."

I stand, guiding Emerson off my lap as I stalk toward Owen, swing my fist back, and land a blow square across his cheek.

I'm not done with him. I'm nowhere near done. "Don't you ever talk about Em like that," I say, snarling as I grab him by the lapels and shove him across the lawn.

We're just feet from the raging fire blazing beside

us, and the three guys seated closest to us jump up to intercept.

Owen pummels me back in the chest, pushing me back, not the least bit interested in walking away.

Good.

Neither am I.

It's an all-out brawl between the two of us.

Jasper grabs Owen, yanking him back, keeping him from lunging forward. It takes both Levi and Noah to hold me back from breaking Owen's face into dozens of tiny pieces.

The other guys on the team stand. "Walk it off," Asher says, his gaze on me like this is somehow my fault. What the hell?

"Daddy." Bristol's voice is soft and filled with concern.

I spin around and find her standing by the door in her pajamas. She's clinging to her stuffed monkey. That toy gives me the creeps with its beady eyes, but she loves the damn thing.

"What is it, sweetheart?" I ask, stalking across the yard and back toward the house.

"The movie ended," she says, staring up with wide, soulful eyes. "Can I watch the mermaid movie next?"

I glance at my watch as I head into the house. I'm

about to shut the door when I look over my shoulder and realize that Emerson is following me. Is it because of what happened outside? I can't deal with her right now.

"Of course," I say to Bristol and follow her into the living room. She climbs on the sofa and curls up under the blanket. She stretches out, laying her head on the pillow and staring at the screen while I switch movies.

Within seconds, I've got *The Little Mermaid* playing, and she's happily fixated on the screen. Oddly enough, she knows how to change the channel and find any movie she wants, but I suspect she wanted to see what we were doing outside.

I drop a kiss on Bristol's cheek, and she pushes me away. "Daddy, I can't see the movie."

"Okay, okay!" I laugh, holding my hands up in surrender. I head for the hallway and notice Emerson watching the two of us.

"Need any help?" she asks, although I suspect she doesn't mean it. She made it clear that she wasn't Bristol's nanny. I can't expect her to help tuck my daughter in or get the kid ready for bed. That's my responsibility.

Emerson is here to protect her.

I run a hand through my hair. The thought is still

strange to me, a girl protecting my daughter, mostly because of her size and stature. But she proved herself in the locker room, and I can't keep testing her as much as I may want to.

"I've got it. She just wanted another movie," I say, and gesture for Emerson to follow me down the hallway toward the kitchen. I'm careful to make sure I'm out of Bristol's earshot when I add the last part. "And I think she secretly wanted to see what the adults were up to."

"What was that—outside?" Emerson asks. She licks her lips and folds her arms across her chest.

"I didn't like the way Owen was talking about you." I step closer, encroaching on her personal space, trying to defuse the tension building around us. She's irritated with me. At least that's what her stance and tone are telling me, and I don't need her getting feisty when all I was doing was protecting her honor.

She scoffs and stares up at me, her gaze never wavering. "I don't need you fighting my battles. I can handle Owen or any of your guy friends."

"No," I say.

I take another step closer, and she steps slightly back, bumping into the counter behind her.

She has nowhere else to go.

"No?" she squeaks. Her voice betrays her. The longer I stare into her eyes, the darker they become. Her cheeks are a faint shade of pink, and her lips part.

Does she think I'm going to kiss her?

I swallow back that thought or any other ones leading to the bedroom. Not that I couldn't fuck her on the kitchen counter, but the shades are wide open, and the guys would get quite the show.

My cock stirs at the thought of shoving my hand up her dress. Are her panties soaked? The flushed look on her face tells me that she wants me.

Although most girls would throw themselves at my feet for a wild night with a professional hockey player.

But from what I've seen, Emerson isn't like most girls. Maybe that's why I'm attracted to her. She doesn't act like she's interested, at least most of the time.

"The guys are watching," I say. As long as we're supposed to be pretending to be in a relationship, I might as well take advantage of the opportunity that's presenting itself.

I don't bother to look at the open curtains to see if the guys really are watching us or if their backs are turned and they're still seated around the campfire.

Honestly, they probably don't give a shit about what Emerson and I do other than to tease the hell out of me because that's what the guys do. Give me shit. I dish it back. It's part of the comradery of being on the team.

"Bullshit," she says, calling my bluff, and as she turns her head to see if there are any sets of eyes on us, I make my move.

My lips crash on hers, hard and fierce. I tangle my fingers in her hair, gripping her to me, pressing my body firmly against hers. I want her to feel my cock through my jeans and know that I want her.

It's all a game.

A war to see who can last the longest and not break.

I want to fuck her right here, right now.

Her mouth opens, and whether she knows the guys aren't watching or not, she gives me what I desire.

Tongue fucking her is fun, but it's not enough. It's not nearly satisfying as I yank her head to the side, and my mouth descends on her neck, biting and nipping at her skin.

I intend to mark her.

I want any man who gets a glimpse of her collarbone to know she belongs to me. If she so much as thinks about going out on a date with another man, there will be questions if they see my mark.

Fuck.

Why am I thinking about her dating another man? She belongs to me.

I paid for her time, her body, and her ability to be my fake girlfriend. That comes with exclusivity, at least from her.

"Kyler," she rasps, and her words are sweet and sultry. They make my cock even harder.

With one hand buried in her hair, I take another forceful bruising taste of her lips, needing to satisfy the craving building inside of me.

I drag my other hand up her thigh, beneath her little black dress, and feel her panties soaked as I dip my fingers inside.

"You're so fucking wet for me." I bite her lips, wanting to make her come.

"It's not for you," she says, denying me any hint of satisfaction.

"Liar." I don't believe her. She's displaying all the signs of arousal. Her breathing is heavier and thick, her eyelids drooping, and her panties are soaked. "If not for me, then who here has you dripping wet?" I grab her pussy, waiting for her to answer.

She presses her lips together, trying to keep her composure.

I plan on tearing it down.

"Your brother," she says with a smirk, and my eyes widen.

I'm sure as hell she's trying to make me jealous and rile me up. Well, it's working. Every pang of jealousy imaginable seeps through my veins. She won this battle.

"You want to fuck my brother, Jasper?" I say. I can't fucking believe her. I spin her around and loosen the button and zipper on my jeans, pulling my cock out. I stroke the length with one hand while I continue to grip her pussy, holding her to me but not giving her the satisfaction she wants.

I'm not fingering or fucking her yet.

"You're going to beg for my cock," I say.

Her hips gyrate against my palm when I don't use my fingers to tease her. I want to. I want to plunge my digits into her warmth and make her scream my name.

My name.

Not my dumbass brother's.

"I swear if you say Jasper's name, I will rail the fuck out of your tight little ass."

"Jealous?" She's thrusting against my palm, trying to get off, and I smack her pussy.

She gasps, and I'm pretty sure that's a chorus of pure pleasure as she rocks against my hand. "Do that again," she whispers.

"Do what?" I ask, my lips against her ear as I smack her pussy and grab my shaft, dragging it over her bottom.

"Oh." She shudders, and I haven't even fucked her.

"Do you like ass play?" I ask, nipping her neck and her shoulder.

"I don't—I don't know," she stammers. "I've never..." her voice trails off when I remove my hand from her pussy and slide her bottom cheeks apart.

"Say my brother's name again, and I'll fuck you hard in your tight little ass," I warn her.

Her breath catches in her throat.

"Unless you like it dirty," I whisper. She tilts her head back to the side, and I bite her lips.

"Fuck me," Emerson says, and I want to, more than anything.

"No, not until you beg for it," I command. I glide two fingers into her pussy, and my thumb grazes her little pink pucker.

Her hips shift, and she grips the counter, leaning forward.

"Fuck," she gasps, and she's not the least bit quiet.

I have half a mind to silence her, but I want the guys to hear her screaming my name. Let them know I'm fucking her. Have them come and watch if they want.

I drive two, then three fingers into her tight pussy, and my thumb circles her pink pucker. She tightens her insides, clenching down as she thrusts against my hand.

"I'll fuck you, princess, but you have to beg for my cock."

"Oh god!" she screams and wiggles her hips and gyrates as she leans farther back, half bent toward the counter, giving me the perfect view of her ass and her pussy lips from behind.

I stroke my cock; the condom's upstairs and out of reach. I won't chance getting her pregnant, fucking her bare won't do either of us any good if she gets knocked up.

"Fuck me." She's clenching down, her insides quivering as the first wave begins to ripple through her.

"Not until you beg for me," I say.

I guide my cock against her pussy lips, teasing her with my head. "Tell me you want my cock in your ass."

She gasps and trembles, her pussy walls clenching onto my fingers as her full orgasm rips through her. She tightens, dripping wet and gasping for breath. Her come is all over me, and I withdraw my fingers, wishing it were my cock. Spinning her around, bringing them to her lips. "Suck," I say, putting my fingers to her mouth.

Emerson opens her mouth, and I guide my two fingers coated in her pussy juices past her lips. She obeys, sucking them clean.

I might actually explode.

My cock twitches and throbs. Watching her suck my fingers, tasting herself, it's a huge fucking turn-on, and most girls refuse my kink.

She's staring up at me, her dress falls back down around her, and other than her messy sex hair and the flush on her cheeks, no one would know what she's done.

"On your knees," I command, pushing her shoulder down, and she instantly falls to the ground, her lips parting as she takes my cock in her mouth.

Her tongue is like heaven as she takes me in past those sassy little lips of hers. My fingers tangle in her dark hair, and my eyes shut as she takes me deeper into her mouth.

My cock throbs and aches, growing closer as the back door swings open and two of the guys, Jasper and Noah, walk in on the impressive blow job.

"Whoa!" Jasper says, covering his eyes. "At least warn a man, like put a sock on the doorknob or something."

Noah is grinning like an idiot when Emerson releases her mouth from my cock.

I'm rock hard, even with two spectators. Three, if you count Emerson staring at my glistening shaft like it's a lollipop, and she wants another taste.

"Out!" I shout at the two men by the door.

"Hey, guys, wanna watch Kyler get sucked off by his new girlfriend?" Jasper shouts over his shoulder at the team.

"I'm going to fucking kill you," I growl at my younger brother.

Emerson stands and wipes the imaginary dirt from her dress. *Don't worry, princess. No one is looking at you.*

I'm going to have the worst case of blue balls. I shove my cock back into my jeans just as several other members of the team come barreling toward the back entrance. "Seriously?" I can't believe them. "Never took you all for voyeurs," I mutter.

"What's going on?" Levi asks.

"What are we watching?" Owen is next, poking his head in behind the other guys.

Maybe they didn't hear verbatim what Jasper said, only that they should come and look, and I want to kick the shit out of my brother for ruining a perfectly good blow job with Emerson.

I'm not sure there will even be a second chance after what just transpired between us. It was fucking hot, but the fake arrangement didn't include sex, finger fucking, or blow jobs.

Emerson sneaks off toward the fridge a few feet away, opening it as she buries her head in there. She's probably trying to cool herself off, or maybe she hopes that they'll forget she's in the room.

"Grab me a water," I say to her, bringing the attention back to her.

"Kill me now," she mutters into the fridge. She grabs two bottles of water, tosses one at me, and keeps one for herself.

EIGHT

EMERSON

IT'S BEEN TWO WEEKS, actually fifteen days, since the amazing orgasm Kyler Greyson gave me. Two weeks since my lips were wrapped around his enormous cock that I surprisingly didn't gag on. That was a first.

And we haven't spoken about it since.

I probably shouldn't have told him I wanted his brother, which was, in fact, a lie. Jasper is a nice guy, but he's not my type.

I was trying to make Kyler jealous, and it seemed to work. He does realize I'm not interested in his brother. Right?

Kyler has been all business for the past two weeks.

With games at home and away, I've been looking

after Bristol without any time off except while she's in school.

Apparently, I did a good enough job convincing the team that I'm Kyler's girlfriend. Getting down on your knees and blowing a guy is a convincing enough act that we haven't had to make any public appearances yet.

I've been keeping a watchful eye on Bristol while Kyler has been interviewing potential nannies for an actual position involving caring for his daughter.

Not that I couldn't care for her, but I can't do an adequate job of watching surveillance footage and making sure that everything is secure while I'm cooking her dinner or getting her ready for a bath before bed.

"We need to settle on a nanny," I say, gesturing to the file folders spread across the kitchen counter. It's been hard to pin Kyler down long enough for him to hire someone else.

"Are you leaving, Emmie?" Bristol asks, glancing up from the picture that she's working on. The kid has a knack for drawing. At six, I was still making stick figures.

"No, sweetie. Your dad and I, we think it would be a good idea for you to have a new nanny," I say, glancing at Kyler and waiting for him to elaborate.

He should be the one explaining to his daughter why he's hiring a nanny. He never should have lied to her and put me in this predicament in the first place.

"But I don't want you to leave," Bristol says, slamming her colored pencil onto the table. "I want Emmie to watch me."

"And Emerson will be here with you," Kyler says, bending down to her level, "but she's my girlfriend," he says, glancing at me.

My stomach has a thousand tiny butterflies fluttering its wings on his admission. Because it isn't real, even if he makes me feel things that seem like they are, it's all a ruse.

And lying again to Bristol doesn't feel like the right thing to do. She'll be crushed when she realizes that we're no longer together because that's the only viable outcome when everything settles down and Bristol is no longer in danger.

"You're dating the nanny?" Bristol says. Her eyes widen, and she glances from her dad to me. "Does this mean you'll be my mom?"

Thankfully, Kyler answers before I have to disappoint the six-year-old.

"No, sweetie. Emerson and I aren't getting

married. We're just dating, like we talked about. The thing you get to do when you're thirty."

Her nose scrunches, and she glances back at me. "Are you sure you want to kiss my daddy? That's gross."

A smile grazes my face, and I try my best not to laugh. "Definitely gross," I say with a wicked grin, "but more importantly, I'm not going anywhere. I'm still going to be here with you and your nanny. But she's going to help make you dinner when your dad is at his away games and when—"

"Oh, so she's like a chef!" Bristol says, her eyes lighting up. "Good, because your cooking stinks."

I never claimed to be the best cook, but I wouldn't consider my food inedible. Bristol had pushed her food around her plate a bit, but I assumed it was because she was picky.

"I don't understand why Emmie can't watch me, and you just hire a really good cook." Bristol is adamant about my culinary skills lacking.

"Emmie is taking care of some important business matters for me when I'm away. She can't do that and watch you all the time." Kyler drops a kiss on his daughter's forehead.

Emmie?

I press my lips together, finding the nickname far

more endearing than M&M. Maybe it'll stick with Kyler.

"Do you want to vet the list of potential candidates?" Kyler asks, gesturing to the manila folders on the kitchen counter.

"I thought you'd never ask," I tease, grinning at him as I take a cursory glance through each one. I'll have to do a more thorough investigation into each potential new hire. More specifically, Eagle Tactical will have to do the background check, but I can stalk the potential candidates on social media and see if any obvious red flags come up with a little minor digging.

Each file has a picture along with the potential candidate's resume. They are far more impressive than my "nannying" experience, but then again, I never was a nanny, and it had only been to convince Bristol of why I was there and watching over her.

We've spent enough time together these past couple of weeks that, hopefully, when I see her off to school and pick her up, she won't think anything of it.

"Are all the new hires young and gorgeous?" I can't help but feel a tinge of jealousy seep into my veins. They're all in their early twenties, the same as me, but they're cute, and I swear they could all be cheerleaders or whatever type of girl chases after a hockey player.

Do they even have cheerleaders at hockey games?

"I didn't notice," Kyler says, and I glance at him, but he's not smirking. He seems genuine in his acknowledgment. "I'll let you pick the top three that meet your expectations for my daughter's safety, and then I'll interview them."

"None of them have decades of experience," I say. I was hoping he'd have picked an older woman, someone he wouldn't think twice about sleeping or flirting with.

Definitely jealous.

"I suppose not, but I thought that Bristol might bond better with someone younger."

I bite down on my tongue because I don't think it's Bristol he's thinking of when it comes to bonding with anyone. I grab the stack of files and shove them on top of one another. Grabbing them from the counter, I push them into his chest. "Find someone more qualified."

"Is that all it is? You don't think they're qualified because I'm confident that with what I'm paying, I'll get the best that money can buy. All of these girls have a degree in elementary education. Some of them have spent the last couple of years teaching grade school."

"You're not hiring a tutor. You need a nanny," I say as if that emphasizes my point, but I don't think it does.

"And they're plenty qualified. But if you don't think they're the best candidates, for whatever reason, I'll contact the agency and have them suggest a dozen more whom you can vet." He runs a hand through his hair and lets out a heavy sigh.

Am I being unfair?

I want what's best for Bristol, and if one of these girls is the best thing for her, shouldn't I look past the fact that they're cute? Maybe one of them is happily married, and I won't have to worry—I wince at my own thoughts.

"What's wrong?" Kyler asks, studying me. I hate how much he's an open book, and although I try to keep my thoughts and feelings buried away, I'm not great at it.

"It's nothing."

He steps closer. "Tell me," he says, his tone stern. "If it involves a nanny or my daughter, out with it."

I inhale sharply and exhale a nervous breath. "I don't want anyone getting the wrong idea when you hire a nanny who's cuter than I am."

"You're jealous," he states. It's an accusation, not a question.

I lower my voice, making sure Bristol doesn't overhear us, as I step closer. "I'm just worried about your image. If you're paying me to be your girlfriend, what will everyone think when you bring home an even hotter nanny?"

His gaze flickers, and he glances me over like he's studying my body, trying to decide if I'm right or not. "I'm not hiring a fifty-year-old woman to watch my kid. Someone older wouldn't be able to keep up with Bristol and all her afterschool activities."

"I'm not jealous," I counter, but my heart slams against my ribcage, and my stomach is a bundle of knots.

He nods slowly, but he's not buying my story. "You're right. We do need to keep up appearances when we bring in the new hire. You'll need to come to a few of my games. No one is going to believe you're my girlfriend if you're never around."

My eyes flicker with concern. "What about your daughter? I can't protect her if I'm at the arena."

"You'll bring her with you, and the nanny can come too," Kyler says with a shrug. "It'll make it more believable if you go out with me and the guys for drinks. Can't bring a kid to the bar, and the nanny can take Bristol home and tuck her into bed."

"I can't protect Bristol if I'm not around her," I say.

Did he forget why he hired me?

His gaze flinches. "Yeah, I know. It's fine if we have Mitchell chauffeuring Bristol and the nanny back to the house. He has Special Forces training and can handle anything thrown at him."

"Why isn't he Bristol's bodyguard?"

"He is when he drives her around, but I need someone who can look out for me too. He can't be in two places at once."

"Wait. He's your bodyguard?" Why didn't anyone mention that Kyler had a bodyguard?

"I don't need anyone protecting me, but I trust Mitchell, and I'd rather have someone on my payroll who has his level of expertise."

"Exactly! That's why I think these nannies are less than stellar. They're too young to have enough experience." The money can't be a factor in determining who he's hiring. He has plenty of it, given his net worth.

"This discussion is over," Kyler says. Shaking his head, he walks out of the kitchen, probably trying to get away from me.

———

I send the list of potential candidates over to Jaxson at Eagle Tactical to run a detailed background and analysis on each of the girls applying for the position. It takes a few days to get the results, but all of them are clean, with not so much as a parking ticket or moving violation, ever.

No criminal records.

They all graduated with honors and have stellar letters of recommendation. It's almost as if they're too good to be true, but I choose three candidates and leave those files on the kitchen counter for him.

Kyler can choose which nanny he wants to hire out of the three. I'll just have to accept that someone else will be in his life. Not that it should matter. I'm hired as his daughter's bodyguard.

But why do I have to keep reminding myself of that fact? It's obvious that Kyler's interest in me is strictly for the sake of his image.

He's up for a new contract at the end of the season, and making himself a household name by putting himself in front of the media helps his career. It doesn't hurt that he's an amazing player too, but being all over the news helps give him an edge. It helps him get a bigger contract.

He's home late after a game, and Bristol is already in bed. I'm sitting on the sofa, reading a hot new romance novel that just released, when he pokes his head into the living room.

"How was she tonight?"

He's got a hell of a bruise on his cheek.

"Disappointed that you didn't get to tuck her into bed. But I got her bathed, teeth brushed, and read her a story. Are you okay?" I ask.

He gestures at his face. "It looks worse than it is. Are you sure you're not secretly the perfect nanny?" Kyler says as he comes to sit beside me on the sofa.

I close my book, leaving the back cover up so that he can't see the title of the steamy romance. "Pretty sure," I say with a faint smile. "I left you three potential nanny candidates on the counter. And they all claim to have culinary skills."

"Perfect. Bristol will be thrilled." He nudges me with his shoulder. "Do you have plans for Friday night?"

"Aside from watching Bristol?" I ask. It'd be nice if he had the nanny start by then so that I wasn't pulling double duty. The only free time I have is when Bristol is at school. The bodyguard job isn't forty hours a week.

"My cousin is willing to keep her for the night. You and I have a party to attend."

"We do?" I ask, and my mouth suddenly goes dry. "What kind of party?"

"The team is attending a charity event, and we're expected to bring a date. Which means you're going to be the highlight of the evening."

"I doubt that," I say with a laugh. "What kind of event? What's the attire?"

"It's fundraising for the local children's hospital. Every couple of months, the team goes to visit the sick kids. We sign jerseys and bring a little light into their bleak lives. The attire for the gala is black tie, super fancy." He tilts his head, glancing at my book.

Kyler tries to flip the book nonchalantly with his finger. But my death grip doesn't let him glance at the title.

He'll tease me until the end of days if he sees what I'm reading.

"Nope." I press the book to my chest, the cover buried against me.

"Oh, really?" His eyes sparkle, and his boyish grin makes my heart flutter.

In a matter of seconds, he has me pinned beneath him as he tries to pry the book with one hand, and his fingers tickle against my stomach with the other.

He's bigger than I am and a hell of a lot stronger. But that doesn't mean I get to fight fair. I've had my share of stronger men at Quantico during training think they can topple me and win.

Looks can be deceiving.

I tangle our legs and flip us onto the floor rather roughly. Kyler lands smack on his back and grunts from the sudden impact. He winces. He wasn't expecting me to fight back.

I'm lying above him, the book nestled between us.

"Don't mess with a girl," I say, staring down at him. I'm straddling his hips, and the position is definitely enticing, with his rock-hard body beneath me.

It takes everything in my power not to wiggle my hips against his and tease him.

"Is that so?" Kyler grins, pretty pleased with himself.

He grabs my wrists and binds them together with one hand, rolling us around and pinning me on my back against the floor.

His hips straddle me, but the book is no longer

pressed between us. It lies unceremoniously against my chest.

"Don't even think about it," I warn.

"Or what?" The grin on his face makes my stomach somersault, and with one hand, he keeps me pinned down, and with the other, he knocks the book to the floor, managing to flip it over.

"Lady porn, that's cute."

I scoff at his suggestion. "It's not porn."

"Then why were you trying to hide it?" he asks. "*Jailed Little Jade* sounds like something that would give you a lady boner."

I knee him in the thighs, careful not to injure his groin or hurt him too much since he has another game tomorrow, and I swiftly roll out from under him.

"What do you know about lady boners?" I laugh, sitting up on the floor, my back against the sofa.

"I'd say I know a thing or two about making a girl moan." Kyler grins, staring at me. "Want to go for round two? This time, no interruptions."

The room is several degrees warmer, and I laugh nervously, glancing away. I grab my book, bringing it back onto my lap as I pull my knees to my chest. "We were just pretending, for your friends' sake," I say.

The harmless crush I feel toward Kyler isn't so

harmless if I catch feelings for him. And that isn't an option.

He's an NHL player. I'm just—me. There are a million girls out there who would tear down his door for one night with him.

I'm not that girl.

Not that I wouldn't love to experience a night with him, but I have to be realistic and not set myself up for failure again.

"Too bad my friends aren't here," he says and sits up beside me, leaning on the sofa. He drapes his arm across the cushions, and I swear it's a maneuver to cuddle me. Except, he doesn't place his arm on my shoulder like I think he might.

I try to mask my disappointment.

"Oh yeah, we have the meeting at Bristol's school tomorrow morning," Kyler says.

Tomorrow happens to be Monday. Way to start the week off head-on.

"The one with the Moretti family?" He'd been trying to schedule the conference with the school, and there were constantly conflicting schedules between his games and the other family not being available.

"The one and only," he says with a heavy sigh.

"I'd like you to be there, but I also want to know Bristol is safe."

"I'll watch Bristol," I say in agreement. It's not really my place to attend the parent-teacher conference.

"The headmaster has asked for Bristol to attend the meeting. I think he's expecting an apology from her." Kyler grimaces and rubs his forehead.

"You're concerned," I say. "About the Moretti family or Bristol?" I ask, sensing his discontent.

He's silent, and the air is thick, surrounding us. It's unlike Kyler not to say what's on his mind.

"Both."

"I'll be there," I reiterate. "I won't let anything happen to your daughter."

"Thank you," he whispers.

————

When the school day ends, Kyler and I head into Briarwood. He's done a decent job covering up the bruise on his cheek and his knuckles. He got into it with someone on the ice. But he won't talk to me about it. Shrugs it off as game stuff that happens during a hockey game.

The kids are bustling out the door with their teacher as she signs them out for pickup.

I'm always on high alert, looking for potential threats. Although the biggest one is where we're heading: the headmaster's office.

We're meeting with the Morettis, and I'm not thrilled with the idea of being in the same room with Antonio, the head of the mafia.

Not that we've had a run-in together other than during pickup time with the kids.

I didn't last very long at the FBI, given the circumstances for why I left, and so at least I never had to work a case involving the Italian Mafia. Which is good, considering he'd find me a threat if he knew who I was in a former life.

But my work with the FBI is behind me. The boys' club, with their sexual innuendos and trying to get the newly appointed women agents drunk and into bed during their own brand of initiation for new agents, sucked.

Fuck me. I thought college was bad.

And maybe I should have done more, but it was *his* word against mine. And *he* was a senior supervisory agent. I was fresh out of Quantico.

Not to mention he was married.

Yeah, I fucked that up for him, at least. I'm no

saint. But she deserved to know the truth about her husband, even if she didn't want to see it.

One last glance, and there's a woman in the distance, standing outside the wrought iron gates. She's watching the school, the teachers, and maybe even us.

She doesn't come inside to pick up her kid. There's something about her, but I shrug it off. I don't sense any immediate danger or threat. But something feels off.

My hairs prick on the back of my arms, but it could also be that we're walking in alongside the Moretti family, Antonio and his wife, Aleksandra. She rests a hand on his arm; it's possessive, and his tight gaze screams that if you mess with him, he'll murder you.

Okay, maybe it's just the fact I know he's killed people for a living that makes me feel uneasy around him.

I stand between Antonio and Kyler, doing what I can to protect him from the Morettis.

Kyler is tall, he's at least six foot, and while Antonio isn't short by any means, he's also not quite built like a hockey player.

"You should let me stand on the inside," Kyler whispers into my ear.

It's difficult to hear him amongst the hustle and bustle of the few kids remaining in school for after-school activities and sports.

He wants to protect me from Antonio Moretti.

That's charming but completely unnecessary.

Kyler reaches for my hand, a sign of solidarity. At least, I think that's what he's going for. He doesn't have a wife to accompany him like Antonio does.

"You're dating the nanny?" Antonio apparently sees the gesture and can't stop himself from stating the obvious.

Kyler beams, his face lighting up as we stop, and he tugs my hand to keep me from going any farther toward the headmaster's office. Apparently, Bristol can wait a little longer for us because Kyler is ready to have a pissing match with the head of the mafia.

This can't be good.

"Is that what you'd call it, *sweetheart*?" Kyler says, staring down into my eyes. He releases his grip on my hand, only to move his hands to my cheeks. His palms are huge as they envelop my face. "I'd say we had him and the rest of the world fooled."

Kyler is grinning, and Antonio raises a curious eye as he stands there, taking it all in.

"I don't give a rat's ass what you two are. You could be felons for all I fucking care. Just keep *your daughter* away from *my son*." Antonio is staring fiercely at Kyler when he says *your daughter*.

He probably would like it if we were dirty. That way, he'd have someone else to do his bidding on his payroll.

"I'm his girlfriend," I announce proudly. "The nanny was a ruse, and your lame ass fell for it."

"Whatever? Who gives a fuck? And why the fuck did you bring the nanny?" Antonio glares at us like we've lost our minds. Maybe we have. The ruse wasn't to convince Antonio of our relationship, but maybe we could convince him that I'm actually Bristol's biological mother.

In which case, any concern regarding Ashleigh would be moot. And since Kyler doesn't seem to give a shit when it comes to tall tales, this one would actually help solve one problem, not create two new ones.

"You don't think it's sweet? The two of us finally rekindled our relationship after all these years. And Bristol is *my daughter*," I say with determination. "I'm her mother."

Kyler winces at first glance, and his jaw is set tight.

Okay, not exactly what I was going for. He looks pissed, but I'm slightly concerned that look is at me and not at the culprit, the man standing across from him.

Aleksandra smacks her husband's arm. "It's kind of sweet. Don't be such a dick," she says to him.

"Her mother," Antonio says and huffs. "You abandoned your kid for years. That's really noble of you. Showing up now, when Kyler Greyson is wildly famous."

"You think I'm famous?" Kyler grins, trying to defuse the situation. "Do you want an autograph? I don't have any jerseys with me, but I'll bet there's a marker somewhere around, and I can sign your arm. I'll even give you permission to get it tattooed forever."

I cover my lips with my hand, trying not to chuckle too loudly.

"Let's get on with the conference," Antonio grumbles, stalking for the headmaster's office. He drags his wife alongside him, and they walk on ahead of us the last twenty or so feet to the main office.

Kyler pulls me back a little, keeping us farther away from Antonio and Aleksandra. He leans against me, his arm brushing mine as he whispers into my ear, "That was quite a bomb you just dropped. Her mother?" His tongue darts out to the side of his mouth as he stares at me, his jaw tight.

"I had to think on my feet," I say.

"We'll talk more after we're done," he says, his arm wrapping around my waist as he accompanies me into the main office.

Bristol is seated by the door, legs swinging nervously as she wrings her hands together. Beside her is a little boy scowling in her direction, Liam Moretti. I recognize him from pickup after school. The boy seems a bit feral, although I'm not sure if that's as much from the dirt on his clothes from recess and a little that's stained his cheek.

"Can we go home?" Bristol asks the moment she sees her father.

"No, we're having a conference with the headmaster," Kyler says, reminding her, although I doubt she needs reminding. It seems more likely that she's trying to get out of it. I can't say that I blame her. I'd be doing the same thing.

"Bummer," she grumbles under her breath.

The headmaster's door swings open just as we arrive. "I'd like to speak with the parents first," he says sharply.

Bristol's eyes widen, and she glances at me for

help. This isn't my expertise, getting her out of that kind of trouble.

"Behave," Kyler warns his daughter before heading into the headmaster's office. He glances back at me as I stall at the entrance. It's not really my place to attend, and isn't it better if I'm at Bristol's side watching over her? "Come on, you're her mother," he says under his breath, tugging my hand and practically dragging me into the conference.

Crap.

Well, I did that one to myself.

"Have a seat," the headmaster says and gestures to the three chairs in the room. It's obvious that he had two extra seats brought in, likely for this very meeting.

"Sit," Kyler commands, nodding for me to take a seat.

"You take it," I whisper. It wasn't like I planned on being in the room, and I can do a better job of keeping Kyler safe if I'm standing and on high alert. As it is, I don't like having my back to the door. I give his hand a firm squeeze, silently trying to tell him I want him to sit without making a fuss over the situation.

His gaze tightens, and then he nods, sitting in the

chair. I stand behind him, one hand on his shoulder. He's tall, and even while seated, he is enormous.

There's an air to him, and when he walks into the room, everyone takes notice. I thought it was because he was a famous hockey player, but the more I come to know Kyler, the more I think it's just him.

He's magnetic.

"I thought we were only bringing in parents to this meeting," the headmaster says, and although he's talking about me, he's staring at Kyler disapprovingly.

Antonio clears his throat. "Turns out she's the kid's mother." The way he says it puts me on the defensive.

"Oh," the headmaster says, his brow knit, and he gives a nod. "Then I suppose it's good for her to be here. Perhaps being in Bristol's life again will help give her a positive female role model."

I want to slap the guy, but instead, I dig my fingernails into my hand, the pain biting me from using my sharp tongue.

"How have the children been since the last incident several weeks ago?" Aleksandra asks. "Liam's teacher hasn't mentioned any further incidents between the kids."

"Their teacher will be joining us shortly," the headmaster says. "But I would like a united front among the parents. It's important that the children see the parents getting along, which might help alleviate some of the problems."

"Excuse me?" I can't keep my mouth shut. What the hell is he insinuating?

The headmaster shoots me a look as if to say that I have no place here, but he continues on with whatever asinine idea he has running through his thick skull.

"It would be beneficial to have both families gather together to get past the differences between the children."

"You want us to invite them over for a barbeque?" Antonio asks, shocked by the suggestion. "We don't entertain people we don't know."

"Precisely," the headmaster says. "I want both of your families to get to know one another. Whatever differences your children have, we need to be able to put them aside. It's a teaching moment."

It's an insane moment.

Thankfully, I'm quick enough not to let my mouth run with that thought.

It's a horrible idea. Letting the Moretti family into our home or vice versa. What the hell is the headmaster up to? He knows the Morettis are part of the Italian Mafia.

With one hand, I grip Kyler's shoulder. He's rigid and tense, and so is Antonio. Neither wants to go through with this arrangement.

"We'll do it, but it has to accommodate my schedule," Kyler says.

Antonio glares at Kyler. "You're not the only one who has important meetings to attend."

Aleksandra reaches for her husband's hand. "Play nice," she warns him. Her voice is soft and coaxing, and he seems to relax under her touch.

Perhaps I should get to know Aleksandra. She might be an ally in this whole predicament that we've found ourselves involved in. That's not to say that she's not mafia, because she is, but her name strikes me as Russian, and that I find even more perplexing because the Russians and Italians do not get along.

NINE

KYLER

EMERSON VETTED the potential candidates for me to hire as a nanny. They have the qualifications, and on paper, they're perfect, but none of them are Emmie, as Bristol likes to call her.

But I can't keep putting the pressure on Emerson to babysit Bristol, and I need a nanny.

Lia is the best on paper and holds up to every standard I could ever expect, but I value Emerson's opinion, and I need to see how she interacts with Bristol as well.

I text Emerson, even though she's just out back with Bristol in the garden. I want both of them to meet this nanny. The others were qualified but didn't really pique my interest in the same way.

Within a few short minutes, Bristol comes

jogging in. Em is just a few steps behind her. "You called, boss," she says with a teasing grin.

"Lia, I'd like you to meet my daughter, Bristol, and my girlfriend, Emerson. Em may be around a little more than what you're used to, just to make sure the transition is smooth," I say, not wanting the nanny to know about any inherent danger in the job.

"It's nice to meet you," Lia says, shaking Emerson's hand and then Bristol's. "What do you like to do for fun, Bristol?" she asks, giving my daughter her undivided attention.

I let the two of them converse, glancing every so often at their exchange. Bristol immediately seems to take to her, and I nod for Emerson to join me on the other side of the desk so that we can speak quietly.

"I think she's the one," I whisper to Em, wanting to get her approval.

Her gaze tightens for only a second before nodding. Her eyes are on Lia and Bristol the entire time while keeping her voice low so only I can hear her. "She's qualified." There's no question. It's a statement.

Both of us had been through the list of candidates repeatedly before settling on three who were the best for the job.

"What do you think about her watching Bristol while the two of us attend the charity gala?" I want Em's honest opinion. I value her input.

She lets out a soft sigh. "I prefer someone with *different* qualifications," Em says, glancing at me, giving me a look to tell me she wants someone who can protect my daughter, not just babysit her.

"Mitchell will be parked right outside, except for when he drives us to the gala."

She presses her lips together, unconvinced. "Yes, to her as the nanny, and maybe, for the charity event? I should be making sure that your daughter is safe, not playing your girlfriend."

Her words strike a chord within me; it hurts, but I don't let on to it. "And I'm paying you to accompany me to these types of events, to be my girlfriend," I say. I glance at Lia, who seems to be focused on Bristol, but this conversation needs to take a different turn. I don't want her overhearing anything about my arrangement with Emerson.

"Daddy, can we hire her?" Bristol asks before I have time to pull my daughter aside and ask her what she thinks of Lia.

"When can you start?"

———

Hiring Lia was a good decision. She's only been with us a few days, but already Em seems not to be so overwhelmed. While she accompanies the nanny to school in the afternoon for pickup, with Mitchell on the premises, it gives her the morning free to herself.

But she's insisted on still being there in the afternoon, which I find oddly satisfying, like she wants to be in Bristol's life. Yes, I know it's just a job —she's hired to protect my daughter—but I can't help but think maybe she wants to be here too.

And with that realization, it dawns on me that Emerson's not going anywhere. She's here to stay, at least while the threat remains on my family and she's my fake girlfriend. If I'm honest, I could drag it out. I rather like having her attention on me, as if I'm the only one in the world who exists.

I'm a selfish bastard for making her play the role of my girlfriend, but it'll be so worth it. Especially tonight at the charity event.

Mitchell comes waltzing in through the front entrance, carrying a garment bag in one hand and a shopping bag in the other. "Mr. Greyson," he says, announcing his presence.

I can see him over the banister from upstairs. I knew the minute he opened the front gate that he was on his way inside, but I appreciate what he was trying to do.

I glance at the garment bag. "Everything go okay at the store?" I don't need any surprises.

"Perfectly. I have what you requested for this evening."

"Great, bring it upstairs." I gesture for him to come on up, and then I lead him to Emerson's room, having him hang the dress on the closet door and leave the shoes in the box on the floor nearby.

"Are you sure it'll fit, sir? You only have a few hours until the event this evening." He's more concerned than I am about the gown and shoes.

I snuck a peek inside her closet while she was away and contacted one of the designers I use to guarantee that the dress and shoes would fit Emerson.

There are some surprises I don't like, and not having the dress and shoes fit on the night of the event is one of them.

"It's fine, Mitchell. She should be back from the park with Bristol any minute." I dismiss him for the rest of the afternoon. He'll be required to drive us to and from the event this evening, and I don't want him getting tired behind the wheel or distracted.

The front buzzer wails and I grab my phone,

letting Lia inside. Unlike some nannies who live with their employers, Lia is more of a dayshift nanny. She helps with Bristol during business hours or when I have away games. There's an extra bedroom for her if she needs to sleep over, but it's not a requirement of the job.

I suppose some of the responsibility still falls on Emerson, but not nearly as much. Lia makes the meals, gets Bristol ready for bed, and, once she's asleep, is free to go so long as Em is home to take over.

It's an arrangement that seems to work for everyone. It gives Emerson more free time, and Bristol is ecstatic to have two people who adore her.

Emerson punches in the code at the front gate when they arrive back from the park. It's a short walk, a couple of blocks away, and with the weather being nice today, I'm happy to see Bristol get out and run around for a bit.

My phone buzzes with a visual of the two girls coming back from the park. I can't help but smile at the sight of them and shove my phone into my pocket. I need to shower and get dressed shortly for the gala, but I want to surprise Em with the gown and shoes that I picked out just for her.

"Hey," she says, opening the front door, surprised

to see me. I'm usually busy buried in the gym working out if I'm home and have a little free time. "No workout this afternoon?"

"I had practice with the guys this morning," I remind her. I'm still a little sore from the beating that I had on the ice the other day. The bruise on my face was nothing compared to the bruise on my chest from James.

I can't even remember when the beef between us started, but every time we're playing the Bruisers, he's always coming at me, and I'm nailing his ass to the wall.

The other day, it felt like we saw more of the penalty box than the ice. Seems neither one of us are willing to forget a grudge.

But the gala is tonight, and I'm grateful for the time away from work. I certainly intend to enjoy Emerson's company.

"I have a surprise for you," I say.

"For me?" Bristol's eyes widen.

"For both of you." I don't want to disappoint my daughter when the surprise is solely for Emerson. I tread carefully, wanting to make this into something fun.

"Oh, what is it?" Bristol's eyes light up, and she hurries over toward me excitedly.

The kid is spoiled rotten, but that's my own doing. I want to give her everything as long as she appreciates it.

"Lia is going to watch you tonight. I had Mitchell pick up some cookie dough so she can make you an extra yummy snack after dinner."

Bristol grins and taps her fingers together excitedly. "Yum!"

I'm relieved that the cookie dough is enough of a surprise to excite my daughter.

"Do you have a treat for me too?" Em asks, a faint smile playing at the corners of her lips.

"Actually, I do. But it's more the kind of surprise that you wear. Come with me." I take her hand and lead her up the stairs to her bedroom.

"What are we—"

Bristol is following on our heels, and Em keeps giving me a questioning glance with our little shadow in tow.

I open the door to her bedroom, and the garment bag is hanging obtrusively from the door.

"What's that?" she asks, glancing from the closet to me and back again.

"Open it," I say. I lean against the doorframe, a smug grin on my face as she saunters into her bedroom and slowly unzips the bag.

She gasps as she unwraps the dress from the bag. "Kyler, it's too much. You shouldn't have. I can't accept—"

"You can, and you will," I say. It isn't a question. "The charity event this evening is extravagant, and I need you looking the part of a hockey player's girlfriend. And it's no secret, my net worth. You can't attend in anything less stunning. It would reflect poorly on me."

"And this is the image that you want, of me, on your arm wearing this?" she whispers in awe.

"Yes, I want everyone staring at you," I confess. I want to make all the men jealous and the women envious of her. It shouldn't be difficult, considering how stunning she always looks in a simple pair of jeans or black leggings and a t-shirt.

"Crap. I'm going to need a pair of shoes—"

"Already done." I point at the box on the floor near the closet.

My daughter grabs the box and hands it to Emerson. "Open it," Bristol says excitedly.

Slowly, Emerson lifts the lid of the box, and I didn't expect her to be even more surprised. "Wow. You've really outdone yourself."

"And everything will fit," I say. I have no doubt she will look amazing in the ensemble.

"Try it on!" Bristol squeals with excitement, jumping up and down.

———————

Emerson looks exquisite. The gown fits her like a glove. It's tight in all the right places, which doesn't do me any favors as she struts down the staircase with her grand entrance.

We need to head out to the event, but I can't take my eyes off her body.

It's hard not to stare as the V-line of the dress dips down into her cleavage, leaving me with quite an eyeful. I'm a man. It's hard not to stare at her assets. I'll have to send an extra-large tip to the tailor who made sure the dress fit perfectly. I owe him big time.

"Is it too much?" Emerson asks. Her cheeks blush, and she pushes a strand of hair behind her ear.

"It's perfect," I whisper. I escort her outside, and Mitchell is waiting for us. He opens the back door, and Emerson slides into the backseat. I shuffle around to the opposite side to climb in beside her while Mitchell shuts her door.

"We're really doing this," she says and bites down on her bottom lip.

Mitchell pulls us away from the house. I glance back, knowing that Bristol is safe with Lia. The security system is armed, and if anyone should so much as open a window, I'll know about it.

I don't worry about Bristol at home. The concern is when she's outside, where I can't protect her.

I reach for Emerson's hand, and she forces a smile.

"You'll do fine," I say and offer a smile, trying to reassure her that she has nothing to worry about.

We can pull this off. We certainly did well with my teammates and friends visiting. Not that I expect her to get down on her knees and put on a show during the gala. Although, wouldn't that be something if she did? It would certainly make the headlines.

I shift uncomfortably. That's not the kind of press I need right now. Coach Malone has been on my ass for showing up late to practice. I'm always on time for game day, but I've been stretched a bit thin before Emerson waltzed into my life.

Another reason I'm doing this gala.

It's punishment for me showing up late. Contractually, we're required to do a certain number of appearances per season, but I got shafted with doing a few extra big events. It's also a cause that I want to support, which is why I'm happy to be such a large donor for the gala.

I don't blame Coach for chewing me out and forcing me to attend this charity function. He didn't have a choice. Malone is a tough ass, but he's fair. It's the owner, Brent Fitzgerald, who has my balls in his grip, and he'd love to squeeze the fuck out of them to torture me.

You would think being a hot-shot hockey player would usurp the issues with Fitzgerald, but my contract is up at the end of the season. And he's got balls of steel when it comes to negotiating. He always gets what he wants, and if he thinks he can hire someone younger and cheaper, I'll be tossed aside.

It's not like I need the money.

I'm a fucking billionaire.

At least that's what everyone keeps saying, and they're not wrong. But I love being on the ice, and playing professionally is a dream come true. And now that Jasper has finally made the team, I don't want to leave the Ice Dragons.

I'd pay to stay on the team.

Fuck. I've lost my mind.

I'm madly in love with the sport. I feel at home, alive, when I'm on the ice. The tension before a game, the adrenaline while on the ice, the screams of the crowd when we make a shot, it's freeing.

Like nothing else in the world exists.

Besides, New York is my home, and the team is my extended family.

So, I'm doing my best to impress Brent Fitzgerald tonight, who will be in attendance. And flaunting my gorgeous fake girlfriend in his face will hopefully make him realize I have the support he tells me I desperately need.

And he's not wrong.

I do need a support system. Depending on my cousin isn't fair to her. She has a family of her own. And my brother can't help anymore now that he's on the team.

"Are you okay?" Em's voice pulls me from my thoughts as she squeezes my hand beside me in the vehicle. "Nervous?" she asks, trying to guess what's running through my head.

She has no idea about Fitzgerald and how his brother and I are rivals on the ice. But James isn't here, just Brent, the owner.

I shift to face her, forcing a smile. "Cool as a cucumber."

She raises an eyebrow, unconvinced.

"How the hell do you do that?" I ask with a laugh.

"Do what?"

"The eyebrow thing. You have to teach me."

She releases her grip on my hand, smiling faintly, and she pushes an errant strand of hair behind her ear. Her hair has been curled, and she has the top part secured in a fancy clip at the back of her head.

She looks absolutely stunning.

I can't keep my eyes off her, and my gaze dips down to her cleavage. Because I'm a man, and her breasts are one of my favorite parts of her body. I try not to leer. I don't want to be *that* guy, the creepy perv who can't control himself.

But she makes me feel like a giddy schoolboy with a crush.

And I do not intend on her ever finding that out.

"I don't think it's something I can teach." She laughs, and her shoulders relax as she nudges me. "Do you want to check the cameras and make sure Bristol is safe?"

I shouldn't be surprised by her level of concern, especially since I've taken her away from Bristol for the evening. I retrieve my phone from my pocket and open the app, shuffling through the video feeds until I find my daughter sitting on the sofa watching a movie, a bowl of popcorn in her lap. I added a half dozen new cameras for inside the house when we hired Lia.

"I think we hired the right nanny," I say and nudge her right back. "Can I tell you a secret?"

She rolls her lips together and nods, her eyes wide as she stares straight into my soul. I'll have to share her tonight with the world, but right now, she's mine and mine alone.

"Bristol isn't the only one in need of a bodyguard."

"What?" Her voice catches in her throat. "I thought you hired me because of the connection to her mother and—"

TEN

EMERSON

I SWEAR he's trying to give me a heart attack. Leaving Bristol alone with Lia wasn't exactly easy. Is that how it feels like for first-time mothers to leave their child with a babysitter?

Bristol isn't my daughter, but it's my responsibility to make sure that she's safe and protected.

Kyler leads me effortlessly out of the vehicle. His hand is nestled at the small of my back. His scent is strong and masculine, and I try not to make it obvious that I want to lean in and take a strong whiff.

What the hell is wrong with me?

I still can't get Kyler's words out of my head that his daughter isn't the only one in need of protection.

From the moment I laid eyes on him, I suspected there was more to it than the story he'd told the Eagle Tactical team.

He's been leaving out details, and I can't do my best to protect him if I'm left in the dark. But right now isn't the time or place to argue and demand answers. There are cameras everywhere, flashing lights, and reporters asking questions as we shuffle inside.

I've always seen the red carpet on television, but I never thought that once in my life, I'd step foot on the plush velvet under my heels.

"Smile," he whispers into my ear. "Pretend that you like me."

"That's a tough sell," I say, leaning in and planting a soft, chaste kiss on his cheek.

He smirks and tugs me closer as the cameras around us flash over and over again, taking in the sight before them.

I try not to give an awkward look, but I'm not used to being in the spotlight. I knew what I was getting into when Kyler suggested that I play his girlfriend, but I didn't think quite so far ahead to realize I'd be in the spotlight with him.

Imagining his arm wrapped around my waist or

my hand on his arm as he escorted me to fancy events was the most I envisioned.

Kyler turns his head, his gaze on me as he dips me back and plants a long and firm kiss on my lips.

I'm startled by the gesture. His mouth doesn't loosen, and his lips tease mine apart. Slowly, my mouth parts, granting him entrance as his tongue glides in past my lips. The world around us seems to melt away.

His hand remains planted at my lower back, keeping me secure to him before he lifts me back to my feet.

I'm sure my cheeks are flushed, and the cameras catch every glimpse of it. What will the headline tomorrow read? Something embarrassing, undoubtedly.

Kyler leads me inside, past the paparazzi, and into the gala. It's being held at the Metropolitan Museum of Art, a private function after dark, allowing only those invited guests inside.

I can't imagine what it cost to host something quite so extravagant.

To say I'm impressed is an understatement. The event alone is probably more than I'd make over the course of a decade.

Okay, maybe that's a little over the top. It seems

like a million-dollar event, but what charity would spend that much to bring in more money? That would be insane.

"Do you want a drink?" Kyler asks, his hand remaining at my lower back as he escorts me toward the bar.

"Yes." I've never been quite so excited to get something to help loosen me up. The atmosphere is regal, and I don't feel the least bit like I belong.

My gaze scours over Kyler. He shifts, a bit uncomfortable in the stuffy suit he's adorned for the night, but he looks handsome as hell. And dare I admit that if another girl so much as looks at him, I'd feel a twinge of jealousy.

I suppose I'm lucky I get to play his girlfriend. It'll keep the vultures away. Won't it?

Kyler escorts me to the bar. "Pick your poison," he says with a smirk.

My eyes narrow with a faint smile, and my grin widens when I see the list of suggested cocktails. They all have ridiculous names for the event.

"I'll have a Code Blue," I say, curious to try the blue cocktail featuring rum, blue Curacao, coconut cream, lemon juice, and pineapple juice.

"Defibrillator," Kyler orders for himself. "Someone has to save you."

My breath catches in my throat, and his stare feels like he's undressing me. Flustered, I glance at the drink menu and discover what his defibrillator features—gin, champagne, and orange liqueur.

"I thought that was my job?" I grin, trying not to show that I'm way out of my league at this type of event. The bartender hands us both our drinks, and I take a sip, the sweetness masking the alcohol.

"To our first date together," Kyler says, holding up his drink for a toast.

"You do know this isn't a real date," I whisper, keeping my voice down so that only he can hear me.

Kyler shrugs and clanks our glasses together. "Feels pretty real to me." He takes a swig of his Defibrillator, and somehow, he doesn't even manage to wince.

Just the smell of it is overpowering and bitter.

"I want to show you off and make all the guys on the team jealous," Kyler says.

Before I have time to object, he wraps his arm snuggly around my waist, pulling me close against him.

I breathe in his scent, and my arms wrap around him, my fingers tangling in his hair.

He invades my personal space, and his lips come crashing down onto mine hard. He backs me up several steps, pushing me against the wall as his fingers inch the hem of my dress higher.

"Kyler," I squeak, my voice betraying me. I don't need to give everyone a show or let them see that I'm not wearing underwear.

"Ever since you put that damn dress on, I can't stop thinking about what's underneath." Kyler nips at my neck, leaving a mark, claiming me.

"I'll give you a hint; it's nothing," I say with a smirk.

His hands are rough and callused, his body firm against mine.

The pads of his fingers trail higher over my thighs as his eyes widen. He pins me with his stare, wanting silently to know if I'm playing him.

Everything inside of me aches for Kyler. My body hums with electricity, but we can't do this here, not with eyewitnesses and vultures with cell phone cameras.

He growls against my neck, and I try not to moan. "I want you so bad right now, Em."

Butterflies fill my stomach, and I inhale sharply. "We should greet your teammates," I whisper, trying to keep this from getting out of hand.

I want Kyler, but not here. Not where cameras

will get an eyeful, and we'll be the front page gossip for the tabloid magazines.

He pulls back, his eyes dark as he stares at me. "You're right," he says. Like he can read my mind, and he knows now isn't the time to fool around, even if we both want it.

He walks me over toward the team.

All the guys are in suits and ties. They clean up well for the event. Freshly shaven, hair trimmed, showered, and impressive. "You remember Jasper," Kyler says, reintroducing me to his brother.

"I never forget the face of a man whose ass I kicked," I quip with a wry grin.

Jasper's gaze tightens, and he smiles, but it doesn't seem as forced as one might expect. "I let you win."

"You really didn't," Kyler says, slapping his brother on the shoulder. "But I still love you, bro. Even though you got your ass kicked by a girl."

Jasper's face turns bright red, and he hightails it to the bar without another word.

"He's pissed at me." Kyler shrugs and doesn't seem to let it bother him.

Is that what brothers do, fight all the time? I have a younger sister, Amber, whom I don't see often enough. I should call her and get together. She lives in the city.

"Coach," Kyler says, wrapping his arm around my shoulders. "You haven't met my girlfriend, Emerson."

"Malone," the coach says, holding out his hand to introduce himself.

"It's nice to meet you," I say, forcing a smile. Kyler doesn't appear tense around his coach, which I suppose is good news. But I don't quite fathom why he needs me here tonight. Where is the threat? Or is it just because he wants the media to eat up the fact that he has a new girlfriend?

"You should be mingling, Greyson," Malone says. "Fitzgerald is already in a mood, and you guys standing around isn't going to help matters."

"He's always in a mood," Owen, one of his teammates, says. I recognize him from the party Kyler had at the house.

"At least he hasn't been riding your ass all season," Kyler says, glancing at Owen.

"There are plenty of other teams to play for," Owen says. "You don't have to take his shit."

"No, I suppose I don't." There's hesitancy in his gaze. His words evoke confidence, but having learned to read people, there's something that Kyler Greyson isn't saying.

What is keeping him in New York? Is it his brother?

Glancing around, my stomach tightens, and I sway on my feet at the sight of Brad Clemens. My stomach flops, and nausea rears its ugly head. He was the leader of the initiation when I joined the FBI. Getting me drunk and taking me home was part of his game.

Bile rises to my throat, and my cheeks burn.

I still hate him for taking advantage of me. But most of all, I hate myself for letting it happen.

Guilt. Anger. Humiliation.

It all resurfaces with one glance in his direction. He took everything from me, my friends, the bureau, and my career that was just getting started.

I was stupid to file a formal complaint.

What I thought would be right only made everything a thousand times worse.

Every friend at Quantico, I discovered, was nothing more than a colleague. They turned their backs, even those who were caught up in the initiation and had been victims. They didn't want to be tied to the same scandal that burned me.

"Emerson." Brad stalks right up to me, his wife

on his arm. He doesn't appear the least bit bothered by the fact that he's slept with both of us.

Although only one of us was conscious enough to let it be consensual.

I remember bits and pieces. Biting down hard on my bottom lip, tasting blood.

She, on the other hand, looks like she sucked a lemon before being dragged over. Not that I should be surprised, I told her what her husband did to me.

Her one-word response on the day I showed up and told her what a dirtbag her husband was and what happened between us.

"And?" she asked, staring up at me like she was waiting for more. As if his forcing himself on me wasn't enough.

Like I was looking for something from her.

Kyler stands taller, if that's at all possible. He wraps an arm possessively around my hip and presses his lips to my temple, making it known that I belong to him.

I want to relax in Kyler's embrace, but I probably look more like a deer in headlights and stiff as a surfboard.

"Brad Clemens," the douche introduces himself, "I used to work with Ryan." He holds out his hand to Kyler.

Kyler pauses a beat, casting a quick glance at me before shaking the douche's hand. He doesn't so much as tell him it's nice to meet him, and while Kyler doesn't know much about my short past with the bureau, he must sense my discomfort. "Kyler Greyson."

"I know. I've seen you on the ice," Brad says. "It's quite impressive what you guys do out there, getting the shit kicked out of you and going back for seconds."

Kyler is steaming and holding me tighter, possessively, like he can read my mind, which I know is impossible.

"Just part of the job," Owen says, chiming in when Kyler doesn't say a word.

The two men are having a stare-down, and I can't help but wonder who will blink first. Or maybe one of them will growl.

It feels a bit animalistic, the heat between them. Kyler pulls me closer, and Brad flinches, his nostrils flaring as he takes in a deep breath of air through his nose.

Brad's wife, Ainsley, tugs on his arm, quietly gesturing that she wants to move on and probably mingle with anyone else.

I don't blame her.

I'd prefer Brad to get lost too.

Why the hell did he show up tonight?

Ainsley doesn't meet my stare, her gaze landing anywhere else.

My stomach roils. How could Ainsley still be with him after I told her what happened? Clearly, she didn't believe me. Just like my friends, former colleagues, and the rest of the bureau.

It was his word against mine.

"Brad." Ainsley's voice is soft as she tugs on his arm. "Perhaps we should meet with some of the other guests?"

Brad flinches and nods curtly. "Of course. It was nice seeing you again," he says, his gaze landing on me.

I don't say a word because if I do, I know I'd tell him off and give him the finger. The minute he turns away with Ainsley and heads in the opposite direction, I exhale a heavy breath I hadn't realized I'd been holding.

"Asshole," Kyler growls a bit too loudly in Brad's direction.

"Excuse me?" Brad spins around, having overheard Kyler's remark.

Kyler lunges at Brad, but Coach Malone jumps

in, along with Owen, to intervene before there's a full-blown fight breaking out at the gala.

"Walk away," Malone shouts at Brad, pushing him backward and in the opposite direction. Ainsley is right on Brad's hip, pulling him farther from Kyler.

"What the hell was that?" Owen asks, stealing my question before I have the chance to voice it.

"Nothing," Kyler huffs under his breath.

"Doesn't look like nothing to me," Coach Malone says after Brad takes the hint and heads off in the opposite direction. "I don't know what the hell is going on, Greyson, but now is not the time to be starting shit with cameras around. Go take a walk."

Several guests have their phones in hand, and I can't help but wonder how much of that interaction was recorded and will be uploaded to the internet.

Kyler grumbles under his breath, releasing his hold from me as he storms off in the opposite direction of Brad. I clear my throat, force a smile, and hurry after him.

He storms out through a back exit, and I'm seconds behind him, following him outside.

The door slams shut behind me with a thud.

There's no way Kyler knows about Brad. I never told him. And while it became watercooler gossip at the bureau, Kyler never worked there.

"What the hell was that?" I ask, catching up to him.

His jaw is terse, and his arms are folded across his chest as he paces the length of the loading dock.

"Nothing."

His demeanor tells me he knows. "Who told you?" I glower, stalking closer to Greyson. "Who the hell told you about Brad?"

"No one had to tell me he was a creeper. His eyes were on your rack during our introductions. Is he the reason you dropped out of Quantico?"

I shift the weight on my feet. "I didn't drop out," I clarify. "I quit."

"Same difference."

"It's not." I'm appalled that he thinks I didn't make it as an FBI agent. I passed Quantico and had a badge and gun. I was an FBI agent for a few months before I botched it by going to the office of professional responsibility. Yeah, all they gave a shit about was covering their own asses and his.

"So, you slept with him," Kyler says, scowling. He drops his arms to his sides. His hands ball into fists.

"Not willingly," I say, as if to excuse my own actions at the time. "I was drunk. I don't want to talk about it."

"He raped you?" Kyler lunges for the entrance

back into the party, and I grab his arm to keep him from losing his shit.

"It was—a bad night. I don't really remember much of it. Maybe I encouraged him before we ended up in bed." I'm making excuses, even though I don't believe the words coming from my lips, but I don't want Greyson to end up arrested for beating the shit out of Brad, even if he deserves it.

Kyler pins me with his stare. His fingers reach mine, intertwining our hands together. "It's not consent unless it's enthusiastic and you're both sober. He should have respected the fact that you were inebriated."

"He's the reason I was drunk. Hell, I didn't even want to drink," I mutter, chewing on my bottom lip. "It was some stupid initiation with the new hires, and that jerkoff was buying all of our drinks, insisting we drink and fuck our superiors or wash out. I went along with it until I told him to stop, and then—" I glance away, tears glistening in my eyes.

"I'm going to fucking kill him." Kyler heads back inside, yanking the heavy door with ease as it flies open.

"Kyler, wait. No." I hurry after him.

I'M LITERALLY SEEING RED. You know the expression; when someone gets so angry all they see is red.

That's me right now after hearing about how that asshole forced himself on Emerson.

She deserves so much better than what that prick did to her and the damage to her career. I knew she left the bureau, she hadn't kept that a secret, and I'd done a tiny bit of digging online to find out why, but most of the dirty laundry had been swept under the rug.

Her reputation had been tarnished by an accusation of sexual harassment against her boss.

The fucking liar tried to destroy her because he

couldn't keep his dick in his pants. My hands ball into fists as I storm back into the gala.

I don't care that there's a party going on with cameras around and the paparazzi are just outside the door.

None of it matters.

I stalk inside and come face-to-face with that chick who had her arm linked with Brad, now shoving her tongue down Noah's throat.

"For fuck's sake!" I yank him off her, shoving him back against the wall.

"What the hell, man?" Noah's eyes flicker, and he pushes me forcefully backward. I stumble but catch my footing.

She clears her throat and saunters off down the hallway like she didn't just get caught sucking face with a member of the hockey team.

"She's married!" I shout, as if that's the worst of it, because it's not. But I can't bring myself to say the words aloud. They're not even mine to bear.

Since when did Noah start sucking faces with married women? He met her husband; it's not as though he wasn't aware she wasn't on the market.

"She cornered me," Noah says, holding his arms up in surrender. "I just went along with it."

"You and your dick." I scowl at him. "Keep it in your pants. There are reporters everywhere."

"Outside, sure. What's gotten into you?" Noah glances past me, presumably at Emerson. "Everything okay in romancelandia?" he jokes.

"Just peachy." I reach behind me, grabbing hold of Emerson's hand, and I tug her to follow me past Noah and back into the crowd. My gaze darts around, looking for Brad, which I know is a bad idea, but I can't stop myself, either.

"Kyler, I didn't confide in you so you'd start a fight." Her fingers graze my cheek, bringing my gaze down to her stare.

Her eyes are glistening, and she tugs her bottom lip between her teeth. There's a smear of blood. It's small and tiny, but I hate seeing Emerson hurt herself.

My thumb grazes her lips, and the longer I stare, the calmer I feel. Like she's a siren, and she's lulling me into the harbor. Except she's not going to make me crash, she wouldn't do that. She's protecting me.

"What was all that about?" Em asks as she sizes me up. Her gaze moves over me with a questioning glance, and I stand taller, trying to shrug off her concern.

"Nothing."

"Nothing doesn't result in shoving your teammate," Em says. She's on point, but how can she not be pissed about what she saw?

"She's married."

"And he's a prick," Em says pointedly. "I'm not excusing her behavior, but you have no business getting into fights with your friends over a girl who isn't your concern."

"It wasn't about the girl," I say a little too quickly.

She nods knowingly and does that cute thing with her one eyebrow raised above the other. "You can't go assaulting Brad or your teammates over what happened. Your friend doesn't deserve it, and he's a big boy. If he wants to make out with a married woman—"

"I don't like seeing my friends get played," I say, clearing my throat. "And she was using him."

Her tongue darts out to the side, and she offers a quick nod of understanding. She doesn't argue with me, and I take that as a win, at least for tonight.

Leaning in closer, my lips brush against her ear. "Do you want to get out of here?" I ask.

"Don't we have to mingle or something?" Emerson asks.

She's right. We've barely made introductions with anyone other than the guys on the team and

Coach. If I leave now, I'm risking renewing my contract, which is up at the end of the season. I have to play nice with Fitzgerald, who I thought was worse than that FBI asshat with a pole shoved up his butt, until I found out what he did to Em.

And now, I'm not keen on introducing Fitzgerald to Emerson, mostly because of Fitzgerald's reputation. I'm not afraid of losing Em to him, I'm more concerned about how he'll treat her, and I'll be stuck between a rock and a hard place when he hits on her. Because undoubtedly, he will.

She looks fricking gorgeous tonight. What man wouldn't stare at her perfect tits?

And while I'm sure she can handle herself, she shouldn't have to be ogled and harassed by decrepit men.

"Fine," I say, relenting because she's right. I want to stay glued to her hip. I wrap my arm around her waist, keeping her close to me, my lips brushing against her ear every so often as I lean in close to make sure she can hear me over the crowd and live band.

Brad glances in our direction and turns on his feet, heading the opposite way. Good, it's one less pig to deal with again. If he so much as glances at Emerson again, I'll knock his teeth out.

Another reason to stay joined at the hip with Emerson. If I let her out of my sight, he'll pounce like the animal he is. And I don't want anything happening to Em.

"Anyone we should mingle with first?" Emerson asks. She scouts the room, but I suspect she's also reading the crowd, getting a feel if anyone poses a danger.

I shouldn't have doubted her at first sight. Just because she's petite doesn't mean she's not fierce. It makes her the perfect undercover candidate because no one would suspect that she's former FBI and a trained agent.

What else has she been trained to do?

I lean in close, stealing a whiff of her perfect vanilla and hazelnut scent. I try not to swoon from the smell as she has the uncanny ability to make me rock hard. "Have you ever killed a man?" I ask.

"What?" She laughs, her eyes widening. "Where is that question coming from?"

Emerson shifts slightly, sizing me up. There's a wry grin on her face, and I can't tell if she's nervous or appalled by my question.

When I don't answer her, she smiles and shifts back into my embrace, letting me hold her for the world to see that she belongs to me. My arms instantly wrap around her waist, my fingers at her hips. Possessively, I hold her, touch her, and press her against me to hide the growing bulge in my pants.

"I've never been in the position while working for the FBI that I've had to kill anyone before," she says with a soft sigh.

There's a sense of dread, of discomfort in her tone. Anyone else might miss the disconnect, but I hear it a mile away. "And before you were an agent?"

"I protected my sister when we were younger. I don't want to talk about it," she says and spins around in my embrace. She wraps her arms around my neck and leans in on her tiptoes, trying to meet my lips. I'm still several inches taller than she is.

I know this routine, trying to silence me with a kiss. I'm not an idiot. I'm a hot-blooded male who would gladly take her distraction and use it to my benefit. I let her kiss me and pull her closer as our lips brush against each other.

It's chaste at first, but that doesn't last for long. I press my tongue at the entrance of her lips, and my fingers tug at her hips. Her lips open, granting me entrance, deepening the kiss. Her body is like a flow of hot, molten lava, burning and exciting me. There's no denying she makes me hard, and while I don't need the entire gala witnessing my erection, I don't mind Emerson feeling my secret pushed up against her belly.

Someone clears his throat beside us, and I feel a rough pat on the back. I hate breaking apart from Em, but I don't feel like there's much of a choice.

"Jasper," I grumble, not the least bit surprised to see my brother interrupting us. "What?" I bark.

"Don't bite off my head," Jasper says, a wide smirk on his face. He's not the least bit afraid of me. The guys probably sent him over to disrupt us. "Fitzgerald just arrived."

"Of course, he did," I mutter. "Who's head has he chewed off thus far?"

"No one. He's saving his coyote teeth for you, big brother."

"Jackass."

"Save it for Fitzy." Jasper grins and smacks me on the back.

I'm no longer hard, which is both good, it won't embarrass me, and bad, I no longer have the distraction of Em's body pressed tightly against me.

"Do you want me to stay with you or disappear for your meeting with the owner?" Em asks. Her hand falls into mine, and she gives it a prominent squeeze.

While Fitzgerald is a huge douche, I refuse to let Em out of my sight. After what she confided in me about Brad, I need to protect her. "You're coming with me," I say, dragging her with me. "We'll make this quick."

Em forces a smile, and I'll do everything I can to protect her, but I also need this contract, which puts me in a tight spot. Not that I'm willing to pimp Em out to get it. On the contrary, I need Fitzgerald to believe I've got a girlfriend who's serious and who will take care of my daughter.

He expects every man with a kid to have a wife. Someone to stay home with the kids while his men are on the ice.

Fitzy is an old man with caveman ideals. That is, if cavemen were running around playing hockey all day. Even so, he's an asshole with the contract that I need signed in his hands. So, I pretend to play the part that he so eloquently wants to keep me in the game.

It's not as though any other team won't have me. They probably would, but I like where I live, I want stability for Bristol, and my brother is on the same freaking team. How much luckier could I get? Finally, I have everything I could ever want. And I don't want to chance it all disappearing.

Right?

"Greyson," Fitzgerald says, his gaze cross, and he sneers up at me. He shoves his hands into his designer pants, an ensemble that shows his worth with his crisp suitcoat tailored with perfection. It's the only thing perfect about him.

He's got a hell of a crooked nose, and I can't help but wonder who did that to him and when? Another player? Someone in his younger days? Perhaps it was more than just one man who beat the shit out of him. He certainly deserves it.

"Sir," I say, forcing the words out past my dry lips. "This is my girlfriend, Ms. Ryan."

"Ryan," he says, glancing her up and down, slowly and methodically, like he's undressing her with his gaze. His jaw is slack, hung agape as he takes every inch of her in with his mind.

I feel like he's fucking her with that disgusting glare, and I step forward, chest held out, ready to shout at him to avert his stare, when Emerson squeezes my hand and forces a smile. "I've heard so much about you, Mr. Fitzgerald. It must be such an honor to have one of the most talented players on your team."

She's good.

His tongue darts out, and he swipes his lips

before letting out a huff. "You call this guy talented?" He jabs a thumb in my direction. I can feel the insults brewing before he even releases the first one, and I bite down hard on my tongue, my jaw terse to keep from fighting back. That's what he wants, isn't it?

"Greyson is past his prime. And when he is dedicated on the ice, he's too busy thinking about that rugrat at home. The kid is a distraction. I don't get why the mother isn't in the picture, raising the little imbecile like a mother should be, but it's nice to see he has a girlfriend willing to do a mother's bidding."

"Excuse me?" Emerson drops my hand, folds her arms across her chest, and steps closer, coming face-to-face with him.

She's a spitfire, my Em, and something about her boldness makes me hot and horny for her. Thankfully, my dick is managing its ability to stay in check.

"Do you not speak English? You've got a nice set of tits, but no one was talking to you, *sweetheart*." Fitzgerald snorts disgracefully at Emerson. "Greyson, keep your woman in line." His attention is on me, ignoring the brunette as if she no longer exists.

I pull my arm back to land a blow to Fitzy's face when Noah and Owen jump in, each throwing an arm around my shoulder, keeping me from making a career-ending mistake.

"This nice set of tits," Emerson says, stepping closer and leaning up to meet his beady stare, "belong to a woman with more class than you could ever have. I suggest you take a course or two on sexual harassment before you end up with a lawsuit on your hands. By the looks of it, you have plenty of money that could make this set of tits even better." She smirks and turns, stepping on his foot with a grin. "You coming, Greyson?"

I'm dumbfounded and speechless by her remark, but my grin doesn't seem to vanish. "You really stood up to that pompous ass."

"Someone had to. I hope it won't hurt your chances at a new contract for next year." She bites down on her bottom lip. "Did I go too far?"

"You were perfect," I whisper, leaning in and brushing her lips with a searing kiss. "I want to take you home."

"In an hour. Do your mingling, and I'll manage on my own for a bit."

"You're leaving me to deal with these vultures?" I'm shocked that she thinks she can disappear without being harassed by wealthy old men looking to stick it to a hot, young girl. She's fresh meat to these guys, like a virgin ready to be sacrificed. And I'm not letting anyone near her, even if she can fend them off herself.

"Oh, come on." Emerson grins. "You'll be fine. There are plenty of cameras and security. Just stay inside. I want to check the footage back at your place and make sure Bristol is safe and in bed by now."

"Shouldn't that be my job?" The staff brings out hors d'oeuvres and champagne flutes, and we're in the way as they shuffle on by us. I back Em against the wall, helping the staff by keeping out of the way. I swear I'm not trying to cop a feel, but it's difficult not to get hard being pressed up against her.

"You need to worry about your hockey career and making sure everything is golden before we leave. Even if that means another round with your favorite vulture," she teases.

I groan. "Please don't make me talk to Fitzy again."

"If you don't, I will."

She'd better be joking, because if Fitzgerald comes anywhere near Emerson, I'll put her over my shoulder and carry her ass out to the car.

TWELVE
EMERSON

WE KISSED QUITE a bit on the night of the gala. It's not as though we haven't fooled around in front of his friends, like the time I dropped to my knees and gave him a blow job at his house. But that was all part of the plan, wasn't it?

Well, maybe not the blow job, but making out with him and pretending to be a couple. It just went a little farther than expected. He's hot, and our hormones got the better of us. Completely normal.

At least, that's what I keep telling myself.

But when we're not in front of spectators or potentially on camera for an audience, we keep our distance.

And the gala was six days ago.

He hasn't been so much as within arm's reach, physically, for nearly a week.

And I hope his avoidance doesn't have anything to do with Brad. I hadn't wanted to tell Kyler the specifics of my leaving the bureau. He wasn't like Brad. Jaxson had assured me that what happened at the FBI would not happen with his men or any of his clients.

And I can't stop thinking about when Kyler's lips grazed mine or when his cock poked into me. It's just a physical reaction, nothing more. Right?

He doesn't actually want to be with me. That's ludicrous.

He could have any girl.

And I'm not the girl NHL players chase after or fantasize about. I'm lucky he even suggested we fake date. Not that I feel very lucky. Our schedules mean we barely cross paths with one another. When he's home, he's practicing every day with the guys or at the gym training.

His schedule is rigorous, and Lia seems a bit confused about why I'm always around, but she hasn't said anything to suggest that I shouldn't be accompanying Bristol to the park or at home when she returns from school.

I corner Kyler late after one of his games when

he rolls in smelling clean, like almond soap. I'm sure he had a shower after his match, but the scent rolls off him, and I can't help but take a step closer, wanting to breathe him in.

"We need to talk," I say.

He laughs half-heartedly like he's nervous.

Do I make him nervous?

"Nothing good ever comes from those four words," he says.

"What's really going on between you and the owner?"

He drops his bag at his feet and cocks a grin. Like whatever he'd been caught doing went unnoticed, and he's relieved by my line of questioning. What am I missing?

"He's a dickwad. You met him. Tell me I'm wrong."

Kyler isn't wrong, but I don't think that's why he's playing the fake relationship angle. "You're a billionaire. Why do you care so much about the contract to play for *his* team? You could play anywhere. Hell, you could buy your own team!"

He glares at me to keep my voice down and grabs my arm, dragging me with him into the library. He flips on the light and shuts the door behind us.

Is he really that worried that his daughter or the nanny might overhear the conversation?

"Money isn't everything, Ryan."

I bite down on my bottom lip. "Of course, it's not. But it helps. What's going on?"

Why the hell is he referring to me by my last name? It's impersonal, like he's trying to add more distance between us when we're just inches apart. He drops his hold on my arm, and I let out a soft sigh, disappointed for the break in contact.

I shouldn't care that he isn't touching me.

This relationship is one hundred percent fake.

He doesn't want me.

He could never want someone like me.

"Tell me I'm wrong, that you're not a billionaire," I say.

He shuffles his feet, staring down at the floor. "It's more complicated than that."

"How so?" I push the issue, wanting to know what the hell he means. I've seen his net worth when the Eagle Tactical guys dug around to make sure there weren't any skeletons in Greyson's closet.

"I don't want it. I'm giving it all away."

I cough, clearing my throat. He can't be serious. "You're what?"

He glances up at me, his eyes darkened and

fueled with passion. "I don't deserve a cent of it, so I'm giving it away."

"To whom?" I can't believe him. Why didn't Jaxson or one of the other guys tell me when they ran background on him?

"Does it matter?"

"It does if you're being blackmailed." Why else would he have handed over more than seven figures?

He steps closer, breaking the distance between us. "I wasn't being blackmailed," Kyler says. His gaze twitches, and I can't quite read if he's lying or just holding something else back.

"No one gives away that kind of money willingly."

"I do," he says. "I don't deserve it."

I grab his hand and pull him to the sofa, forcing him to sit beside me. "What do you mean you don't deserve it?" I shift on the sofa to face him, giving him my undivided attention.

"I mean, all it's done is lay a huge curse on my family since landing in my account. My cousin immediately got a cancer diagnosis the day I cashed the funds. Two weeks later, my brother fell off a ladder and nearly killed himself. Then, the following week, my daughter was in the hospital for nine days with pneumonia—"

"Those things happen. They're a part of life."

Does he really believe he's cursed?

"I lost every game, Ryan, until I started giving the money to charity. The childhood home that Jasper and I grew up in burned down, my car was stolen, and on the last date I went on, she stole my credit card and went on a shopping spree while posting pictures that she photoshopped of the two of us together on the internet."

"So, you got a stalker and had a string of bad luck."

"Oh, I'm not done," Kyler says. "There's more—"

"You feel guilty. That's understandable. It happens with lottery winners—" But I can't fathom why he feels guilty.

"That's not the same thing," he says, clearing his throat. He stands, unable to sit still, as he begins pacing the length of the room. He's uneasy, his hands bunching into fists at his sides as he speaks. "I earned the money, every cent, but money doesn't equate to happiness. And the more that I acquired, the worse things got. So, I began donating it to charities, like the gala you attended. I hosted the fundraiser."

"You paid for the gala?" I try to hide my shock, but I'm sure it's evident all over my face. "That isn't your responsibility, Kyler. It's wonderful that you want to help, but it shouldn't all fall on your shoulders."

"I know, and that's why it was an event to encourage other donors to help fund the children's wing at the hospital," he says. There's a weak smile on his face. "I've met those kids, and I'm telling you, every cent I've donated is worth it."

"That's wonderful," I say, staring up at him. "Does that help alleviate the guilt?"

"Of course not. The money I used to acquire the wealth was from my share of my parents' life insurance policy. When they died, I got drunk and stupid. I tossed it all on a gamble with digital currency. Turns out, it blew up, and I became stupidly rich."

"And what about Jasper?"

"He kept his in a high-interest savings account until he was old enough to buy a house. But do you think I let him use his money?"

"So, you let him use yours, the cursed money?"

"Hell, no! The money that I've earned from hockey, it's helped pay for his place, education, and living expenses. I'm not giving him cursed funds. What kind of a monster do you think I am?" He runs his hands through his hair, clearly frustrated with the situation.

I can't help but smile. "The generous kind?"

He glares at me, and I can't help but stand and stalk toward him. "And what about me?"

His brow is furrowed, unclear about my question. "What about you?" Kyler shakes his head, waiting for me to elaborate.

"The money you were giving me to play your girlfriend. Is that money cursed?"

He smirks and glances away. "Maybe. But I'll find a way to pay you—"

"I don't believe in curses, Kyler. And you shouldn't, either. I think it's generous that you want to donate all your money to charity, but don't do something you might regret. You have a beautiful house and a daughter who goes to a private school, and you'll want to fund her education when she goes to college. Those things cost money."

"Bristol will be taken care of. It's why I need the contract with Fitzgerald to go through for next year."

"Does he know about the curse?" I ask, trying to see things from Kyler's point of view. If Fitzgerald realizes that Kyler is desperate to stay with the team, then the jackass could easily take advantage of him.

"It's not something I go around advertising," he

says. "But he picked up wind of it from Coach Malone. He overheard Malone telling me I'm out of my fucking mind for giving it all away."

"I have to agree with your coach on this one," I say.

He huffs, and his nostrils flare. "You haven't seen what that money can do, Ryan. How it tears people apart."

I step closer, reaching for his hand. My fingers tangle with his. "Your parents were already deceased when you chose to invest that money. It was yours," I say, reminding him that he wasn't stealing something that didn't belong to him.

"I know, but I was also seeing someone, and she became interested in what I could buy her, a car, a penthouse suite, anything she could get her hands on made her magically tell me *I love you*. It was disgusting."

"They have a name for that, gold digger."

"But she wasn't like that when we started dating. She was actually really good with Bristol and helped me change diapers and was there for me—"

"Until she wasn't," I say, cutting him off. "Any chance she could be holding resentment? Could she be behind the threats to Bristol?"

"She'd never hurt my daughter. Bristol was like a

daughter to her." He pulls away from me and opens one of the books, retrieving a half-torn piece of paper with a note written in blue ink. "This isn't in her handwriting, but it's the reason I need you to keep Bristol safe."

Kyler,

Make one wrong move, and your little Bristol will meet the same fate as your parents. Lose the next six games, or pick out a casket for your little one.

X

I inhale a sharp breath. "How long have you had this note? Why the hell didn't you show it to the security team you hired or to me?"

"It was only six games. I couldn't take a chance that someone would hurt Bristol." He folds his arms across his chest. "We play eighty-two regular games a season unless we make the playoffs. Losing six sucks, but it wasn't going to kill our record."

"Until they ask you to lose more." I study the lettering, the note, and the way the pen bleeds against the paper. Someone took their time penning such a simple threat as if they were trying to disguise their handwriting. "It makes sense that the mafia would be behind something like this," I say.

"Why, because they're involved in illegal activities like gambling?" Kyler doesn't look nearly as convinced. "We still have dinner with the Morettis coming up, and I doubt either one of them has ever seen a hockey game in their life."

"Doesn't mean they don't run a gambling ring and want to ensure they're keeping the odds in their favor. Is this the only threat that you've had against Bristol?" I wave the paper at him, still dumbfounded that he kept this from me. By now, he's played dozens of games, and he's lost more than half of them. I can't help but wonder if it's been on purpose.

"There may have been more. I burned them," he says, glancing away from me.

"How many more?"

"There's practically a new one every week, instructing me to throw specific games."

"And you've been following through with his orders? How am I supposed to help you if you're keeping secrets from me, Greyson?"

"I didn't ask for your help. I hired you to keep my daughter safe in case this wanker decides to go after Bristol even though I've followed his orders."

"You could get kicked out of the NHL if anyone knew what you were doing."

Kyler steps closer, backing me up against the wall. "No one can find out. If you tell anyone, Ryan, we're done. You won't get a cent."

"You think that's all this is to me? Money? I'm trying to protect Bristol. I can't do that if you're not honest with me. Jackass," I mutter, smacking him on the arm as I push him out of the way and storm out of the library.

"We're not done, Ryan," he says, calling after me, expecting me to do as he pleases.

Well, he's got another thing coming if he expects me to fall in line like his teammates. He may be the captain of his team, but he's not bossing me around.

"We're done." I storm out of the library, and he grabs my wrist, pulling me back to face him. His hands land on my hips, keeping me from moving out of his grasp.

If I really wanted to slip from him, a swift kick to his groin would have him toppling to the floor. But I don't feel threatened by his presence. He wouldn't hurt me.

"This isn't over," he says, his gaze darkened and his grip rough against my skin. "You don't get to walk away from me because you don't agree with what I'm saying."

"I'm pissed that you are more concerned with keeping secrets from me than letting me protect your daughter. All this time, I could have been helping look into the threats. Instead, I've been going at this like the only real threat is the mafia!"

"I'm sorry. I should have told you—"

"Save it." I hold up a hand, not ready to hear his apology. "You're right. You owe me the respect of being honest. If you want me to protect Bristol, I need to know everything."

He nods slowly and takes a step back, releasing his hold on me.

"Do you have any other threats that you've saved? Anything on your cell phone?" I ask, waving the piece of paper at him.

"Just that one note is all that I kept."

"And how are they being delivered?" They mustn't be coming to the house, or else the security cameras would have captured the footage.

"They're always hand-delivered to my private mailbox at the arena."

"They must be sent via courier unless it's someone on the inside—"

"It's not," he answers a little too quickly. "My teammates would never threaten my daughter, nor would anyone else I conduct business with, and I've tried the courier angle."

"What do you suggest? Threats don't arrive by carrier pigeon."

He huffs, not pleased with my brand of snarkiness. "There are hundreds, if not thousands, of employees who have access to our mailboxes. Nothing is locked, it's all open and available for anyone to tamper with, and there aren't any cameras. I've checked."

"Someone knows how to play detective," I mock.

His lips land hard on mine, crashing against my mouth, silencing me. I open my lips to protest, and he only takes it as further encouragement, his tongue pushing its way inside.

Kyler's hands graze my hip, pulling me closer, the pads of his fingers teasing the hem of my shirt, grazing my bare skin as he inches the material higher.

Fuck, the man knows how to kiss.

His lips move a path down my neck, sucking the sensitive skin that drives me absolutely weak at the knees.

"Stop," I say, and it's the only word he needs to hear. He yanks himself back, blinking down at me, his breathing heavy and ragged.

"Shit," he mutters, taking a step back. He runs a hand through his hair, flustered. "I didn't mean to take advantage—" His face reddens, and he backs himself against the wall, trying to get as far away from me as possible.

"You didn't," I assure him. He's not Brad. He's never done anything to hurt me or force me into anything I'm uncomfortable with. And he stopped the moment I told him to, but he's also my boss. I work for him. "But this isn't going to happen, Greyson."

I need to put up a wall between us, making it clear that this can't occur unless it's part of the job, pretending to be in love.

Because if we keep kissing, it won't be pretending. Not for me.

"Right." He shakes his head like he's clearing the cobwebs. "No audience. No making out. My mistake." He takes a step this time for the door, like I'm fire, and he's too close to getting burned by the roaring flames.

Before I can say anything further, he's out of the library, down the hall, and gone. He hasn't left the house. The cameras haven't alerted me that anyone has come or gone from the residence, which means he's probably up in bed, which is where I should be.

My own bedroom.

But I'm not tired.

Kyler has a way of making me wide awake at the

most inopportune times. I'll have to be up early tomorrow to investigate the note and figure out who might have a grudge against Greyson. The threats could be anyone, from some mobster running a gambling ring to an addict trying to get rich by betting on Greyson's team losing a game.

Did I mention I hate hockey?

THIRTEEN
KYLER

EMERSON IS AVOIDING ME. Is it because I kissed her while we were arguing, or because she's pissed at me for hiding the stupid letter?

She's asleep, or at least in the shower, every time I try to get a word with her, but it's near impossible to get a moment alone with her. And Lia isn't exactly helping. She's been going to Emerson for advice on what to make for dinner or if she should take Bristol to the park after school today.

Bristol is my daughter. The nanny should be coming to me, not Em.

But Em has been around more than I have lately. It's like the two of them are becoming friends, and I'm not sure I like that—they both work for me.

I wait for Em to emerge from the shower, sitting

on her bed. We have a game tonight, so at least I'm not going to be late for practice.

The shower turns off, and I'm silent, not wanting to alert her that I'm waiting for her in her bedroom. She won't be thrilled, but if she's going to avoid me, then I'll do whatever is necessary to get five minutes alone with her.

The bathroom door squeaks open, and steam emanates from behind her as she steps out in only a towel. Her hair is wet, dripping down her shoulders, making her skin glisten.

"Kyler! What are you doing in here?" She clutches the towel tighter across her chest.

If only she'd drop the towel and let me ravish her. We both need it; the sexual tension between us keeps growing. I shift against the bed, hoping she doesn't realize how hard I am for her.

"We're having a home game, and I want you to come—in the stands. I want you there." I feel like a teenager all over again, blabbering and nervous. It's not like she hasn't seen my dick when she was sucking me that night the guys were over.

I should have another night with the team over if that's what it takes to get her down on her knees. It was pure heaven. She knows how to use her tongue and throat. I groan when she interrupts my thoughts.

"Fine. I'll be there. Get out!" She points at the door, wanting me to leave.

I take my time, slowly standing from the bed as I waltz toward the door. My dick hardens as I steal another glance at her over my shoulder.

"Can you move any slower?" she huffs with wide eyes. "Out. Now!"

———

Once again, the feisty brunette avoids any time alone with me. She's focused on her tablet, which gives her access to all the security cameras and anything else that she needs.

Bristol has the day off from school, and Lia is on her tail, making sure she's changed, fed, and cared for. She's attentive to Bristol's needs, which is incredibly important, while she doesn't have the faintest idea about the threats to our family.

"Mr. Greyson," Lia says, closing the fridge after grabbing the carton of orange juice. "When I picked up Bristol from school yesterday, her teacher mentioned you're supposed to have dinner with one of the other parents."

"Right. I'll have Em call and schedule the dinner for our place."

Emerson glances up at me, one eyebrow raised higher. How the hell does she do that?

"Are you sure that's wise? It might be better if we go out to eat," Em says, glancing briefly at Lia. She's trying to talk around the nanny and not alarm her about the Moretti family.

I highly doubt the Morettis are the ones threatening me, leaving notes behind for me to fall onto. It's not like the mafia to leave a threat unsigned. I'd expect them to hand deliver it or, more likely, make the threat to my face.

This leaves me pondering who the hell is behind the threats to my daughter. I've never been involved in any gambling rings or met with any bookies. Jasper is just as clean. The boy is a saint. He spent his years after Mom and Dad passed away focusing on school, his grades, and hockey.

The threat is coming from somewhere else.

I glance at Lia and give a forced smile. "We'll follow up with them and make dinner arrangements. Thank you for bringing it to my attention."

Lia gives a puzzled look but shrugs it off and helps Bristol clean up after breakfast.

Em seems to sense Bristol and Lia are getting ready to leave the kitchen, and she grabs her coffee and tablet, prepared to follow after them. I appreciate her shadow-like abilities, but they're safe inside my home.

I grab Em's arm, not letting her disappear just yet. "Tonight, I want you at the game."

"I know. I heard you after my shower. I'll be there. In the meantime, I need to make a few calls and find out what I can about that note." She glances me over. There's a look of disappointment that crosses her features. "You should have told me sooner."

I lower my voice to keep the echo down to a minimum. I don't want Bristol or Lia to overhear the conversation. "I told you what you needed to know. I did what I needed to do to keep my daughter safe."

"We could have put all of this behind us a whole lot sooner if you'd have just turned over the note and let me investigate its origin."

"And you'd have been at the hockey arena instead of keeping your eyes on my daughter. Bristol is the priority. Send whatever you need to Jaxson and his team. But your responsibility is protecting my kid."

Her gaze tightens, and her tongue swipes across

her top lip before jutting out slightly to the side. "You don't have to remind me how to do my job. I know what I was hired for."

"Good." I steal her fresh cup of coffee, untouched, and take it with me outside. I need some air and a few minutes away from Emerson.

"Bastard," she mutters under her breath on my way outside.

I choose to ignore her remark, stepping out and shutting the door behind me. I need to get my head screwed on for game night.

————

I don't see Emerson again before heading out to catch up with the team before the game. Bristol is at the park with Lia and Em. I'm sure they're fine, but I really wish I'd installed some sort of tracking device on the nanny and my fake girlfriend's phones.

At least if something happened to them, I'd know their last known whereabouts.

"You seem distracted," Jasper says, pulling me aside in the locker room. There's a lot of noise and commotion, the team getting ready to take on an undefeated champion for the season. "Is it because the guys are groaning about our last four losses, and we're about to get our asses kicked?"

I'm not looking forward to playing the Island Bruisers. Every time we play their team, James and I get into it on the ice. We throw insults back and forth as often as the puck, and we both end up beating the shit out of each other until we get thrown into the penalty box.

I don't want Em or Bristol to witness that tonight.

I huff at his remark. "Hell no. We're not going to lose tonight. Em's going to be in the stands."

"You didn't give her tickets to the private box?"

I glance at my younger brother. "No. I want her to experience the game like it's meant to be."

Jasper grins. "Do you even know if your girlfriend likes hockey?"

I avoid his question, unsure about the answer. Although she's never really swooned over the fact I play for the NHL or the sport, and I can't even recall her asking me a single question about hockey.

"I want her to see me up close," I say, smacking him on the back. "She can't do that from those private boxes."

"Right." Jasper's eyes narrow as he studies me. "Is Emerson really your girlfriend? I mean, I know the whole nanny act was a cover. Is that what this is too?"

Fuck. If Jasper doesn't believe that Em is my girlfriend, then no one else is going to believe it, either. I have to convince him, no matter the stakes.

"Are you asking because you want a piece of her? Because she's mine," I growl instinctively. The thought of him or anyone else so much as taking her out on a date makes my stomach knot and my hands bunch into fists.

Jasper tosses his hands up into the air. "Just checking, bro. She's cute, but the two of you haven't really been seen at any after-parties, and she hasn't been invited to the wives' room. I assumed parties weren't really her thing, but the guys talk—"

"You've been talking about Em?" The room feels several degrees hotter, and I scour the room. "Who else?" I want to know what they've been saying about *my girlfriend*. Even if it's fake, no one else knows the truth.

Jasper shrugs and shuffles his feet, avoiding the question. "Just the guys." He doesn't give me a straight answer, and I grab him by his jersey, shoving him up against the wall.

"Who?" I growl.

"Whoa!" Noah shouts as he jumps between us,

pushing me back and keeping me from pelting my brother.

Owen jumps in, protecting my little brother. He's twice the size of Jasper and not the least bit apologetic in his tone. "Save it for the ice," Owen says. "If you're going to break someone's neck, do it to that asshole James Fitzgerald."

"Walk away, Greyson," Coach Malone says.

Coach refers to most of us by last name, especially when he's pissed at us. But given that I was on the team before Jasper, I'm Greyson. And Jasper is always Jasper.

There's no question which one of us he's referring to, and I let out a huff before heading out of the locker room for a beat.

I don't expect anyone to follow me, but a minute later, the doors open from behind, and I hear heavy footsteps.

"A word." Coach Malone is standing there, arms folded across his chest. "Do you want to tell me what the hell is going on? Or should I ask your baby brother?"

My top lip twitches at the mention of Jasper being my *baby brother*. Tell me something I don't already know. I've helped raise that kid since our parents passed away. I've looked out for him. I helped make sure he got a fair deal when he got drafted.

I trudge back toward the coach, wanting to keep this between us. "It's nothing," I say and glance away. It's hard to ignore the steely gaze of Coach Malone. "I'll walk it off."

"You'd run laps if it were up to me, but I need you in game shape in under an hour. Get your head screwed back on, Greyson. If this is about your daughter—"

"It's not," I say and breathe a sigh of relief. Bristol is at home with Lia, and I don't have to worry about either of them because I know without a doubt that the security system is top-notch, and if anyone came within several yards of the house, I'd be notified, as would Emerson.

"Then it's about the girl." Coach Malone's eyes tighten. "Is your brother in love with her or something?"

"I'd kill him if he were," I growl a little too quickly, and Malone's gaze widens.

"Don't let some girl come between brothers. There are a lot of fish in the sea, Greyson."

"She's not just some girl," I say, and I inhale sharply at the realization that as much as Emerson gets under my skin, it's because I want to be around her. I think I might actually be harboring real feelings for her.

He smirks, and his shoulders sag as he glances me over. "Is that so?"

"I'm just not sure she realizes that yet, how much she means to me. Can I—" I glance at his wedding band. It's plain and simple, and yet it would be perfect for a ruse. "Can I borrow your wedding ring?"

Coach Malone squints at me, fiddling with his wedding band. "Are you sure about this, Greyson? Don't be stupid over something your little brother said or did."

"This isn't about him," I say.

The guys clearly don't realize I'm serious about Em, and if I can't convince them that our relationship is real, how am I going to convince the rest of the world?

FOURTEEN
EMERSON

"WHAT THE HELL do you wear to a hockey game?" I glance over my shoulder at Lia and Bristol in the doorframe, waiting on me to hurry up.

I've tossed open every drawer in my bedroom, pulled apart the closet, and left clothes scattered on the bed, floor, and hanging over the bathroom door.

"A jersey," Bristol says, matter of fact. She's wearing an Ice Dragons hockey jersey that's a little big but clearly a youth size. That won't work for me. I have nothing to wear.

"Did you check Mr. Greyson's closet?" Lia asks.

"No," I gasp. Lia and Bristol part ways, letting me hurry across the hall.

They both follow close behind as they watch me tear apart Kyler's closet.

"I don't know much about hockey," Lia says as she opens his dresser drawer and pulls out a jersey that I'll be swimming in, "but this jersey definitely has the NHL logo."

Bristol's eyes widen, and she bites down on her bottom lip before grinning wildly. "You should definitely wear that. Dad will—" She snaps her mouth shut, and I hurry into his bathroom and close the door.

I slip into the jersey and wear black leggings to go with the ensemble. Lia has helped put everything back into place in Kyler's room. Although he'll know I borrowed the jersey, I'm sure he won't mind.

"Are you sure these are for the same team?" I ask, glancing at the different emblem and colors.

"It's vintage," Bristol says. "Dad always goes on about how the old jerseys were so much cooler. Trust me. You'll make him blush."

I glance from Bristol to Lia. "What has gotten into her?" I laugh and pull Bristol to me for a hug. "You'd better be right."

Lia hurries out with Bristol ahead of me. I shut and lock the house, climbing into the vehicle and letting Mitchell take us to the game.

"Are you sure you guys are ready?" Mitchell asks, glancing at us in the rearview mirror.

"It's game time," I say with a wry grin. The hockey game hasn't started yet, but I'm looking forward to it.

Mitchell shrugs and pulls away from the house, taking us to the arena.

Bristol is seated beside me, and Lia is up front, having a nice and quiet discussion with Mitchell. I can't quite make out what's being said, but they're having a good laugh.

"Who is playing the Ice Dragons tonight?" I ask. I know next to nothing about hockey, but I'm looking forward to watching Kyler on the ice. Actually, seeing him play, it's a bit exciting, not that I want to admit that to him.

"The Island Bruisers," Mitchell says. He laughs under his breath. "Maybe I should get a ticket and join you guys in the stands."

"You should. Kyler would love to see all of us there, cheering him on."

Mitchell shakes his head, but I can hear the laugh as he pulls up near the stadium. Traffic is heavy, and there are lots of people crossing the street, heading for the stadium. "You'll want to check in at the box office. Show them your I.D., let them know you're with Kyler Greyson, and they'll have seats available for the three of you."

"You're not coming?" I ask, surprised. He sounded interested moments earlier.

"I would love to see Greyson's face, but I don't want to be blamed."

"Blamed?" I ask. He pulls up out front near the box office, and we climb out of the vehicle. Bristol takes my hand, walking beside me.

Lia is a few feet behind me, and she gasps.

"What? Do I have toilet paper on my shoe or something?" I ask, glancing back at her.

"Holy Mackerel," Lia gasps.

"Nice save, but that was an intended curse. You owe the jar back home one dollar," Bristol says.

"She drives a tough bargain," I say, glancing at Lia. We hurry up to the front as the line moves fast, and within a matter of minutes, I have three tickets in-hand and three VIP lanyards with golden tickets.

"You can't—we have—oh my gosh." Lia is trying hard not to cry from laughter.

Bristol glares at her. "Shushy your facey."

"That's not even a word." I glance at Bristol. "What has gotten into the two of you? Did you guys punk me? Is this a jersey for another team?" I can't see the back of the jersey, but the crowd thickens, and we're pushed forward toward the entrance.

I show our tickets, and they scan all three, letting

us inside. We follow the signs for our section, and Lia grabs me before we make it down to the floor. "You should probably look to buy a jersey with Greyson's name on it."

"He would like that a little too much," I say with a laugh, and grimace, realizing I'm supposed to be his girlfriend. Of course, I'd have a jersey with his name on it.

Shit.

Lia seems way too kind or unsuspicious; I'm not sure which it is. If she suspects anything between Kyler and me isn't real, she hasn't let on.

"Can I have popcorn?" Bristol asks, pulling me in the opposite direction of the stand with the merchandise.

"Of course," I say.

After the snacks and drinks are handled, we head down to our seats, which are directly behind the team bench.

It isn't long before the game starts, and the players come out onto the ice.

There's a panel of glass between the team and us, and Bristol climbs onto her chair, waving at her father. "Daddy!" she squeals excitedly.

While on the ice, his focus is entirely on the game. I'm not sure he's even seen that we're in the stands, but that's probably for the best. I don't want to be a distraction to him.

I'd love to get Kyler alone for a moment and find out if there were any more recent threats sent to him or if he has any other suspects in mind about who might want to hurt his daughter.

There is plenty of security at the arena, and sitting just behind the bench with glass between us, I don't get the feeling that anyone from his team is involved. But there are plenty of others who could be responsible.

Bristol leans against the glass pane, shoving her face against it, making faces at the players in an attempt to get their attention. Most of them are too busy focusing on the game, but Noah is on the bench and gives a smile and waves to Bristol.

She waves back excitedly and spins around to face me. "Did you see that? Noah waved to me."

Before I have time to answer, Noah is pointing at me and shaking his head in dismay. "What the hell are you wearing?"

"It belongs to Greyson. Take it up with him," I shout back.

Noah grins. "I know. We gave it to him as a joke. You're not supposed to wear the other team's jersey.

He's going to kill you when he sees what you have on."

I exhale a hearty laugh. "I guess it's a good thing I'm behind the glass." I tap the partition and give a little wave when Kyler skates by, a frown on his face when he catches a quick glance in my direction.

Greyson shouts something, but he's gone long before Noah or I hear whatever it is that's on his mind.

"I'm telling you, take that off before he loses his fucking mind," Noah says, glaring at me. "You can't be supporting the other team!"

I scoff at his suggestion. "I'm not a—whoever they are—fan."

"Bruisers," Noah says. "And you're wearing their jersey like you're in support of them."

"I'm not a fan. It was the only jersey I could find. Why the hell would you give him this as a joke?" I ask, pointing at it.

"Swear jar!" Bristol says, pointing at both Noah and me. "One dollar each!"

"Oh my gosh," I groan. "Hell isn't even that bad of a word."

Bristol's jaw drops. "Two dollars! No arguing."

The kid is all sass; I give her that. "Fine, when we get home, I'll put two dollars into the jar."

"You too, Noah. You owe me a dollar."

"How about I buy you a soda?" Noah asks.

Bristol shakes her head. "I know you and Daddy get stuff for free. Besides, I can't buy a unicorn with a soda."

"Huh, a unicorn?" Noah smirks and shakes his head. "Good luck," he says, staring at me.

I'm not sure if he's referring to the fact that Bristol is six going on sixteen or that the jersey I'm wearing might start World War III.

Noah heads onto the ice when Kyler skates off and to the bench. The coach is blasting him about missing some easy play, but honestly, I can't imagine any play is easy.

Did he miss on purpose? Was there another threatening letter left behind for him, instructing him to throw the game?

It's not a question I can ask here where anyone might overhear us.

Greyson grumbles and glances over his shoulder at me. "Are you trying to make me bleed?"

"What?" I ask.

"You're cheering on the Island Bruisers?" Greyson's eyes are wide. "I can't believe my girlfriend is supporting the other team."

"This is your shirt—" I refrain from calling him *dumbass*, although it does cross my mind.

His eyes widen, and he gestures for me to spin around. It's not a dress.

"Not happening," I say. What's the big deal?

"Take it off," Kyler says, and his top lip snarls. "My girlfriend isn't wearing *that* tonight."

I laugh nervously. "Yeah, that's not a good idea."

"And wearing a jersey for the Bruisers is?" he snaps.

"I'm not wearing anything underneath." That's not a complete truth. I am wearing a bra, but I don't think everyone would appreciate me removing the jersey, and quite frankly, it's a bit chilly only to be wearing a bra and leggings.

He shoots a look at Lia. "Go buy my girlfriend something else during intermission."

"That isn't necessary," I say.

"Daddy, I told her to wear it." Bristol beams, giving her thousand-watt smile at her father.

He laughs. "You, little devil, are the reason that the guys are giving me hell?"

"Always," she says and blows her daddy a kiss. "And another dollar in the swear jar!"

We both groan in unison.

Kyler glances behind him at the guys and the

game. "This isn't over. Go put that jersey on inside out."

"Not happening. Take your jersey off, and I'll wear that one." I'm joking, but if he wouldn't get in trouble, he'd probably take it off and toss it to me over the glass partition.

"You're trouble, Ryan."

"I know, and you love it."

There's commotion on the ice, and Kyler shuffles around to watch the action. Hopefully, the coach won't give him too hard of a time for talking to us in the stands.

Several minutes pass before he's back on the ice, scoring goal after goal. He's on fire tonight until he gets into it with another player on the Island Bruisers' team. I can't see what's happening, with the guys standing up in front of us shouting animatedly.

Kyler is tossed into the penalty box along with the other player he was fighting. I glance at Lia.

"What's happening?" I ask her.

She shrugs. "It's a hockey game. Fights break out. It's common."

I hope she's right, but I don't like seeing Kyler fight with anyone. It makes me sick to my stomach.

The Ice Dragons are down, and the buzzer

sounds. The teams retreat to the locker rooms, and the guys on the bench head out.

"Is the game over?"

Bristol grins. "No, silly. It's intermission time."

"Oh. Like half-time."

"More like thirds."

Apparently, the kid knows her fractions. I try to play it cool, like the six-year-old beside me didn't just point out that she knows more about the game than I do. But for the record, her father is a professional hockey player. I'm sure this isn't her first game.

"Lia, will you take me to the bathroom?" Bristol asks.

"Of course. We'll be right back," Lia says and stands. Taking Bristol's hand, they walk down the aisle and up the stairs to the restrooms.

There's a lot of hustle and bustle. The Zamboni comes out and repairs the ice for the next period.

Standing, I stretch my legs as I catch sight of the coach heading back toward the benches. He's carrying something in his hands and grumbling under his breath.

"Ryan," he says, nodding at me.

"Yes, sir?" I'm not sure why I'm addressing him

quite so formally, but it comes out before I can say anything else.

He tosses a white, long-sleeved t-shirt over the glass at me. "Your boyfriend wanted you to have this. Go change before you wreck our game."

I laugh under my breath. "Seriously?"

"Do I look like I'm joking?" the coach asks.

I shimmy off to the bathroom. The line is out the door, and I don't actually have to pee. I just need to get changed. But at the current rate, I don't know how long the intermission is, but it's likely I'll miss the next part of the game if I'm standing in line.

Bristol is hopping from one foot to the other, seemingly attempting to hold her bladder. There are at least a dozen women ahead of them.

"I have to pee!" Bristol squeals. "Can I use Daddy's bathroom?"

"I don't think that's allowed," I say. I doubt security would let us into the locker room. While we were given VIP lanyards to wear, it's unlikely they're going to let us ladies into the men's locker room during the game. It's probably for a private suite or afterparty.

"Please," she whines. "I can't hold it any longer."

Lia frowns. "Sweetie, if we get out of line and

can't use the bathroom anywhere else, we'll have to start waiting from the back and start all over."

Bristol groans and wiggles, like the kid has ants in her pants. Her nose scrunches, and I swear she's about to start crying.

"Fine." I grab Bristol's hand and glance at Lia. "Do you want to take a chance coming with us or hang in this line?"

"It's moving, but it's slow. I'll just wait it out," Lia says. "If you can't find a bathroom elsewhere, maybe you can make it back here in time."

I'm not sure Bristol can hold it that much longer. The girl looks like she's about to burst, based on her potty dance. Which I thought was reserved for toddlers, but she's hopping from one foot to the other and grimacing the entire time.

"Let's hurry," I say, escorting her away from the bathroom. With one hand gripping hers and the other holding the white t-shirt that Coach Malone tossed at me, we hurry down the corridor and are stopped by a set of security guards blocking a back entrance.

"Sorry, no access," the taller of the two says. They're both big and burly. There's zero chance of skirting past them without being tackled. They could have been retired football players.

"We're VIPs," I say, showing him our badges. "And this little one has to use the bathroom."

The taller of the two laughs at her awkward dance. "Sorry, the team is in the locker room. I can't let you in while they're there during intermission."

"Daddy!" Bristol shouts over the roar of the crowd. Is she hoping he can hear her? We're not anywhere near the locker room door. We're at one end of the hallway, and it's at least at the opposite end, if not around a corridor. I can't quite tell from where we're standing.

The guard smiles at the little girl. "Who is your daddy?" he asks, bending down to her level.

"Daddy, obviously." Bristol rolls her eyes and snaps her fingers. "Tell him I need to see him."

The kid is all snark. I laugh. "Kyler Greyson is her father."

"You don't say." The guard chuckles. "I can see where she gets her attitude. And who are you?" he asks, glancing me up and down.

"Greyson's girlfriend."

"Isn't he lucky?" The guard grins. He glances at his buddy, who doesn't appear nearly as interested in conversing with the two of us. "Watch the post," he tells him and holds up a finger for us to wait.

"You could get fired if you interrupt them, Chris,"

the other guard says. He clearly has zero intention of helping us.

"Let me handle it," Chris says.

Bristol is still hopping and groaning, her nose scrunching, which would be adorable if she didn't have to pee quite so badly. I'm impressed she's managed to hold it as long as she has, given the circumstances. Truthfully, she probably would have been better off staying in line with Lia.

The guard stalks back, and in the distance, I can see him waiting outside the door. He doesn't knock. He just waits. How long does he plan on standing by the entrance?

It's only a few seconds before the door swings open, and Coach Malone steps out. Chris accosts him long enough to explain our story before pointing in our direction.

"Let them through," Malone says, gesturing for us to go on back. "You're going to have to cover her eyes," he warns, nodding toward Bristol.

With one hand gripping her hand, my other covers her eyes with the shirt.

"This smells like Daddy," Bristol says as we waltz inside the men's locker room. The guys are mostly geared up and ready to go back on the ice.

A few of them are lacing their skates and putting

on the final touches to their gear. I'm not sure why he insisted that I cover her eyes until we get to the bathroom with urinals and the shower is running. One of the players has his back to us, and there's not a lot hidden from view.

I usher her quickly into one of the bathroom stalls and slam the door behind her.

"Someone couldn't wait for the restroom upstairs," I say when the water shuts off for the shower, as if I'm trying to explain why I'm in the men's locker room with a kid.

I stand with my back to the showers, doing my best to give Owen privacy. At least, that's who it looked like from the quick glimpse I got while ushering Bristol inside.

"Where's the boyfriend?" Owen asks, his footsteps thudding over the floor as he approaches.

I'm grateful, when I glance warily in his direction, that he's wearing a towel around his waist. "I haven't seen him," I say. But I also wasn't looking for Kyler. My focus has been on Bristol and getting her to the bathroom without getting an eyeful.

"He's here," Grayson says, coming up from behind. "And why the hell are you still wearing that damn jersey?"

"Another dollar in the swear jar!" Bristol chirps from behind the closed bathroom stall.

"I swear, kid," he sighs and shakes his head. "Change shirts. Now," he growls, his eyes pinning me, making my stomach flutter.

"Umm, okay." I shuffle into an empty stall, not wanting any of his teammates to get an eyeful when I change. I'm quick, shucking the jersey in a matter of seconds. I pull on the white shirt and take a deep breath. Bristol was right; it does smell uniquely of Kyler.

It certainly beats the smell of the locker room, which isn't ideal.

Stepping out from the stall, Kyler grabs the jersey from my hands. "Did you think wearing this was funny?" he asks, flipping it around for me to see the back and all the scribbles and crude caricature drawings in thick black permanent marker.

"Oh my gosh," I gasp. "Bristol!" I can't believe Bristol and Lia let me wear that jersey out.

Bristol flushes the toilet and steps out to wash her hands. "What? It was funny. There's a penis on the back of the jersey!" Bristol giggles like it was the funniest joke in the world.

"I don't know how you even know what that is." Kyler shoots Bristol a pointed stare.

"You gave me a book about the birds and the bees, Dad. I'm six. I'm not a baby."

"Right," Kyler mutters under his breath. "Well, six-year-olds still need plenty of sleep." He glances at the clock on the nearby wall. "Where's Lia?"

"Upstairs, in line for the bathroom," I say.

"She should probably take Bristol home and tuck her into bed."

"Daddy, no!" Bristol wails, and I swear the entire stadium can hear her outburst. "I don't want to go home. I want to watch you play. Can't I stay for the whole game this time? Please?" She bats her eyes up at her father. They're wide and soulful, and I swear he's going to cave any second.

"No."

I'm surprised she doesn't have him wrapped around her little finger. "You can watch for a few more minutes, but before the next intermission, you ought to be on your way home."

We shuffle out of the bathroom, and the team is on their way back out. I escort Bristol out of the locker room, and the security guard stands outside the door, waiting for us.

"Thank you," I say.

We head back to our seats, and Lia is already

waiting for us. "I take it you managed to use the bathroom?" she asks.

Bristol beams with excitement. "Daddy let us use his in the locker room."

"Oh, is that so?" Lia asks with a laugh. She glances over at the new shirt I'm wearing. "I see you've changed."

I glare at Lia. "Yes, thanks a lot for letting me wear that jersey out in public!"

"I didn't actually see the back until we got to the arena," Lia admits. "And I suggested that we buy you something else, but someone distracted us with snacks." She stares pointedly at Bristol.

"Guilty!" Bristol says with a grin. The girl is cheeky.

"Kyler asked that you take Bristol home before the next intermission and get her tucked into bed."

"Of course. You should stay, see the full game and enjoy a little quiet time without us," Lia says.

I'm not sure I'd describe a hockey game as quiet, but I appreciate that she's offering to take Bristol back on her own, although I'm sure Mitchell will be chauffeuring them home. I text Mitchell and wait for his reply when he arrives.

The game goes by rather quickly, especially with Kyler on the ice for most of the period. He gets tossed into the penalty box again. I'm not sure who started the fight, but it's clear he's got an issue with a player on the opposing team.

The Ice Dragons manage to score three goals and are in the lead, but it's a relatively close game.

Mitchell texts a few minutes before the period ends, and I escort Lia and Bristol to the car. I don't want to risk anything happening to his daughter. I'm sure she's fine, but I prefer handing her off to Mitchell, who is capable of protecting Bristol.

Lia is sweet and great with Bristol, but I don't think she could fend off anyone dangerous. She's not trained in self-defense or combat. Perhaps I should suggest to Kyler that he send Lia to a course or two. Even I could teach her a few maneuvers.

I hurry back to my seat just as the second period ends. The team hustles back to the locker room, but one of the players heads toward me with a wink. "Greyson wanted me to tell you to come around to the bench and have a seat."

"That's allowed?" I ask with a nervous laugh.

He shrugs and smirks, not really giving much of an answer. Turning around, I glance at his jersey. *Jameson* retreats to the locker room.

I stand from my seat, and I have to walk up the stairs and back around by the locker room to join the guys on the bench. It seems weird, but this time I have no trouble at all getting through security.

The guard recognizes me and nods for me to head on back through the hallway.

There's hustle and bustle behind the locker room doors. I can hear the noise and camaraderie among the players.

No one stops me as I pass the locker room doors and head down to the bench by the ice. There are no guards on watch, and the players haven't emerged yet.

I hope this isn't some elaborate joke from Kyler's buddy trying to get me in trouble or embarrass Greyson.

A few minutes pass before the guys start to reemerge from the locker room. They took a shorter break since there's still eleven minutes left until the game starts.

"Hey, M&M," Greyson says with a grin when he sees me sitting on the bench. I straighten up, and my eyes widen, worried that maybe I shouldn't have listened to his buddy *Jameson*.

"We don't usually allow girlfriends on the bench," Coach Malone says and clears his throat. "But your man here had something he wanted to say during intermission."

I glance from the coach to Greyson, shaking my head, confused.

What is he talking about?

Greyson's wearing his skates and swings open the door to step onto the ice, giving me a look. "Are you coming, M&M?"

"Not if you keep calling me that." I laugh nervously. "And I don't think I'm supposed to just walk onto the ice."

He gives a half-hearted shrug. "They still have to Zamboni the ice."

"Did you just use Zamboni as a verb?"

The grin on his face widens. "You know more about hockey than you let on, M&M."

"Seriously, Greyson, that nickname has to go." I scowl at him, but I'm not the least bit mad. He takes my hand and guides me carefully onto the ice.

"I never asked, but do you know how to skate?"

"Now you ask? And not in tennis shoes." I feel my feet slipping, but he's keeping me steady, his arms around my waist. We're only a few feet from the door to the bench, which has now been shut by another teammate.

"Ice skating lessons for a future date," he says more to himself than anything else.

I don't remind him that we're faking dating, but

ice-skating lessons don't sound like a bad idea, mostly because the thought of spending time with Kyler makes my stomach flutter and my heart race.

I enjoy spending time with him, even if it's entirely related to the job.

"Right, planning our dates already?" I tease, and my feet slip, but he pulls me close. His arms wrap around my waist, and my arms instinctively move around his neck in an embrace.

"That's not the only thing I've been planning with you, Em." The way he says my name steals my breath. It catches in my throat, and I tremble in his arms. Is it the cold? My nerves? Maybe I'm just freaking out because there are thousands of eyes on us in the arena.

Except no one else hears his words. They're meant solely for me.

"Is that right?" Another nervous laugh, and I really wish I had my emotions under control. It's suddenly warm, and my cheeks are heated. I can feel the flush like a fever coursing through me.

Jasper skates onto the ice, carrying a microphone with him.

I glance between brothers.

What the hell are they up to?

Jasper skates off the ice, leaving Greyson in my

arms. He pulls back only slightly, making sure I'm not going to fall before he releases his grip from me. With one hand, he takes the microphone, and in the other, my hand is in his.

"Kyler, what are you doing?" I whisper, staring up at him with wide eyes.

There's a smirk on his face, fueled with passion and mischief, like whatever he's got planned, nothing and no one will stand in his way.

Shit.

My stomach does a belly flop.

"Kyler," I warn, and already, he drops to one knee, and I swear my eyes practically fly out of my head. "Get up," I whisper to him, and he chuckles.

"Not until you hear what I have to say." Those words are meant only for me. He brings the microphone to his lips. "Ladies and gentlemen. May I have everyone's attention, please?"

I can't speak, only stare at Kyler Greyson, my mouth agape and my eyes like two saucers. There's nothing pretty about looking speechless. A bug could fly into my mouth, and I'd still be standing there dumbfounded.

His eyes stare straight into my soul. I swear he's stolen my breath, and I blink rapidly before I realize I need to inhale and exhale, or I might pass out. The microphone moves away from his lips, again making it so that only I can hear him.

"I need you to say yes." He stares at me, his eyes boring into mine.

My head is in the clouds like a misty fog, and the moment feels incredibly surreal. "What?" I whisper, trying to comprehend what he's saying because my mind and my heart are thoroughly confused.

"When I ask. Say yes." It's like a set of instructions, a manual I have to follow, and I'm not even sure what the hell I'm building. Except I know. My stomach tenses, and my hands tremble because there's no other reason that an NHL player gets down on one knee during intermission and holds a pretty girl's hand unless he's asking her *that* question.

He brings the microphone to his lips. Everyone probably thought he gave me a sweet private speech. Instead, it was a list of his demands. Say yes. Okay, actually, one demand.

I should have asked for more money if I'm putting up with these shenanigans.

Kyler speaks into the microphone loud and clear, making sure everyone hears him. "Emerson Ryan, will you marry me?"

FIFTEEN

KYLER

THE PLAN WENT EXACTLY how I wanted it to, and then it imploded. Not the proposal. At least not publicly.

Em said yes, just like I asked her to before I made a formal proposal for all to see and hear. I wanted it to be the headlines on the news and in the paper.

I wasn't disappointed with her answer. And I'm sure that tomorrow, the news channels will be all over it. I'm pretty sure if I turned on the television to one of the sports channels, they'd be talking about it.

It was what happened after the proposal that has me dumbfounded.

She stayed for the rest of the game, insisted on

returning to her seat, and then Emerson high-tailed it out of the arena the minute the game ended.

Not so much as a goodbye. I headed off the ice to the bench, and she was gone. In the locker room, I texted Mitchell, and he assured me that he was taking her home.

I didn't want to read into anything. Traffic is always awful after a game. Maybe she wanted to get out before reporters tried to hound her with questions.

But when I stepped in through the front door, she was nowhere in sight. She's not answering her texts, and now she's locked herself in her bedroom, refusing to speak with me.

"You can't ignore me forever. I'm your boss." I knock once again on her bedroom door.

The girl is practically steaming when she finally throws open the door. Em folds her arms across her chest. "That was a dick move, even for you, Greyson."

So, we're back to a last-name basis. That isn't exactly good, but the guys on the team refer to me as Greyson, so maybe it isn't all bad. I'm trying to see the silver lining.

"Asking you to marry me?" I know it's fake, and

while my feelings for her are slowly becoming real, I pushed things too far.

"We should have discussed it first!"

"I like you—"

"You like your career," she spits back. "I'm just trailing in third." She slams the door in my face.

I'll let her sleep it off. Maybe tomorrow, we can have a genuine conversation, and I can apologize for throwing her off and making her uncomfortable with the arrangements. But she agreed to be my fake girlfriend. It's just one more step to proving we're an item.

And after seeing her today at the game, I want her there beside me all the time. I have no qualms about her bringing Bristol into the locker room today, but she wouldn't have had to do that if the guys knew I was serious about Em.

She hasn't been invited to the wives' room yet. It's reserved for the wives and serious girlfriends of the team to hang out. There's even a place for the kids to play, which would be great for Bristol.

But I can't just give her an invitation.

It's a sacred place among hockey wives, even though I'm the captain of the team.

Hopefully, by proposing, the ladies will see how serious I am about Emerson and invite her into their inner circle. I don't believe any of them would be behind the threats to Bristol's safety, but maybe they've seen or heard things.

The group, I've been told, is gossipy but also incredibly close and protective of their inner circle. And getting Emerson an invitation isn't an easy feat. I can't just ask them to invite her. It doesn't work like that.

I head off to bed, deciding that riling up Em any further isn't going to help. She's tired. I'm beat. A good night's sleep may fix things.

Could I be that lucky?

I strip down to my boxers and climb under the warm blankets. I try not to envision her curled up in my arms, but it's impossible. I still smell her on me, even after the game and the shower in the locker room.

Her scent is intoxicating, and it's invaded my senses from the inside out.

The kiss on the ice, the fans cheering, and her arms wrapped around my neck are imprinted on me forever. I could die a happy man.

If only it had been real.

If only the kiss had meant for her what it means to me. The proposal may be fake, but the feelings behind the attraction are one hundred percent real.

I'm not ready for marriage with Em or anyone else yet. But I want her solely in my life. No strings and no other attachments. The thought of her so much as looking at another man fills me with an intense rage of jealousy.

I toss and turn, unable to sleep.

And talking to Em isn't going to help put me out for the night.

She's mad, or at the very least, disappointed in me, which makes me feel a thousand times worse, because I do like her.

And not just as a friend.

I'm trying to bury those feelings, but the more time we spend together, flirting and talking, the more I see her for who she is, and I like it. I like her.

Fuck.

Did I screw up by pushing the fake relationship into a fake proposal?

Sleep eludes me. The clock on the bedside table taunts me.

My thoughts are entirely of Em.

Her body, her mouth. Her tongue teasing my cock.

Fuck, it's been too long since I've gotten laid. Having Emerson under my roof has been a distraction. The perfect titillating distraction who gave me the best blow job of my life until the guys interrupted.

I have wanted her since that night, but she's been distant, and I've had to focus on my career and protecting my daughter, which means keeping Emerson at arm's length. She's here for Bristol, not for me.

Talk about complicated.

Because a part of me wants her here for me, and it isn't a small part. It's my dick, and it's acting based on my heart, which is not the least bit logical for me.

I like Em, and I don't want to screw things up because, like she said, I'm her boss. But it's more than that with her. She's not just my daughter's private bodyguard. She means so much more to me, and she doesn't have the slightest notion of how I feel.

Because I haven't told her.

How can I, without screwing things up further? I've already made a mess out of what we have going on between us.

The clock reads half past three, and I'm not about to get any sleep when I'm restless and having thoughts of Emerson.

There's only one way out of this mess. And my

tenting boxers are indicating to me the obvious answer.

I keep my breathing as quiet as possible as I reach down inside and stroke my length. It's hard not to picture Emerson when we were on the ice together. Except for this time, I'm in control of the fantasy, and I have her wearing nothing but my jersey.

And I mean nothing.

It rides up, barely covering that pert little ass of hers, and I want to steal a taste, push her up against the glass, and drop down to my knees to tongue fuck her. I'd show her what it means to be with a real man. A man who worships every inch of her body and takes her over the edge repeatedly.

That's what she deserves, nothing less.

I imagine it's her hand on my cock as I pump harder and faster. Her name spills past my lips as I try to stifle the urge to control myself.

My breathing is labored and heavy. I should flip on the ceiling fan and do something to drown out the sounds coming up from me in the stillness of the night. But I don't care.

Let her hear me.

Warmth runs through my veins, and I wish it

were her wet tongue on my cock or her tight pussy trembling around me.

I imagine her sneaking into my bed, finishing the job.

"Emerson," I grunt, grabbing a tissue from the nightstand as I feel the flood of heat seep out of me.

But it's only my imagination as I'm trying to catch my breath. My eyelids are heavy, and finally, sleep wins over, but for how long?

The soft patter of footsteps awakens me, along with the light streaming in through the curtains. It's evidently morning. My alarm has yet to go off, but I'm certain it will soon enough. I roll over to ensure it's off before it startles me or anyone else.

I stumble out of bed, use the bathroom, yank on my boxers, and then head into the hallway to make a pot of coffee.

Emerson's gaze moves down my body. I neglected to put on anything else, half-asleep and too exhausted even to care. "You're in your underwear," she says, and her cheeks redden as she adverts her eyes.

"Pajamas," I correct her, but she isn't wrong. I'm not wearing a shirt, and if it were anyone else, I wouldn't be walking around in my boxers for the world to see.

But it's just Em.

Bristol is asleep, and the nanny didn't stay the night. She must have gone home once Emerson came in after the game.

"That's not pajamas." She laughs under her breath. "Do you make a habit of walking around in your underwear?"

Em does a decent job of meeting my gaze, not staring at my bare chest or my low-riding boxers. I can't quite read her this morning, which only makes me more puzzled. She could have just walked away or given me the cold shoulder, but I'm glad she hasn't done either.

Her cheeks redden as she holds my stare, and I've yet to answer her. I want her to look, to take it all in. I'm proud of what I have to offer her. And it isn't like she hasn't seen the goods.

Hell, she took it for a bit of a test drive.

My cock begins to stir at the heated memories of her lips around my shaft. Fuck, I cannot get hard while she's staring at me and things are finally getting back to normal after last night.

Hockey.

Pucks.

Fights on the ice.

I try to throw random hockey thoughts into my head to keep my dick in check.

"You shouldn't have proposed to me on the ice, not without first discussing it."

There's a chill in the air, and it's coming entirely from Emerson. That's one way to crush a man's ego and his boner.

Not that I thought it was a real proposal or that she was in love with me. But the kiss on the ice had been spectacular.

"Will you marry me?" I ask, holding the microphone with one hand and gripping her hand, staring up into her eyes.

She smiles and nods, and for a moment, it feels real. The happiness behind her gaze appears one hundred percent genuine, and if I didn't know any better, I'd think she was as ecstatic as I was.

I slide the ring onto her finger. It's a simple gold band and far too big, but she doesn't say anything about it.

I stand and wrap my arms around her waist, crushing her lips against mine. My heart pounds against my chest, the drowning of the crowd hushed by the heat building between us.

She opens her mouth, her fingers playing at the back of my neck, tangling in my hair as I deepen the kiss.

The world fades away, it's as though it's only the two

of us, and I pull her tighter, closer. My clothes are thick and hard between us, making it nearly impossible to feel her body against me.

But she doesn't seem to care or notice. Her tongue glides past my lips, and I want to explore every inch of her body from head to toe on the ice.

A loud thud jars us apart, and I realize I've dropped the microphone, forgetting it was in my fingers with her body pressed tightly against mine.

Emerson is staring at me, waiting for a response as to why I proposed without discussing it with her first. Because I knew she'd never agree to it.

"I was just emphasizing our fake relationship."

"You don't emphasize by proposing," she says. "Or by moaning my name in the middle of the night. Were you seriously fantasizing about me while jacking off?"

"Daddy, what's jacking off?"

Neither one of us heard Bristol climb out of bed and sneak into the hallway with us.

SIXTEEN

EMERSON

I COULD DIE OF EMBARRASSMENT. That is not an exaggeration. And if looks could kill, I'd already be dead from the death glares Kyler shoots in my direction.

I take it upon myself to answer, to try and minimize the damage. "It's when you're bouncing on the bed and jump off."

Bristol's eyes widen. "You were jumping on the bed without me, Daddy? You never let me jump on the bed."

I can't tell if he's relieved or even more agitated by my answer.

"And you're not going to start jumping on the bed. Emerson didn't literally mean jump on the bed."

"Then what did she mean?" Bristol asks with wide, curious eyes.

He groans and runs a hand through his hair. "I need to shower before practice. Can you watch her until Lia gets here?"

I force a smile, sliding the ring off my thumb. It was far too big for my ring finger, and whoever it belonged to, they probably wanted it back. "Of course. Come on, let's get you breakfast. Head on downstairs," I say.

Bristol hurries down the stairs. "Are you coming?"

"Just a sec," I call back.

I hand the ring to Kyler. "Next time, maybe don't use your finger to measure an engagement ring."

"Thanks," he says and palms the ring. "It belongs to Coach."

"I kind of figured it wasn't for me." I head down the stairs, not able to take the pain of staring at him, at the ring, at all of it, without feeling more than I should.

Why do I feel torn up inside when I know it's all an act?

He's always made his intentions clear that this is a fake relationship. I probably just need space to clear my head and collect my thoughts as far away from Kyler Greyson as possible.

Hurrying down to the kitchen, I get Bristol situated with breakfast and put on a pot of coffee. The surveillance system indicates that Lia has just arrived and is entering through the main gate.

The front door squeaks open. "Hi!" Lia calls out, announcing that she's arrived.

"Hi, we're in the kitchen," I say, grabbing a cup and waiting for the coffee to finish brewing before I pour it.

Half an hour later, my tablet pings, but it's not from Kyler leaving. It's an alert that someone is at the front gate. He's still lacing up his sneakers by the door.

It's not Mitchell because he's inside the property, waiting out front.

I grab the tablet and open the app to check the surveillance footage. It's a woman with dark hair, wearing a baseball cap and sunglasses. It's almost like she's trying to be inconspicuous, but it's not going over real well.

"Everything okay?" Greyson glances up at me when he sees me studying the tablet. He's got a cool exterior, calm and collected. Like he isn't worried, and I'm not sure if it's because he trusts me or he doesn't think the threat can touch him inside these four walls.

Well, he's wrong.

The surveillance isn't foolproof. It's helpful as an alarm system, but it's not about to shoot someone or throw stones at them if they breach the property.

My job is to protect Bristol and Kyler. Yes, he may have hired me solely to protect his daughter, but if they're both around, I intend to keep them safe.

"Know her?" I ask, showing the screen to Kyler.

She pulls back the shades and pushes the buzzer.

"Yeah, you can let her in."

That's all he says. Kyler heads for the front door and yanks it open. "There's no game tonight. Just practice."

Bristol hurries toward him to give him a hug and kiss goodbye. "Bye, Daddy!" she says, waving as he exits the front door and heads toward Mitchell.

He's out the door before I have time to ask who the hell she is. Well, I'm about to find out.

I step out onto the porch, not wanting this strange woman anywhere near Bristol. Even if Kyler isn't concerned, he hasn't answered any of my questions about who she is and what she's doing here.

She stalks down the length of the private driveway in heels. The woman is all class, but... Why the hell didn't she drive in past the gates?

She cranes her neck, getting a full view of the property before landing eyes on me. The brunette smiles, but it feels forced.

"Emerson, right?" she asks, glancing me up and down. She looks a tad disappointed by what she sees. I'm still in pajamas. I wasn't expecting visitors.

"Yes, that's me. Can I help you?" My back is to the house, keeping her from the front entrance, shielding Bristol and Lia inside.

In her right hand is an envelope, sealed with wax, and in calligraphy, my first name. She hands it to me and purses her lips. "If you decide to come, it's required that you wear your fiancé's jersey."

Without another word, she turns and heads back down the road.

I didn't even get her name. I wait until she's outside the property and the metal gate closes before sauntering into the house.

"Was that Kate James?" Lia is still peering out the window when I step inside. "She's Asher's wife. He's the enforcer for the team."

His wife isn't familiar, but I know Asher. It's my responsibility to know all the players, but their wives

I haven't studied up on because I didn't think of them as suspects. Maybe I should.

"What'd she bring you?" Lia asks, glancing at the envelope in my hand.

It's formal. Fancy. I carefully open the thick envelope to reveal an invitation to a private event hosted by the hockey wives.

"You have to go to that," Lia says. "And tell me everything afterward."

"I thought you weren't into hockey?" I frown, putting the invitation back into its envelope.

"My high school boyfriend used to blab on about the sport. I really don't know much, but she did a full spread in one of those scantily clad magazines, and I remember catching him—"

I nod vaguely toward Bristol, who is watching the two of us eagerly.

Lia's eyes widen, and she blinks repeatedly, shutting her mouth, perhaps realizing the conversation needed to end, and quickly.

"Let's get you ready for a fun day at the zoo," Lia says.

"What were you two talking about?" Bristol asks.

"It's time to get you upstairs and dressed," I say, changing the subject and trying my best to distract Bristol. The kid is smart, and I don't need her blabbering on to Kyler about anything she overhears.

I text Kyler while he's en route to the guys for practice.

Invitation received. She mentioned wearing your jersey. Should I grab one at the store?

He immediately responds via text.

Absolutely not. That isn't acceptable. I'll bring you one of mine to wear. When's the get-together?

I don't feel ready for an event with the hockey wives, but I'm going to have to pull it off if I want to be invited to the wives' room, where the ladies gossip before the game and during intermission.

Tomorrow. I text him back.

Food drive?

How did you know?

He doesn't text me back. It isn't overly important, he probably arrived at practice with the guys, but a 'see you later' or 'goodbye' would have been nice.

I put my phone away and hurry upstairs to get showered and dressed so that I can accompany Lia and Bristol on their outing.

"You don't have to come with us," Lia says. "I promise I can handle Bristol on my own for a day."

Is that what she thinks? That I'm spying on the nanny or something? Of course, that would imply that she doesn't know I'm joining her, and I don't make a habit of stalking Lia and Bristol.

"I know, but I like spending time with you guys." I'm confident Mitchell could handle any situation with Bristol, but he's driving them to the zoo, not accompanying them throughout the entire park. "It's really no bother."

"Don't you have work to do?" Lia asks, her brow pinched.

She's asking too many questions, and I'm grateful when my cell phone interrupts us. Except it's my sister. And I haven't talked to her since before I started working for Kyler.

"Hey, Amber," I say, and I can already feel the prickly heat of electricity coming from the other line.

"You didn't tell me you were seeing anyone! And now you're engaged?"

I suck in a sharp breath. This isn't a conversation I want to have in front of Bristol, although she's bound to find out eventually. She and the nanny may have missed Kyler's big announcement on the ice when he got down on one knee, but word travels fast in this city.

And the moment Lia hears the news, she's bound to comment on it. Which means I should squash it far before she gets wind any other way. Except she isn't supposed to know what Kyler and I have is fake.

I groan. This has gotten out of hand and far too complicated. I don't want to disappoint Bristol or put her in the middle, making her think that I'm going to be her mother one day. That isn't fair to her.

But Kyler should never have suggested it, either.

We're both to blame. It's not entirely his fault. I went along with it.

"It's kind of a new thing," I say, feeling Lia's stare on me. She's ready to go, and now they're waiting on me. "Can I call you back?"

"Fine, but you owe me details. Even the juicy, filthy ones!"

I end the call with my sister and follow the girls out to the vehicle. Mitchell is already back at the house after dropping Kyler off for practice this morning.

"Where to?" Mitchell asks as Bristol climbs into the backseat, and I make sure she's buckled before securing my own seatbelt. I let the nanny sit up front. For some reason, it feels natural, sitting next to Bristol, like she's my daughter.

It's also the best way for me to protect her; by keeping her close.

We spend much of the day exploring the zoo,

filling up on popcorn and sweets before returning to the house to make dinner. Mitchell swings by to pick up Kyler on our way home from the zoo.

He yanks open the back door, surprised to see us all stuffed inside. I scoot over, squeezing up against Kyler. Not that I mind.

"What were you guys up to today?" Kyler asks, yanking his seatbelt on while Mitchell pulls back out through the lot and into traffic.

"We went to the zoo," Bristol proclaims, shoving her penguin across my lap for her dad to see. She doesn't relinquish it into his hands, though, gripping it tightly before bringing it back to rub noses with.

"I'll bet you two spoiled my little Bristol."

"I'm not little," Bristol says, staring at him pointedly.

"Of course. I'm sorry. My mistake," Kyler says with a wry grin. He shifts in the backseat to get comfortable, but he's tall, and his legs are up to his knees. The front seat is typically shoved all the way forward when we get in, making Lia push it back. I suppose I now see why.

"How was your day?" I ask, nudging him.

"Good. Practice went well. Nothing too exciting. Yours?" He glances at me with a genuine smile, and my stomach flutters. It's hard to keep the feelings straight, the ones that aren't real, when he looks at me as if nothing else matters, and his eyes stare straight into my soul.

My breath catches in my throat. "Just an ordinary day at the zoo." I want to talk to him about Amber calling and how Lia is bound to overhear the gossip. We need to address this before Bristol hears about it.

He must sense my hesitation because his brow knits, and he reaches for my hand, intertwining our fingers together.

We're not on display. Lia isn't watching, and we're far from the stadium, his teammates, and the hockey wives.

"My sister called this morning," I whisper, keeping my voice down. The radio helps give us a hint of privacy, although Bristol is seated beside me.

"Yeah? Anything special?" Kyler asks.

"She watches television," I say, hoping that's enough of an indicator of what we need to discuss when we get back to his place.

He shrugs nonchalantly. "That was inevitable. Someone you know would find out about us, *babe*." He squeezes my hand. "Relax."

How can I relax when I was too naïve to think about the agreement that far ahead? I mean, sure, I figured I might be in a few pictures with Kyler, but I never thought my sister would see the headline. I never thought he'd propose at a hockey game for everyone to see.

Mitchell pulls up to the house, and we all climb out of the car.

I head inside first, making sure the house is still secure. Kyler is right on my heel, with Lia and Bristol following behind.

I slip out of my shoes and head up the stairs.

"Where are you going?" Kyler asks.

"I'm just going to start dinner," Lia says as she helps Bristol out of her sneakers. "Do you need me to do something first?"

"I was talking to my fiancée." Kyler pins me with his stare.

The air rushes out of my lungs, and Lia's eyes widen. "You two are engaged?" She doesn't seem to get the message that Kyler is focused entirely on me, and for the first time, it scares me.

"What does that mean?" Bristol asks, peering up at us as she's seated on the bench beside the front door. She kicks her feet wildly and wiggles her toes, bare of her shoes. Her socks are mismatched, but the kid doesn't seem to care. Knowing Bristol, she probably insisted on wearing one unicorn sock and one bunny sock.

Lia quickly zips her lip and ushers Bristol into the kitchen. "How about you help me with dinner?"

"I don't want to cook," Bristol whines. "That's your job."

"You can draw me a picture while I cook?" Lia suggests as she guides her out of the hallway and into the kitchen, affording us a tiny bit of privacy.

"I was trying to avoid that," I say and gesture toward the kitchen with Lia and Bristol.

"Upstairs." Kyler is short and even-tempered. He grabs my hand on the way up the stairs, and I have half a mind to push him away, but I don't.

I'm not sure what game he's playing at, and even worse, I hate the fact that I may actually like it.

Well, not the games. I like Kyler. At least, I think that's the reason for the butterflies in my knotted stomach. I chew on my bottom lip as he pulls me into his bedroom.

It smells like Kyler. Warm, woodsy, and thick. I try not to inhale, but it feels like I'm taking a hit. Kyler Greyson, the newest drug on the block. And I want to bring it to my lips and breathe it all in.

"Sit." His one word is a command, and he untangles his hand, gesturing for me to approach his bed.

That is definitely not a good idea.

"I'll stand," I say. My mouth goes dry, and my tongue swipes out, trying to save me from embarrassment when I speak.

Kyler shrugs like he doesn't really care whether I sit or stand. He's trying to make me comfortable. Well, nothing about this conversation is about to be comfortable.

"We just told your daughter we're engaged. Actually, technically, you did," I say. I'm not usually one to point the blame, but this time it was all him.

"And I'll explain it all to her later. But I had a good day, and I wanted to celebrate it with you."

My voice betrays me as it comes out more like a squeak. "In your bedroom?" I'm confident my cheeks are flushed, and I shuffle backward, trying to keep ample distance between us. Not because I don't trust Kyler. The truth is that I don't trust myself.

How can I when I heard him last night?

He moaned my name.

And I thought maybe it was in his sleep. He could have been having a bad dream, but then I quietly opened the door, and he definitely wasn't asleep.

Thankfully, he didn't see me.

Walking in on your boss doing *that* and moaning

your name is non-negotiable. If he caught me watching, I'd have to quit.

It's not like I haven't fantasized about Kyler. But there's the fantasy world locked tight up inside my head and the real world. Those two can't collide.

"You look terrified," Kyler says, and the smile fades from his face. "Shit. I didn't think—I'm sorry." He backs away from me, giving plenty of space between us.

Frowning, I shake my head. "What are you talking about?"

"I don't want you to think I'm like that creep Clemens, who—"

I cut him off. I know what he did. I don't want a reminder or for him to feel sorry for me. I fold my arms defensively across my chest. "That thought never even crossed my mind, Greyson." He looks hurt. I thought he'd look relieved. "What?" I ask, wondering why he's staring at me.

"You call me Greyson when you're trying to put distance between us."

"I hadn't noticed." He's probably right. "You call me Ryan."

"Rarely," he counters.

I don't argue because, this battle, he's won. I

stand by the window beside his bed. "So, what now?" I ask.

"Tell me the truth, Em. Do you have any feelings for me at all?"

I let out a heavy breath. "That's a loaded question," I say.

"It really isn't. Do you have feelings for me, Em?" he asks again.

"You're my boss." I avoid answering the question. "We're in a fake relationship. It's easy for it to feel real." I shuffle my feet and glance away. "Why? Do you have feelings for me?"

Kyler doesn't back down. I swear the man has no fear, no sense of dread, or the fact that how he answers might screw everything up. "How could I not? You're gorgeous, funny, and great with Bristol."

Those could easily be traits between friends. I breathe a sigh of relief. At least he's not throwing around the L word.

That would be crazy. Wouldn't it?

"I'm also your daughter's bodyguard," I remind him.

Kyler shrugs. "Yes, I hired you. I know that. It doesn't mean I don't have feelings for you, Em. But if you don't reciprocate them, just say the word. I'll compartmentalize what we have and keep it professional until we're in the spotlight."

"You're putting me under a lot of pressure," I say.

"Got it." He nods and opens the bedroom door, letting himself out.

I exhale a heavy breath and glance around the room. What the hell just happened?

SEVENTEEN

KYLER

EMERSON HAS BEEN distant since I cornered her in my bedroom. Maybe I should have chosen a different room, but I doubt the outcome would have changed.

I wasn't asking her to actually marry me, just admit if she harbored feelings for me.

Her non-committal answer was enough of a blow to make me realize that this relationship is entirely fake, just like I asked for it to be.

I did it to myself, one hundred percent, suggesting that we fake date and then blindsiding her when I fake proposed.

Not my finest hour in terms of communication, but at least she's still speaking to me. I mean, she texts me that everything is as it should be with the house, no new threats, no suspects.

I haven't received another letter at the arena, but it's only a matter of time. I doubt the threat is over when he can so easily manipulate me into doing what he wants because I'd do anything to protect Bristol.

We have the food drive today, and I tossed one of my jerseys in Em's room after our blowout. Not that it was a huge fight or anything. It was more of a standstill. Two steps forward, a thousand steps back.

She gave me the cold shoulder at dinner, focused entirely on Bristol, and then claimed she was tired and went to bed early. Which I know was a lie. Her bedroom light was on past midnight.

I could see she was logged onto the internet and on the tablet doing work, hiding from me.

And I should give Em her space. Clearly, she needs it if she's avoiding me, but I also don't like her being mad at me.

I get dressed and head downstairs for a cup of coffee.

Em is standing in the kitchen with her back to me. She's wearing my jersey with a pair of black leggings, and I can't help but feel a swell of pride inside.

That's what I wanted when she came to the game. I won't make the same mistake twice. She'll keep the jersey and wear it to every game she attends, so everyone in the stands and on the team will know she belongs to me.

I walk up beside her and grab a mug from the cabinet, pouring myself a steaming cup of coffee. "You look good in my jersey."

She laughs nervously and spins around, raising an eyebrow.

"Wear it to the next game you attend. And the one after that. And so on."

"You mean you don't want me wearing the dick jersey?" she asks with a laugh and shoves her face into her hands. "I can't believe I had that on. Were there any reporters who took pictures?"

Thankfully, they weren't aware of who she was until after the proposal, and at that point, I'd already had her change into one of my white undershirts.

"We lucked out. Whose idea was it really to wear it?" I ask. I don't believe that Em would ever lie to me. Had she thought it would be a funny prank like the guys did when they gifted it to me?

"Your daughter," she says. "I swear she insisted that I wear it, and I didn't even think to check the back. I wasn't even sure it was the team you play for, but Lia assumed it was and that it was one of those old-style jerseys."

"Throwback?" I ask with a laugh. "Yeah, I probably have one of those around somewhere that would fit Bristol. I don't usually keep a stack of jerseys on hand at home."

"You should. For visitors," Emerson says and grabs a cup of coffee for herself. "Or for any potential dates."

"I'm not dating anyone else. That would look bad, with us being fake engaged." I smile at her, hoping that she'll lighten up.

She sips her coffee and nods. "Right. I should get ready and head out. I don't want to keep the hockey wives waiting. Are you sure Bristol is okay with Lia today? Can Mitchell keep an eye on them since I have to cover this event?"

"I've got it covered. You worry about yourself. Remember, we're madly in love." I wrap my arms around her waist, and she freezes. Her body tenses beneath my touch.

At least we don't have to pretend today in front of others. Although, to be honest, I kind of want to do that with her. Maybe I'll show up after a couple of hours to see how everyone is treating my fiancée. Then I can steal a kiss from her.

"Right, madly in love," she says with a heavy sigh. "I should go." Em slips from my embrace, and it's like the room dropped several degrees. Her body heat and being pressed against her had warmed me from the inside out.

When the hell did I become a man obsessed with a woman? Let alone my daughter's bodyguard?

I run a hand through my hair and hurry down the rest of the coffee in my mug. I should be avoiding caffeine with the way that she makes me feel inside, but maybe one small hit isn't so bad. After all, it's not like I'm going to see her for at least a couple of hours.

Bristol comes tearing down the stairs, not the least bit quiet. The nanny has today off—I can't expect her to work a seven-day schedule. Even if she were willing to accommodate the over-time, I don't want her to burn out.

I should probably give Em more time off too.

"Daddy!" Bristol squeals as she slides across the kitchen in her fluffy pink socks. "Can we go ice skating today?" she asks.

"Let me think about it," I say teasingly and offer a huge grin. "Yes!"

The kid loves the ice, but I'm not sure if she's just trying to follow in my footsteps because she thinks that's what she's supposed to do. Last year, she joined a hockey team for kids, but she wasn't too fond of chasing the puck or being competitive.

It might have to do with the fact that one of the other girls whacked her with the stick. It wasn't on purpose, but hockey is a bit more aggressive than my Bristol is used to.

After that game, she preferred dancing with the hockey stick on the ice, which made her coach unpleased, and somehow, he thought it was my fault.

When hockey wasn't such a hit, I suggested ice skating with other kids or competitive figure skating, and she stuck her tongue out at me and told me no.

I don't believe in pushing her too hard. Some kids that works for, but not Bristol.

"Can Emmie come with us?" Bristol asks. She plops herself at the kitchen counter, waiting for breakfast.

I make a batch of pancakes, taking my time this morning, enjoying a bit of quality time with my daughter. It isn't often enough that it's just the two of us anymore. Not that I'm complaining. I enjoy having Em around a lot, and it's nice Lia can help with some of the added stress and work that needs to be done.

"Emmie has plans for today," I say, mixing the pancake batter while Bristol quizzes me.

The smile on her face grows. "Doing what? Is it a date?"

My stomach churns at my daughter's question. "What makes you say that?"

"She's pretty," Bristol says with a shrug. "But aren't you dating her, Daddy?"

I bite down on my tongue. Now isn't the time to reveal to Bristol that Em and I are just faking this whole relationship for the world. But eventually, I'm going to have to tell her. I'm nauseous just thinking about the disappointment she'll feel when she realizes the only reason Em is around is that I've paid her to be.

"Liam, at school, he said that Emmie is my mom. I told him he's wrong, that daddies can have girlfriends."

"Liam, as in Liam Moretti?" Isn't this the kid whose parents we're supposed to have dinner with, a meal that I've been avoiding? Thankfully, my schedule has been a good reason for not making plans, but I'm not sure how much longer that will last.

Bristol keeps jabbering on. "He's the boy in school who's stupid, who bullied me. He thinks that because his dad is big and tough that he can say whatever he wants. I told him he was a liar. Emmie isn't my mom, but he keeps saying he heard it from his mom and dad."

I exhale a heavy breath and turn on the stove, heating up the pan to make pancakes. How do I explain this to my kid without outright lying to her? Am I a shitty father for already hiding the truth about Em to her?

Fuck it.

I may not want to scare her regarding the threats, but I can't keep up this charade. "Em isn't really my girlfriend," I say, hoping that Bristol can understand.

Her brow tightens. "Is she my mommy?"

"No, sweetie. Your mom lives in another city, far from New York," I say. "But we may have told Liam's parents that Emerson is your mother."

Bristol's eyes widen, and she gasps, covering her mouth with both hands. "You lied!"

She doesn't seem particularly upset that Em isn't my girlfriend. She's more transfixed on the lie that I told.

"You're right. I shouldn't have done that. Lying is wrong." I don't want Bristol to think that it's okay to fib.

Bristol points at the stove for me to remember to

work on the pancakes. I drop some butter on the pan and then watch it sizzle before adding a few scoops of batter. "Can Em be my mommy? I like having her around. She's really nice. I like Nanny Lia too, but Em is so funny. She makes me laugh until I pee my pants."

I chuckle under my breath. "Is that why Lia has been doing extra laundry?"

"I'm kidding, Daddy. I'm not a baby."

We finish up with breakfast, and I take Bristol to the ice rink. She's been skating on her own since she was three, and she's mastered skating backward and twirling with ease. She's bundled in a scarf, hat, and thick parka. It's not really that cold, but she insists on dressing for the rink weather.

"Does Em know how to skate?" Bristol asks as she gives me her hands and wants me to twirl her in circles as fast as I can.

How does she not get dizzy?

"I don't know," I admit. I had asked her that question and then had brought her onto the ice for a proposal. She never really answered me when I was going on about how she had to say yes. "You can ask her that after we're done. We're going to swing by the food drive."

She giggles while I help her twirl in circles until I

finally stop. There's a squeal of delight, and her cheeks are red from the cold. She lets go of my hand and skates in circles, staring up at the ceiling, arms straight out.

The kid looks absolutely free and blissful.

Eventually, she skates over to me and puts her hands on her hips. She has a pointed look on her face. "Why did you tell me Emmie was your girlfriend?" Bristol asks.

I'm not quite sure where the attitude comes from, but I smile, surprised she finally decided to address it. For a minute, I thought that it had gotten by her when she'd focused entirely on the other lie I told.

Nothing gets past my kid.

"Is it because you like her?" Bristol guesses.

I do like her, but that developed after our little agreement. And how do you tell your six-year-old daughter that she has a bodyguard without worrying her? That is one secret I don't want to share. I'm worried about what it will do to her, the fear and concern making her constantly look over her shoulder.

"I do like her," I say. "But do you remember how the owner of the team is a big stinky poo?"

Bristol giggles and nods, staring up with bright eyes. "Those are my words." She beams proudly.

"He doesn't like the idea that you don't have a mommy around. He believes in a traditional family, with traditional roles."

Bristol shrugs. I'm not sure that she's comprehending everything that I'm saying to her. "He's stupid," she says.

Ordinarily, I would correct her because that isn't nice, but Brent Fitzgerald *is* stupid. He's an asshole. "Yes, so Em promised me that she'd play pretend for a little while until Fitzgerald leaves us alone."

"Like how we play house?" Bristol asks. "Does that mean Emmie is going to move out one day?"

I exhale a heavy sigh. "I don't know, sweetie. Let's just focus on one day at a time, okay?"

"I like Emmie." Bristol grabs my hands and skates backward, bringing me with her. "She's nice to me. And makes me smile. You seem happy too, Daddy. When you're around her, she makes you happy."

"You make me happy," I say, staring at Bristol.

"It's not the same."

The kid is wise beyond her years.

"Can you keep this little chat just between the two of us?" I ask. I hate making her keep secrets, but

I don't want her saying anything to the kids at school or even the nanny.

Bristol grins wickedly. "No promises."

I give her a pointed stare, telling her I mean business.

"Okay, but only if you answer this, Daddy. Do you love her?"

EIGHTEEN

EMERSON

THE MINUTE I put on Kyler's jersey, I'm surrounded by his scent. The jersey doesn't stink, at least not like he wore it for several games without washing it, but it does smell uniquely of Greyson.

It's musky, woodsy, and thick. I try not to breathe in deeply, like I'm getting high off wearing his jersey.

What the hell is wrong with me?

Thankfully, no one is around to notice. I'm out of the house as quickly as can be, and Mitchell drops me off at the food drive with the hockey wives.

To say I'm nervous is an understatement.

It shouldn't be a big deal. It's just another assignment to get close to these ladies, find out what they know, and who might be threatening Kyler and Bristol.

But the minute I pull up to the event, they're standing outside wearing their husbands' jerseys, and some of them, nothing else underneath. Maybe boy shorts or boxers. It's hard to tell. A few of them have jeans on, and I feel oddly dressed, donning Greyson's jersey.

He's supposed to be my fiancé, but it's all an act, and I'm not sure how long I can keep up this charade.

Don't get me wrong. The money is golden right now. Having worked for nearly two months with Greyson, I've got a hefty balance in my checking account.

I haven't thought far ahead about what I'll do with the full million dollars after we part ways. And I don't believe that it's cursed. That's complete superstition.

The women have designer shoes and handbags. Their makeup is spot on, and their hair looks like it took all morning for a professional to do it before attending the food drive.

I feel out of place other than the jersey I'm wearing. The outside air is fresh and cool. It's still early, and while the sun is up, it hasn't battered the day with its warmth.

Wearing Kyler's jersey is like a warm bear hug. If I could sleep in it and he wouldn't make fun of me, I totally would.

But he's going to expect the jersey back when we get home.

I'm just borrowing it, and it's covered in his scent. I swear if he bottled it up like a fragrance, he'd be the wealthiest man in the world.

But knowing Kyler, he'd want to give it all away because he's undeserving of it—or so he says.

I don't believe him, at least the undeserving part. I believe he'd give it all to charity, but I don't think he should. Donating is nice, but not at the expense of giving away your entire wealth.

That's insanity.

Or I'm just seeing it from a different perspective because I haven't accumulated the wealth that Mr. Greyson has acquired. I've never been able to toss money at engagements and galas to help people. There's something freeing and strangely hot in his generosity and philanthropy.

Although at what expense?

"Emerson, you came," Kate says, and she's wearing that fake smile that she had when she handed me the invitation. She's cute and tall, and I can't make out almost any of her body because she's swimming in her husband's jersey. She also has dynamite legs because she is showing them off by not wearing any pants.

"Of course, thank you for inviting me."

I'm quickly introduced to the other hockey wives, and it's a polite interrogation as they ask me a hundred and one questions about how Kyler and I met and what I think about him playing professional hockey.

"You don't just marry your man," Ava says. "Your life will become living and breathing everything that is hockey. You're marrying him and the sport." She's Parker Montgomery's wife, whom I've yet to meet off the ice. I caught a glimpse of him during the game, and he was good, but so was the entire team.

It's not like I know much else about the sport other than they toss a puck around and hit it into the goal. But I'm careful not to spoil that secret with the wives.

I spend the next hour chatting with the wives as we pack together boxes for the food drive and handing them out. There's a press crew who stops by for a few minutes to get photos for their article.

They're writing down everyone's name, making sure to get the correct spelling, when Kyler comes up from behind, wrapping his arms around me. His breath tickles my neck as he nuzzles my skin, sending warm tingles all throughout my body.

"I like the jersey on you," Kyler whispers loud enough for the other hockey wives to hear.

I imagine he's doing it on purpose, putting on a show for everyone.

The woman with the press snaps a few extra pictures of the two of us, smiling brightly like we've just made her day.

Wonderful.

Except, I don't feel ecstatic because I'm concerned that our picture will be the highlight at the top of the article. The last thing I want is for these other wives to get jealous or start a catfight.

"Smile for the camera," Ava says with a grin and steps out of the shot.

Kyler spins me around in his arms and dips me back, kissing me passionately, taking my breath away.

I hear the *snap, snap, snap* of the camera watching the two of us. There's no such thing as a private moment when your fake fiancé is a professional hockey player.

"You didn't have to do that," I say, glancing at Ava.

The photographer steps back, checking her work with the digital camera before heading away, clearly done for the day. She got the shot she needed.

Ava is genuinely smiling and happy about letting us be front and center for the photo. "Oh, please. It'll make good press for the team, and that's one thing you should know about us. We're sisters. We protect each other and look out for our families. We're not competitive with each other, ever. There's enough of that on the ice amongst the other teams."

"Good to know," I say, exhaling a laugh. I want to relax, but being wrapped in Kyler's arms just makes the butterflies take flight.

"Hi, Emmie," Bristol chimes from around the opposite side of the table. I didn't see her, with Kyler stealing away my attention. She's wearing her Ice Dragons jersey, but instead of it reading Greyson on the back, it reads Daddy. She leans on the table and rests her hands on her chin with a wicked grin. "Daddy says you've been faking it with him."

I cough, shocked by the words coming out of Bristol's lips.

Can the ground swallow me up and bury me?

I am not ready to deal with Bristol and her sassy little comments. And does she even know what she said or what that sounds like?

She's six. Of course, she doesn't know what *faking it* means. But every hockey wife is staring at me, mouth agape, eyes wide.

And I just want to die.

Kyler peels his arms off me and climbs over the table, not bothering to walk around to the opposite side.

"I haven't been faking anything," I say to the ladies. Forcing a smile, the only relief I find is that the reporter isn't still here because, heaven help me, Kyler's image would probably be ruined.

I don't even know how to respond to Bristol's little outburst. Does she think what she said is funny? Did someone put her up to it? Who?

Kyler grabs Bristol and tickles her mercilessly, returning the sentiment of torture that we're both enduring because of her words.

"Daddy, no!" she squeals with laughter and squirms in his grasp.

The hockey wives don't seem phased by the endless tickles to Bristol, only with the words that spilled past the kid's lips.

"Don't worry," Ava says, smiling, and I can tell she's trying not to laugh. "What I said still stands. We don't gossip about each other. Once you're invited to the wives' room, you're one of us for life."

But I haven't gotten *that* invitation yet. I've only been invited to the hockey wives hosting a food drive, not the main event.

Kate chuckles under her breath. "Like we all haven't faked it before meeting our husbands?" She chews her bottom lip and wrinkles her nose. "Please tell me that he's brought you to O—"

"Oh, please stop," I say, wanting this conversation to end. I appreciate that they're trying to be friendly, but they're not helping. At least Kate isn't. If she's trying to offer pointers or something, maybe let's not do it during the food drive when there are guests walking up to the table to take boxes back to their car.

Kyler finally releases Bristol from his clutches, putting her feet back down on the ground. "No more embarrassing me. Got it?" he says to his kid.

She sticks out her tongue. "Daddy, you didn't answer my question at the ice arena. That was payback."

He's raised an adorable little monster, and if this weren't all part of the job, I'd laugh it off. But no one can find out that our engagement is as fake as our relationship.

We finish up at the food drive, and Ava pulls me

aside as Kyler and Bristol head to the car. Mitchell is waiting for us.

"The next game you attend, you're joining us in the wives' room," Ava says.

"Wow, thank you." I wasn't expecting the invitation today. I thought that maybe the ladies would discuss it at the next game or social event when they got together. "I would love that."

"Bring Bristol with you. There's a playroom for the kids during intermission and a bathroom. We heard about what happened during the last game." Ava chuckles and embraces me in a hug. "And don't worry about Greyson and having to fake it. We'll talk next time when he's not around. Get to the bottom of it."

"I promise our sex life is perfect," I say. Well, I imagine it would be with him. It's not like we've actually done the deed yet.

"It's okay if it's not. You don't have to lie. And I promise, we'll keep it between us girls." She releases her hold on me and waves before heading to her awaiting vehicle. None of the ladies drove themselves. They all have chauffeurs escorting them to the event.

"But I didn't lie," I mutter to myself.

I head for the vehicle, and Greyson steps out,

letting me climb into the middle seat beside his daughter. "She's testing my patience," he grumbles under his breath.

"And that's a first?" I slide into the backseat and try to buffer some of the tension between father and daughter.

"Do you love my daddy?" Bristol asks as soon as I sit beside her in the back. I buckle my seatbelt and glance at Kyler.

"I love all sorts of things about him, like how he's good with you. And he's kind. He also has a great sense of fashion," I say, gesturing at the jersey I'm wearing.

Bristol's head is tilted as she stares at me. "Daddy told me you're faking it."

Kyler relaxes in the backseat beside us. "Fake dating," he corrects his daughter. He doesn't seem phased by addressing it in front of Mitchell.

Was he aware, or does Kyler not want his ego to take another hit?

"That's what I said." Bristol jabs a finger in her father's direction, giving a scowl and a playful pout.

"You told her?" I ask, glancing at Kyler.

"Yes, she also found out from Liam that we told his parents you're her mother."

"Oh." I inhale a sharp breath. That one was entirely my doing.

"It's fine. I mean, I think she knows to keep it between our family," Kyler says, "but I also told her not to talk about our fake relationship."

Bristol shakes her head. "No. I promised if you answered my question, and you didn't answer."

"What question was that?" I ask, glancing between them. I can't even fathom how this conversation between them came to pass.

Kyler is glaring at his daughter, silently warning her not to answer my question.

"I asked Daddy if he loved you."

Kyler exhales a heavy breath, and I feel the exact same way. Well, maybe not the same. I don't know how he feels about me. Only Bristol asked a very loaded question that neither of us is ready to address.

He can't love me because what we have isn't real.

That's the truth, but I don't want to voice it, either. I don't know why it stings and makes me sad, but it does.

"I'll turn on some music," Mitchell offers, and I can't tell if he's trying to help the situation or just give the three of us privacy in the back.

"Good choice," Kyler mutters.

————

Lia is off for the day, so Kyler preps dinner, and I keep an eye on Bristol to make sure that she's not getting into any more trouble.

I head into the kitchen to grab us both some water when Kyler's peering into the fridge, distracted. He doesn't seem to notice me.

"Can you grab us two waters?" I ask.

"I didn't hear you come in." He grabs the bottles of water from the fridge and hands them to me, shutting the door.

"Everything okay?" I ask. The air between us feels stuffy and overly complicated. Not that either of us did anything overtly wrong to make it that way. It's been a trying day. Tomorrow will be better, I'm sure of it.

"Yeah, just thinking." He glances at the oven where he's got dinner, and he's just hanging out in the kitchen.

Is he avoiding me?

"Don't do something that might hurt too much," I joke.

He snorts and folds his arms across his chest, leaning back against the kitchen counter. "I've been working you hard. You should take more time off."

His comment surprises me. "What?"

"You work seven days a week, Em. You should take some time for yourself. Go out. Get away from Bristol and me for a few hours."

My brow pinches. "Even if I wanted to do that, I can't go out without being seen. People know who I am," I remind him. Every paparazzi and tabloid will have my face on the cover if I'm out in public.

I've caught a few photographers trying to get pictures of Bristol, and I've shielded her from the limelight as best as possible, skirting her into a store and even going out the back exit to avoid being harassed.

"Does that bother you?" he asks, and he opens the fridge, grabbing himself a beer. He pops off the top and takes a swig.

The kitchen is a bit stuffy, and his heated stare does nothing to cool me off. Quite the opposite.

"I don't mind the attention. It's not like I want it, but it doesn't bother me."

"It did the other day when your sister called." He reminds me of my discomfort when Amber reached out to tell me that she had heard about our engagement.

He has a point. "I don't like lying to my sister. And it's not just a little white lie."

"Any other family?" He takes another sip of his beer.

"I didn't realize there'd be another inquisition," I say. I grimace, realizing my tone is too harsh. He doesn't deserve it.

"Just curious how you'll handle it when they all find out about the engagement. You talked with your sister, but you didn't call anyone else to explain."

"I don't have to explain myself to anyone."

His gaze tightens. "No, I suppose you don't. I just thought if you wanted to go out shopping or meet up with your sister, I'm giving you the night off."

With not much notice. "I don't think Amber will be available tonight." I open my mouth and quickly shut it. It's hard not to run my gaze over every inch of him. He's gorgeous, and I hate that my body is beginning to realize the attraction between us.

"What is it?" he asks, noticing my hesitation.

"You want me gone for a couple of hours. Do you have a hot date?"

"With my hand."

My eyes widen, and Kyler chuckles. "It's a joke. Relax. Who could I even date, Em? The press is all over our fake engagement. My social calendar isn't exactly booming." He takes a swig from his beer.

"But it could be," I say. "You're a hot commodity

in the dating world." I should keep my mouth shut. I'm not doing myself any favors by telling him what I think. It's only going to complicate matters between us.

"How do you figure?" He tilts his head, his gaze never leaving mine. It's like he's staring right into me, and it makes my insides warm and gooey. Like nothing else in the world matters but me, right in that very moment.

"Do you really want me to list all the reasons?" My cheeks heat at the thought of baring my innermost private thoughts to him. He knows he's good-looking, but the real reasons I'm attracted to him go beyond his sex appeal.

The corner of his lips turns upwards. "I kind of do," he admits. "The way I see it, this hot commodity has a career that takes all of his focus and is only second to his kid. The ladies aren't interested in single fathers."

"You'd be surprised."

He laughs under his breath. "I would be." He steps closer, and I feel the air sucked out of my lungs. His gaze is on me. It's hot and primal.

There's a hum of electricity between us, charging the air, making my insides tingle as he steps closer, into my personal space.

It's the reason I've avoided him, and him me, after our little romantic encounters. At least, I assume that's why, and it doesn't have anything to do with him not being attracted to me. I can feel his attraction, his desire poking me, and I gasp softly.

"Are you going to list the reasons?" he asks, his voice gravelly and sexy.

My body reacts to him. Like a magnet, I'm drawn toward him. Even if I don't want to be, the gravitational pull is undeniable. And by the heavy look in his gaze, he wants it too.

"The reasons I like you?" I say, and I'm not sure that was exactly what he was asking, but somehow my mouth has run rapidly on its own, and I ought to snap it shut.

"We could go with that," Kyler says. "You called me a hot commodity."

I'm confident that I'm blushing because the room is several degrees hotter, and his attention hasn't left me. I'm not sure it will until I answer him.

"That I did," I say.

"You're avoiding the question." He pushes me gently to tell him and takes one step closer. His hands encircle my waist, and he backs me up against the wall.

I'm grateful for the wall. It's practically holding me up right now. "So I am," I say with a smirk.

His lips fall to my ear, sucking the lobe, his breath tickling my neck. My eyes close, relishing the feeling that he bestows on me, the heat and warmth as it floods my body and senses. "Answer the question, M&M."

I chuckle at his nickname. I thought we were over that, but I don't argue. Maybe it's his term of endearment toward me? "You're kind," I whisper as he kisses from my ear to my neck. "Generous."

"M'hmm." He nuzzles my neck as his lips move across my collarbone.

My fingers graze his neck and his back, wanting him closer.

I'm tingling inside. Warm and relaxed, as his fingers skim my hips, slipping under my shirt. The pads of his fingers tease my skin, caressing my lower back. "You put your daughter first. Some women find that attractive."

"What else?" he whispers, letting his fingers glide across my stomach as his lips continue teasing my neck.

I want him to kiss lower, to take off my shirt and pants and have him explore every inch of me.

My eyes fall shut, and I revel in the warm

feelings that tingle across my body. Not staring into his intense gaze makes it easier for me to voice my feelings.

"You're passionate in everything you do," I say, and he guides my thighs apart, pushing his leg between mine.

My mouth parts, and I gasp as the friction from his cock rubs against my core.

"Passionate?" he mumbles against my ear, his breath warm and tingly. He hasn't kissed me, but dry-humping me against the wall definitely takes the cake.

Each word comes out raspy. I'm already finding myself breathless as I speak, answering his question. "With hockey, your kid, everything." It's becoming harder to talk as my head becomes foggy.

He nibbles on my neck, grinding against me, and my hands fall to his ass, gripping him through his jeans as he thrusts into me.

My head falls forward as the warmth spreads through me, making my insides ache and throb. "Fuck," I mutter under my breath.

"Not yet," Kyler whispers, grinding and thrusting with our clothes still on. With one hand, my fingernails dig into his shoulder, the other at his ass, gripping him tighter.

I whimper, and I'm not sure if it's because he means we're not taking this to the bedroom right now or he doesn't want to let me come yet. Either way, it's torture as I'm deliciously on the edge with him, and he's bringing me closer to oblivion.

"You want to come?" He nuzzles my neck, his breath in my ear.

I'm nodding and gasping for breath. His hips gyrate and tease me.

"Look at me," he commands.

My eyes lazily open. It's a struggle to focus, to see what's right in front of me, when I'm close to the brink and he's thrusting with his rock-hard cock pressed against my pussy.

It takes all my measurable strength to let my eyelids flutter open, staring up at him. "You're mine," he whispers, covering my lips, capturing my mouth, my tongue, pushing into me like it's his cock as his tongue fucks me.

His hips thrust, and the friction between us is like fireworks as my body trembles and my inside walls clench down, seeking out his cock. "I want you, in me," I rasp between kisses.

He grunts and tenses, and the world around us disappears.

"That's the hottest thing anyone's ever said to

me," Kyler whispers, pressing a kiss against my neck, cheek, and finally, my lips.

I don't want to doubt his words, but no one's ever said anything hotter. Really? He's a professional hockey player. I'm sure he can have any girl he wants. And even if he wants me, I'm sure he has more experience.

He untangles his knee from between my thighs, but he doesn't let me go. I'm not sure if he's worried I'd run or if he wants to savor everything a little longer.

Kyler moves his finger to my chin, lifting my gaze to meet his stare. His breath is heavy and thick as he kisses me lazily and out of breath.

"We should clean up," I whisper, resting my forehead against his. "Dinner will be ready soon." My eyes close as I drink in his scent, his touch, the afterglow of the orgasm with him.

"Daddy." Bristol skips into the kitchen, her tablet in hand. "It's frozen."

While he untangles from my embrace, he doesn't back away. "Give it here," Kyler says.

Bristol hands him the device, and he does a hard reboot when the power button fails to work.

His daughter stares at me, tilting her head

curiously as she waits for her tablet back. "Were you kissing my daddy?"

Guilty as charged. I bite down on my bottom lip.

Do I have to answer? She's staring at me, waiting for me to respond, and the words have disappeared from my vocabulary. I can't even nod. I'm like that tablet, frozen.

NINETEEN

KYLER

MY DAUGHTER HAS IMPECCABLE TIMING, although we're lucky she didn't walk in any earlier. I keep my back to Bristol as much as I can because I'm not sure that my pants aren't actually evidence of what we just did.

"Daddy was kissing Em," I say, answering my daughter's question. I'm done lying to her, and while I don't know what Emerson and I have going on between us, the spark is real. I can't just walk away from it.

Not when we're pretending to be engaged.

I'd regret it if I don't pursue something with her.

I hand my daughter the tablet that's been rebooted and is now ready for her. "Go play. Dinner will be ready in under an hour."

She scurries off with her tablet. She's been fixated on a number of new apps, which I usually wouldn't encourage, but the nanny assured me that they're highly educational, and her teacher had requested the kids download them to work on their skills at home.

"Now, where were we?" I say, returning my attention to Em.

"I was about to use the bathroom and clean up a bit," she says. She scrunches her nose and drops a kiss on my lips before skirting past me.

I wait until Em is upstairs changing and my daughter is preoccupied before I waltz into the laundry room. I grab a fresh pair of sweatpants from the dryer. My back is to the door when it swings wide open, and Em stares at me.

"Sorry!" she says, quick to apologize, and slams the laundry room door shut.

I open the door, half-naked, and grab her arm. "Get in here," I growl, pulling her inside with me and shutting the door behind her. There's no lock, but there's less chance of Bristol finding us in the laundry room than anywhere else in the house.

It's not as though Em hasn't seen me naked. My cock has had those sweet, luscious lips wrapped around it, but that was far too long ago.

"What are you—"

I cut her off when my lips crush hers in another searing kiss. She drops the dirty clothes she was holding onto the floor. Her arms wrap around me, pulling me closer, tighter.

"You make me feel like I'm a teenage boy," I whisper against her ear.

She glances down at my growing cock. "Already?"

"What can I say?" I smirk. "You make me horny."

"That is what every girl wants to hear," Em teases me and pulls back, dropping a kiss on my lips. "I came in here to do laundry."

"Are you sure you weren't stalking me?"

She laughs and bends down, grabbing her dirty clothes and mine on the floor and throwing them into the washing machine. I can't help but stare at her ass the entire time. She turns on the washing machine before spinning around to face me.

"You caught me. I followed you in here so that I could have my way with you," Em says.

"Woman," I growl, my heart hammering against my chest.

"What?" She wears that smile with pride as she steps closer, closing the gap between us. Her lips are parted, and her soft breath teases me as she stares up into my gaze.

Does she have any idea how turned on she makes me? The feelings she stokes are like a raging fire that's burning down an entire city.

My fingers tug at her waist, pulling her against me.

"Put some pants on," she teases, tossing my sweatpants at me that she grabbed from the top of the dryer.

I release my hold on her and pull the black sweats on, choosing to go commando.

She watches and exhales a heavy breath. "I need a cold shower," she confesses. "I have to make it through dinner with your daughter sitting at the table oblivious to this." Em gestures between us.

"I think she kind of already knows."

"That we kissed," Em says. "Sure. But the fact that I want to jump your bones?"

I already know the answer, but I like hearing her say it. "You want to have sex with me?" I ask.

Her cheeks turn crimson as she nods. "Yes. You're not going to make me wait for the wedding, are you?"

The fake engagement.

For a moment, all of it felt real, and what we

shared, it wasn't fake. But her words jar me back to a sharp reality.

The smile falls as I shake my head. "No, Em. I'd never make you wait. I wouldn't want to deny you of any type of pleasure, ever."

"Is that a promise?" She shuffles her feet, and while she's staring at me, I can sense the hesitancy creeping in like a thick fog.

I've been around Em enough the past couple of months to read her. She's an open book, even if she doesn't realize it. "After Bristol's in bed, I'll prove how much I want you."

"I'd like that," she whispers. "A lot."

———

Dinner seems to drag on for hours, and Bristol refuses to go to bed. I swear it's like my daughter has it out for me not to get laid.

In the past, when I wanted to hook up with a woman, I made sure Bristol wasn't home, or I banged a chick at her place.

Neither of those is an option, and the second doesn't appeal to me anymore.

"I'm not tired. I want to play a video game,"

Bristol says. "There's this paintball game which looks like so much fun. Can we download it?"

"Absolutely not!" I can't believe Bristol's suggestion at this hour.

"Please, Daddy. It's almost my birthday. It can be a birthday present."

"Your birthday is six months away." I can't believe this kid. I swear, she's just trying to get under my skin tonight. Does she have a radar that detects that I want adult time?

"Upstairs, now!" I snap at her.

She grumbles and stomps up the stairs to her bedroom.

"Brush your teeth!" I shout upstairs at her.

Em is reading a book or at least pretending to feign interest in it. I don't think I've seen her turn the page in twenty minutes, but I've also been distracted by a three-and-a-half-foot monster.

She glances up from her book. "Do you want me to help?" she asks.

It's not her responsibility to discipline my daughter, but right now, Bristol doesn't want to listen to me. I'm not sure if she's testing her limits or just my patience.

"No, just give me a few minutes." I follow Bristol

upstairs, checking to make sure that she's in the bathroom doing as told.

"Five more minutes, Daddy?" she asks, batting those pretty blue eyes.

"It's already past your bedtime." I don't bargain with her, and eventually, she listens. I get her tucked in and the bedroom door shut before quietly making my way back downstairs.

Em is still curled up on the sofa with her book.

"Bristol is finally in bed," I say, stalking over toward Em.

She holds out a finger, indicating that she wants me to hold on a second. She flips the page and then dogears it, which makes me cringe.

"You're one of *those* people."

"And you're not?" Em closes the book, holding it to her chest.

I stare at her, trying not to smile. "I don't think I can sleep with someone who dogears pages in a—" I try to catch the title, but she's hugging it to her chest.

"Is that so? I promise it's not your book that I dogeared."

Her legs are curled up around her, and I pull them out from under her, forcing her to lie on the sofa as I straddle her. "Let me see what you're reading," I say, pulling it back just a few inches, but I can tell the genre by the half-naked book cover. "Looks spicy."

She giggles, and I can tell she's nervous. She doesn't have to be with me. I toss her book onto the floor, and she gasps at my mishandling of her novel. The same book that she dogeared. My hips push hers into the sofa, pinning her beneath my weight. I adore the feeling of her body under me.

Her face is flushed, and her eyes are wide as she stares up at me. "You're a monster," she laughs. "I can't believe you threw my book!" The smile that covers her face makes me desire her lips on mine.

I lean down, kissing her, tasting her. I relish every moment alone with Em. She is like a drug, and I'm slowly becoming addicted to every hit that I take when my lips graze her warm skin.

We take things slow, exploring each other's bodies. I don't want to rush anything with Em. There's no reason to when I want to spend the rest of my life with her.

She isn't just a girl I'm looking for a good time with or a romp in the sheets. I want to know everything about her.

Em moans as my lips trail down her neck and her body, and she lifts and removes my jersey that she's been wearing, giving me a full view of her gorgeous tits. She wasn't even wearing a bra underneath.

I groan. I swear I wasn't planning on fucking her tonight, but my body has other ideas. Lowering my mouth over one breast, my other hand plays with her nipple.

She moans and gasps. The sweet sounds fill the night air. We should probably move this to the bedroom, but my daughter is likely still trying to fall asleep.

At least downstairs, there's more of a buffer zone for noise. And Em isn't the quietest right now.

I'm definitely not complaining. I tug her leggings down with her panties, admiring her as though she were a piece of art.

"Quit staring," she says with a grin. "Get naked, or I'll make you pay."

I can't help but smile down at her. "Is that a threat?" I tilt my head, curious about what she might do if I don't disrobe quickly. "Tempting offer, M&M."

She leans up toward me and bites my lips playfully, wrestling us around. I let her have the upper hand; I like seeing this dominant side of Em. There's something highly arousing in watching a woman take charge. Especially one I'm falling in love with.

I moan as she captures my mouth and lets my bottom lip go. She straddles my hips and tugs at my shirt, working it free, tossing it across the room.

"Tit for tat," she says with a smirk. "You've seen my tits."

I groan. "I love it when you talk dirty," I whisper, staring up at her. My fingers move for her tits, and she grabs my palms, pushing them into the sofa.

"Not until I get a taste of your cock."

I moan, and just hearing her talk filthy makes me even harder. "You're torturing me," I whimper.

"I doubt that." She smiles and lifts her hips, helping me out of my pants and boxers, freeing my erection.

Em runs her tongue over her lips before leaning down, bringing her mouth to my cock.

"Holy fuck," I mutter, and my head dips back. My fingers thread through her hair. I'd forgotten how amazing it feels to have a woman's mouth and tongue wrapped around my cock.

I swear Emerson gives the best head I've ever had in my life. She teases the crown with her tongue, licking and sucking in just the right way, with the perfect amount of pressure.

Words are lost on me as she takes my shaft deeper, and her fingers play with my balls. I'm trying to hold on, to keep this moment from ending too soon.

"Em," I growl at her as the feeling toward oblivion nears. "I'm going to—you have to stop," I warn her.

I don't want her to stop, but I'm not ready to end our night just yet, either. The last thing I want is her disappointment or for her to tell the hockey wives that she never even had to fake it because I came first and left her hanging.

She releases her mouth from my cock and climbs up my body, teasing me, hovering, and making me want to plunge inside of her.

I slide my fingers between us, teasing apart her folds. She's soaking wet and ready, but I'm not about to deprive her of anything yet.

Em smiles down at me, her eyelids half closed as she struggles to focus. "Kyler, that feels amazing," she whispers and kisses me. "But I want your cock inside me."

"I want that, too," I whisper.

"Condom?"

I climb out from under her on the sofa and hurry to grab a condom from the other room. I didn't plan this. Having one available downstairs wasn't even a forethought this morning. I tear open the foil packet and sheathe the condom on my cock.

This time, I take the lead, my lips on hers, pushing her down onto the sofa, our foreheads pressed together, already gasping for breath.

"Are you sure?" I ask, not wanting to push her too far if she's not ready. After all she's been through, I'd never want to force her into anything.

"I'm sure that I want you to fuck me already," Em says. She spreads her legs and leans forward, reaching for my body.

I run two fingers over her slit. She's soaked, and I dip them inside her wetness, making sure she's ready.

"Please," she whispers, and it sounds almost like she's begging me to fuck her.

I glide my cock slowly into her warmth. She's tight, and Em grimaces. "Keep going," she says when I stop.

"I don't want to hurt you."

"You couldn't ever hurt me," Em says.

I crush her lips and push harder, deeper inside of her.

She wraps her legs around me, taking every inch of me inside her warmth.

My heart pounds just feeling the connection, the closeness with her. I'm falling for her.

Slowly, I withdraw before slamming back into her pussy, filling her completely with me. Her fingernails scratch at my back, my shoulder, my buttocks. She's gripping me, tugging and pulling me deeper.

"More." Her soft rasps encourage me.

Each breath is loud and vocal. I cover her lips with mine, quieting her as we both near the edge. We have to be silent. We're not the only ones in the house.

Her insides tremble, and she clenches onto my cock, moaning into my mouth as I push deeper and feel her come undone.

I'm right with her, tumbling over into oblivion, coming inside of her.

————

We fall asleep on the sofa, tangled in each other's arms.

The morning light wakes me, as does my phone buzzing in my pants pocket on the floor. I untangle my body from Em's.

"Sorry," I apologize, hating to wake her. We

should get dressed and be decent for when Lia comes in or Bristol tramples down the stairs.

I grab my phone and clear my throat, attempting to sound as awake as possible when I read the caller ID. It's Fitzgerald.

What the hell does he want at this hour?

"Hello?" My voice comes out gruff as I answer the call.

"Don't tell me I woke you, Greyson." He doesn't sound pleased, and I'm not surprised. He's never in a good mood. The man wears his bad attitude like it's part of his ensemble. It only comes in black.

"What can I do for you?" I ask. I'm not about to admit that, yes, he woke me. Normally, I'd be up getting a run in before dawn or working weights to get the blood pumping. But last night with Em was enough to make my heart race wildly, and I was catching up on some much-needed sleep.

"I need you in my office in thirty. Can you do that?"

Mitchell isn't scheduled until later, and I'm not sure I can get him to pick me up in time. I'll have to grab the keys and drive one of the vehicles in the garage. "Yeah, I can do that."

I don't ask what this is about. Honestly, I have no clue. It could be about the contract. I'm hoping that he's offering me another year at minimum, although I'd prefer it to be a solid three-year deal. I've never bothered with an agent. I'm probably the only player who has chosen to forego an agent because the last agent and I didn't see eye-to-eye.

He was trying to get me a contract for the most money. I just wanted to play hockey with the Ice Dragons. It was as simple as that. He wouldn't listen to the client, me, so I fired his ass.

I'm quite capable of negotiating the contract on my own. But this is the first time I've had to do that. The offer last time came in, and we argued about the deal until I went to Fitzgerald on my own and signed it behind my agent's back.

That didn't go over well.

And looking back, that might have been the start of the beef between Fitzgerald and me. I don't cave under the pressure of authority. I make my own path.

I hang up and grab my boxers from the floor, yanking them on as I grab my clothes and toss Em's clothes at her as she sits up. The throw blanket from the sofa drapes over her naked body.

"You're in a rush this morning," she says, watching me curiously.

"Fitzgerald wants me to meet with him in thirty."

"Can you get to the arena that quickly? It's across town."

I grimace, and I don't have time to even answer her question as I'm heading upstairs to change clothes.

She yanks open my bedroom door as I pull my jeans on. I'd have opted for a suit if I knew without a doubt that this was a contract meeting, but we also have practice in a couple of hours. And when I get done with practice, I'm going to want something comfortable to wear.

"Should I reach out to Mitchell? Or maybe I should go with you and make sure Fitzgerald isn't up to something sinister," Em says.

"You'll stay here with Bristol." I grab a black t-shirt and yank it on before sitting at the edge of the bed to pull on my socks. "I'll take the truck and drive myself to the arena."

She's watching me, silent and curious.

"What?" I ask, standing and running a hand through my hair. I pop into the bathroom real quick to brush my teeth and make sure that I look like I didn't just roll out of bed or off the couch.

"My stomach is in knots," Em says.

"Why?" I shut off the light in the bathroom, breezing past her.

"It's probably nothing, but I don't think it's normal for him to just call you into his office at six in the morning." She glances at the clock on my bedside table.

I head out of the bedroom with a brisk pace, down the stairs, and grab my sneakers. "It's fine. I'm sure it's part of his usual being a dick routine."

"Will anyone else be there?" Em asks.

I glance up at her as I grab the keys hanging on the wall near the garage. "It's the ice arena. There are plenty of people there, even at six in the morning. I'll be fine." I give her a quick kiss on the lips. "Relax. Look after Bristol, and I'll call you when I figure out what the hell is going on. Okay?"

I hurry out into the garage, hitting the button for the doors to open.

Em is watching me from the doorjamb. She's leaning on the frame, arms folded across her chest. She doesn't look pleased.

Yeah, me either. I'd have rather stayed curled up against her this morning.

I jump into the truck and head out through the main gate, hightailing my ass toward the arena. I'll be lucky if I make it there in thirty minutes.

I park in the private garage, and while I don't typically use the space, I have an access card that lets me inside. My pace of walking is more like running when I hurry through the garage and inside. I use my keycard to enter the building and hurry through the hallway and down several corridors until I reach Fitzgerald's office.

My pace slows only when I'm two doors away so that I don't look like I've been running through the hallways. It's all about composure and looking calm and collected. I don't feel any of those things, but I refuse to let him see through my charade.

Fitzgerald's door is open, and I give it a knock as I step into the doorway. "Sir," I say, and the words are bitter on my tongue, trying to mask my disgust for the man.

"Shut the door and come in and have a seat." He gestures to the empty chair opposite his desk.

I quietly close the office door. He doesn't thank me for coming in so quickly or at all. Not that I'd ever expect to hear the words 'thank you' from his lips.

"Do you know why I called you into my office, Greyson?"

His tone makes me feel like I'm in the principal's office. It's condescending, and I'm ready for a scolding from the man.

I don't feign to know why. "No, sir." I force the

words out, trying to give him the respect he wants, even if he doesn't deserve it.

"Care to explain this?" he asks, and pushes a piece of white paper across his desk. It's scribbled in the same handwriting as before.

Another threat.

Throw the game, or Bristol dies.

TWENTY

EMERSON

LIA TEXTS me that she's running late and stuck in traffic.

It's fine. My job is to keep Bristol safe, so I'm not overly concerned. Bristol has the day off, and I'm trying to figure out what to do with her this afternoon.

Maybe when Lia gets here, she'll have a suggestion. We've done the zoo, the art museum, and the park recently. With the nicer weather making it possible to enjoy a few outdoor activities, we've been doing what we can to enjoy it.

I'm busy in the kitchen making pancakes for Bristol when my phone rings.

"Is that Nanny Lia?" Bristol asks with hopeful eyes. She's not keen on my pancakes, but I swear I follow the box directions when I make them. They're just not as crispy as Lia's.

"It's your dad." I hit accept on my cell phone and take the call. "Hello?"

"Em, it's me." There's a lot of noise and commotion in the background. Is he in the locker room?

"What's going on?" I ask, feeling a sense of urgency in him calling. If it were nothing, he'd have texted me to tell me that Fitzgerald is a douche.

More background noise and chatter follow before I hear his words clearly, and the noise behind him dies down. He must be taking the call in another room. "I need you to come down to the arena."

"Yeah, sure. I can call Mitchell and have him bring me down there this morning as soon as Lia gets here. She's running late."

"I think at this point, just bring Bristol with you. And I also need you to bring that note."

"*The* note?" I repeat, glancing at Bristol, trying to keep things as discreet as possible so as not to scare his kid.

"Yes."

A heavy breath slips past my lips. "Was there another threat?" I ask. My stomach tenses with the dreaded possibility that another threat has been left for Kyler.

"Yes." He's a man of few words this morning.

"I'm making Bristol pancakes this morning. They're just about done—"

"Turn off the stove and leave it. Lia can clean it up. I'll get Bristol something to eat when you get here."

The urgency in his tone is unmistakable. "Okay."

He ends the call before I can ask anything further.

The pancakes are half-cooked. "Go upstairs and get dressed. Your dad needs us at the arena this morning."

"Why?" Bristol asks.

I shake my head. "I don't know."

"What about breakfast?" she asks.

"If you hurry and get dressed, I'll have these done, and you can take one with you."

Bristol doesn't seem convinced, but she rushes up the stairs, her patter of footsteps thumping up the staircase. I turn the heat up on the stove. I'll have to rush to get dressed when the pancakes finish, but I don't want to leave the stove unattended. And I know Kyler told me to turn it off but listening to Bristol complain about how hungry she is on the ride to the arena isn't a good plan, either.

The front entrance buzzes, and the tablet indicates a guest opening the front gate. I grab the tablet and check the surveillance footage to see who has arrived first.

Mitchell.

That's probably for the best. I can text Lia what's going on when we leave with Mitchell.

I flip the pancakes as they're starting to burn, and Bristol comes tearing down the stairs. "I'm ready!" she squeals proudly. She hurries into the kitchen wearing a polka dot t-shirt and leopard print pants.

Bristol is gripping her unicorn socks which she puts on while seated at the kitchen table. I grab some napkins and a bottle of water for her and text Mitchell.

Can you come inside?

The front door clicks. "Everything okay?" Mitchell asks.

"I need to get dressed, and the pancakes need another minute on the stove."

Mitchell finds his way into the kitchen. "I've got it." He glances me over. "Go get ready. Greyson is waiting for us."

I race out of the kitchen, and Bristol is giggling. I hurry upstairs and into my bedroom, stripping down out of my pajamas and into a pair of black yoga pants and an oversized t-shirt.

I need to do laundry, which I was planning on working on today. I grab the note that Kyler asked me to bring, which is enclosed in a clear plastic envelope. I had it sent to the Eagle Tactical team to check for fingerprints or any DNA that might be on the paper.

It was clean. Not even a partial print. They sent me back the original, should I need to compare it to another sample.

That must be why Greyson wants me to bring it to the arena.

I would have thought that he'd discuss it at home between us, unless someone saw something. Is it possible Fitzgerald is behind the threats?

I toss the envelope into my purse, keeping it out of Bristol's sight. She's old enough to read, and I don't want to frighten her.

Kyler has gone out of his way to keep this from his daughter, and I agree with him. She doesn't need to know there's a monster out there threatening her life.

I hurry downstairs, and Mitchell is ushering

Bristol into the hallway. He's holding her pancakes and a bottle of water while she puts on her sneakers.

"Ready, ma'am?" Mitchell asks as I take the stairs two at a time.

I'm not thrilled with being called ma'am, but I don't argue. I'm not an old lady. "Yes." I just need to put my shoes on as well. I sling my purse over my shoulder and grab my shoes, slipping them on and stretching them as we hurry to the car.

Once we're in the backseat, I text Lia to let her know we had a change of plans and to meet at the ice arena. Maybe she can pick Bristol up from the stadium and spend the day with her exploring the city.

Traffic is heavy and slow on the way to the arena. It gives Bristol time to finish her pancakes, although she repeatedly complains about how they taste better with syrup and when Nanny Lia makes them.

We pull up at the back entrance of the stadium, the private entrance, and when we go to enter, there's a security guard and a police officer who glances us over. "We're here for Kyler Greyson."

The security guard glances at his sheet. "Names."

"I'm Emerson Ryan, and this is Bristol Greyson, his daughter."

"I need to see identification for you, Ms. Ryan," the officer says.

Mitchell is waiting in the car. He hasn't pulled away yet, making sure that we get inside before he leaves.

I dig into my purse, grab my wallet, and show my driver's license to the police officer. "Relation to Mr. Greyson?" he asks.

"They're with me," Kyler says, coming up from behind the officer.

"Just doing our due diligence." The officer steps aside, letting us into the building.

"What's going on?" I ask, keeping my voice low. He picks up Bristol, carrying her in his arms, protectively holding her as we walk alongside one another down the hallway.

"Bristol, sweetie, I want you to keep Uncle Jasper company. Can you do that?" Kyler asks as we approach the locker room.

"Of course, Daddy." He carries her into the locker room, and I stand at the entrance of the door. The guys are sitting around chatting, but none of them are undressing or changing into gameday attire.

Confident that Bristol is cared for, he takes my

hand and leads me down the hallway. "What's going on?" I ask, relieved to have him alone for a minute.

"Fitzgerald found another note."

The air is sucked from my lungs. I had suspected there might be another threat. What other reason would there have been for him to ask me to bring the first note? But it hadn't crossed my mind that someone else might have found it first.

"What did he say?"

"Not much. He's gotten the league involved and the police."

I curse under my breath. "What does this mean for your career?"

"When they find out I threw one of my prior games to protect my kid, it will cost me everything."

"And you told them this isn't the first threat that you've received?" A small part of me wishes that he'd lied for his own sake.

"I told them everything, Em. About how I hired a bodyguard to protect my daughter. The league, the police, Fitzgerald, they will want to speak with you."

There isn't much new information that I can give them. I sit down with Fitzgerald in his office first. He's available and ready to shoot questions at me like I'm the goalie, firing shot after shot at me.

"Why didn't you go to the police?" Fitzgerald

asks.

Kyler is outside in the hallway, speaking again with the police, showing them the note that I brought.

It's just me and Fitzgerald in his office. So far, he's been less disgusting and horrible than I thought, considering the way Greyson speaks about the man.

"I'm also part of a team who does private investigations. I trained at Quantico. Calling the police would have put Bristol in more jeopardy. That wasn't what Kyler wanted, sir."

"That wasn't up to you," he says sharply. He stares at me as though he's waiting for me to spill some other secret.

I'm not discussing our fake engagement with him. It's none of his business. And whether he's caught on to it or not, it's irrelevant regarding the threats.

Finally, Fitzgerald opens his mouth. "I saw who delivered the threat to Greyson's mailbox."

"What?" My eyes widen, shock evident in my features. There are times I can keep my cool, pretend I'm not surprised by news, but this revelation has me jumping out of my seat.

I'm standing, staring at him like he's lost his

mind.

"Did you tell Greyson? The police? Anyone?" I ask.

"I did not because it puts me in a predicament. Sit back down," Fitzgerald says and gestures with his finger at the chair. The man's hair is slicked back, greasy, and his overpriced suit is one size too tight. Like he's trying to make up for something.

I don't want to sit, but I also want every detail, and I'd prefer if Greyson heard it as well. At least one other witness, because if he denies it later, then I'm screwed.

I can't record our conversation with my cell phone. That would be illegal.

"Who delivered the threatening note?" I ask, hanging on to his every word.

A slimy grin curves at the edges of his lips. "Wouldn't you like to know?"

My stomach churns. "That's what I asked."

He taps his fingers together, relaxing in his chair. The smugness rolls off him like a fog, and it makes me sick to my stomach without even hearing his request.

"Who delivered the note?" I'm not playing games. This is Greyson's future on the line, and his daughter's life is being threatened.

He pushes his chair back. "Come sit on my lap," Fitzgerald says.

"Excuse me?"

"I'm not asking for a blow job. Just sit on my lap."

"I'd rather not." What a creep!

"Oh, come on. You're sticking it to Greyson on a regular basis. You can't tell me that's real. I can show you a good time. No strings attached. Unless you like to be tied up, baby."

I stand, unwilling to take his sexual harassment a moment longer.

"Sit your pretty little ass down if you want me to save Greyson's career."

My mouth hangs agape, and I put my butt back down on the chair.

"That's a good girl. I like that you follow my orders."

"You're a fucking pig." I'm not playing these mind games with him or fuck games. Whatever he wants to think of them, as I'm not going to indulge his disgusting fantasies.

Fitzgerald shrugs, not the least bit appalled by my suggestion. "You will sit, and you won't move your pretty ass if you want Greyson to play for the Ice Dragons next year."

He unzips his trousers and pulls out his cock.

"Put that away," I demand. If he comes anywhere near me with his dick, I'll grab the letter opener and stab the fucker where it counts.

But he doesn't move other than his hand, with which he pumps his dick as he stares at me.

I can't take his level of shit. I stand and head for the door. "If you leave this room, Greyson won't be playing hockey for any team ever again." His breathing comes out labored as he continues to give himself a hand job.

"I'll report you for sexual harassment," I say, and slide my phone out of my purse, snapping a picture of his hand on his dick.

"It's your word against mine. I'll tell them you came on to me and begged to watch me pleasure myself. Some no-nothing girl with a reputation for crying wolf during sex," he taunts. "I read about your little stunt with Clemens."

My blood runs cold, and I stiffen.

"I see I've struck a nerve," Fitzgerald says and smiles. His eyes are on me while he continues to pump his cock with his fist. "I can destroy Greyson's career. The league is interviewing him today, and me. All it takes is for me to tell them he threw a game, and he'd be tossed out for good."

He grunts, and I glance away, refusing to watch his pathetic act of sexual harassment.

"I have you on camera," I say, shaking my phone in my hand. "Your word against mine or not, it would still make a hell of a headline. NHL General Manager for the Ice Dragons gets caught with his hand on his dick while discussing threats to a six-year-old girl."

"I'm not a fucking pervert," he growls.

"No, you're just a sexual predator. Because that's so much better," I say sarcastically. I snap one more picture. "Enjoy being on the news, because your career is over."

I head for the door, my back to him, my hand on the door handle.

"Wait!" he shouts at me.

I grimace, really wanting to get the hell out of his office.

"It was my brother."

"What?" I spin around and grimace when I see that he's still got his hand around his dick, but it's grown flaccid. "Put that tiny pickle away." I gesture toward his dick.

He snarls and shoves it back in his pants. "The threat. It was from my brother, James Fitzgerald."

TWENTY-ONE

KYLER

I FINISH SPEAKING AGAIN with the police. The members of the league are arriving at noon to fully discuss the situation.

They've been made aware of the threats to my daughter, but that's all they've been informed of. The rest is to be discussed in detail.

Emerson storms out of Fitzgerald's office.

That's about right with how shit goes down with him whenever I'm forced to meet with the jackass.

I wasn't thrilled to leave her alone in the room with him, but he's mostly harmless.

She slams the door of his office when she leaves, and her cheeks are flaming. I glance her over. Her hands are trembling, and she folds them across her chest.

"Show me to the bathroom," she says. It comes out more like a demand, and I'm not sure she isn't going to be sick.

"This way," I say, hurrying down the hallway, and she's right at my side. Even with her shorter legs and smaller footsteps, she easily keeps up with me. It's clear that she's in a rush.

I escort her to the ladies' room door, and she hightails it inside. I wait for her, wondering what's going on. I give her a few minutes of privacy before I knock on the door.

"Em?"

No response.

I knock again and poke my head inside. I haven't seen any other women go in.

She sniffles and stares at her reflection in front of the mirror.

"What happened?" I ask, sensing hesitation on her part.

Her eyes twitch, and her jaw is tight. She doesn't answer me, and I'm not sure if her silence is any better. Because now, I can't stop thinking about what Fitzgerald might have said to her.

"Did he harass you?" I ask, stepping fully into the women's bathroom and letting the door shut behind me.

Em glances at me, and her silence tells me yes.

There's hurt in her eyes, pain radiating off her in waves that make it clear to me something bad happened in that asshole's office. "Did he touch you?" I growl, stepping closer to Em, and she freezes.

Her body goes rigid, and I see the look of shock and fear on her face.

"I'm going to fucking kill him," I growl and spin around on my feet, heading out of the bathroom and down the hall.

"Wait." Em's voice is soft and fragile as she races to catch up with me. "Please, don't do anything stupid."

"Stupid?" I repeat. I stop walking and stare at her. "What did he do to you, Em?" I can tell she's keeping something from me, and rage burns bright through me, needing to protect her. She's like family to me.

"He didn't touch me," she says.

"He better not have!" I can't keep my voice down or the anger that runs through my veins. I keep walking, my footfalls heavy as I stalk down the hallway.

"Please, don't. He'll ruin your career!"

"I don't care about my fucking career, Em. I care about you!"

She grabs my arm. Her touch is soft and soothing

as she pulls me to stop walking and face her. I'm staring deep into her gaze, transfixed and calmed by her presence. But one fleeting thought of Fitzgerald and I'm back at one-hundred-percent-ready to beat the shit out of him.

And I don't even know what he did other than it went beyond acceptable. I've never seen Em look quite so broken and fragile. And she wasn't like that before stepping into his office.

"Don't go after him," Em says, her voice soft. There are a few officers at the end of the hallway. Our privacy is disappearing, the longer we remain in the hallway, several doors down from Fitzgerald's office.

She carefully retrieves her cell phone from her purse. "If I show you this, I don't want you to freak out."

"Freak out?" Now she's actually scaring me. "What is it?" I demand, snatching her cell phone from her hands.

"Fitzgerald did something inappropriate while I was in his office," she says. Em looks skittish and presses her lips tight together. "I can take this to the police, file charges. But if you lay a finger on him, they'll arrest you," she warns.

"You don't have to look out for me," I say. "I can

handle myself." Her cell phone is locked, and I show it to her, waiting for her to unlock it.

"Promise me you won't fight him or lay a finger on him when you see the photo," she says.

I won't make a promise I can't keep. "What's the code to unlock your phone?"

"Promise me, Greyson." Her eyes are filled with pain as she stares up at me, and my heart shatters into a million tiny pieces.

"I love you, Em. I'm not promising anything that I won't follow through with."

Her breath catches in her throat. "You love me?" she asks.

I didn't even realize the words I said until she repeats them. I rub the back of my neck nervously. It is true my feelings are stronger for her than anyone else, outside of Bristol, and that is a completely different kind of love.

I smile and avoid the question. I'm not ready to say it again. "What's your phone passcode?"

She offers a lopsided smile through the hurt in her gaze and shakes her head. "I don't want you to start something with Fitzgerald."

"If it's that bad, then just tell me." I hate being kept in the dark. I stare down at her, pushing a strand of her hair behind her ear. "Just tell me what happened."

"I don't want to," she says, and her cheeks burn even brighter. "I know who did it."

Em pulls back out of my grasp and hurries down the hallway in the opposite direction of Fitzgerald's office and the police officers who are investigating the recent threat.

"What?" I'm not quite understanding her statement unless it has to do with Fitzgerald, and that's why she's so shaken up. "Who?" I need confirmation from her before I lose my mind.

"Fitzgerald's brother."

Bile roils through my stomach, making me nauseous as it churns again and again. I'm grateful I didn't put anything else in there this morning. I haven't even had coffee yet. This day keeps getting better and better.

"What the hell do you mean? His brother was behind the threats to Bristol?" I ask, staring at Em.

"James Fitzgerald."

My stomach drops at *his* name. I should have realized the connection. Maybe I didn't want to see it? "He plays for the Bruisers," I snarl, disgusted at the man who would think it's acceptable to threaten a six-year-old girl.

Sure, we hockey players make threats on the ice, get into fights during a game, but we never go after anyone's kids.

That's a line that should never be crossed.

"Who the fuck does that?" I growl, "Threaten a kid?" I'm steaming, and I want to punch someone's face. Right now, the closest target is the owner and his brother, Brent Fitzgerald.

Emerson doesn't let me skirt past her in the hallway. She's small but mighty as she blocks me squarely, not letting me pass. "You'll regret it," she says. "There are a half-dozen cops ready to have your ass arrested if you try anything."

"It's his fault! Fitzgerald gave his brother access," I seethe between clenched teeth. My top lip twitches in a snarl, and my hands ball into fists at my sides.

"We're going for a walk," Emerson says, and grabs my arm, dragging me in the opposite direction down the hallway.

"Let go of me," I snap and yank out of her hold. "He deserves—"

"What does he deserve, Kyler?" she asks, her eyes meeting mine, never wavering. "Do you want to punch him? Is that it? Beat the crap out of him? Then what?"

My jaw ticks, but my silence is all I can give her

without shouting and storming past her for Fitzgerald's office.

"I want to kill him," I growl, unafraid to voice my anger. She knows the fear that's rattled me for the past several months while I've been worried about my daughter.

"You're not the only one," she says, but her voice is softer, calmer. She takes my hand, intertwining our fingers together. Her touch is soothing, and I exhale a ragged breath, the anger slowly dissipating from her touch alone.

Dammit.

"The police are going to want to talk to you," she says.

"I know. I've already told them everything I know." I lean against the wall and shut my eyes. "The league is going to kick me out."

"What?" Em's fingers graze my cheek, and my eyelids slowly flutter open, staring down at her. Her body is just inches from mine, trapping me against the wall.

"It's against the league's rules to throw a game," I say.

"You didn't have a choice."

"Sure, I did. I could have gone to the police months ago when the first threat was delivered.

Instead, I hired a bodyguard and followed through with what the notes demanded of me."

Her gaze tightens, and she presses her lips together. "But you love hockey. What are you going to do if the league doesn't let you play?"

TWENTY-TWO

EMERSON

I HEAD to the locker room to find Bristol while the league is interviewing Kyler. I give a firm knock. "You guys better be decent," I say, pushing open the door.

Bristol is seated on the bench, giggling when she sees me enter with my eyes half-covered. I'm peeking through my hands, making sure I'm not about to walk into something I can't unsee.

But given the fact a six-year-old girl is hanging out in the locker room, I'm assuming it's okay for me to come in.

"How'd it go?" Jasper asks. He's seated next to his niece, and they're knee-deep in a mean game of hand slap.

She rests her hands on his, and as soon as he goes to flip them over, she shoots them back. He's definitely giving her an advantage, moving slow enough to make sure she wins.

"My turn." She grins wickedly, and Jasper groans.

"Again?" He puts his hands on top and pulls them away too slow, constantly getting his hands smacked by Bristol.

I raise an eyebrow. "That doesn't look like a very nice game, Bristol."

"It's not," Jasper mutters.

Bristol grins. "But it's fun!"

"Hitting your uncle is fun?" Jasper groans as he tries to move his hands away. But he's too slow. "Maybe I should wear my hockey gloves for this game. You're going to leave bruises."

"Don't be a baby," Bristol says. She sticks out her tongue and then jumps off the bench, running down the locker room hallway.

"Where are you going?" I call after her.

"Bathroom!"

Jasper shakes out his hands. "I was letting her win until I realized the kid hits as bad as her dad. Kyler and I used to play this game as kids, and he'd always win. How is he doing?"

"He's holding himself together. He's with the

league right now, explaining everything. How much do you know?" I ask.

"I knew there was a threat against his kid, and that was why he hired you, but the actual threat he kept a secret. He wouldn't tell me what was going on, and I assumed it had to do with Ashleigh. I never liked her."

"Why is that?"

Jasper stretches and glances back in the direction of the bathroom. He probably doesn't want his niece to overhear our conversation. "She was a bit too judgmental for my taste. But I never thought she'd be a suspect."

"The good news is we actually have a suspect," I say.

"Suspect for what?" Bristol asks, skipping back to the bench.

I exchange a quick glance with Jasper. This is a conversation that needs to change fast. "For our murder mystery game," Jasper says. "Remember that game I bought you for Christmas last year."

"You bought it for Daddy," Bristol says. "And I'm too young to play."

"Right. Right," Jasper says with a nod. "Maybe in a few years, kiddo." He ruffles her hair and stands.

"I'm going to gear up and skate. Do you want to join me?"

Bristol's eyes light up. "Yes!"

"What about you?" Jasper asks. "Do you want to join us?"

I inhale nervously, and my breath catches in my throat. "I've only ice skated once, when I was a kid, and I wasn't great at it."

"I can teach you," Bristol says. "It's easy."

"What size do you wear?" Jasper asks.

"Eight," I say.

He mentally does the calculation and returns with a men's skate for me to wear and a pair for Bristol as well. Hers have stickers and are lavender. Mine are black with white laces.

We lace up our skates, and Jasper tosses me a sweatshirt from Kyler's wood locker, throwing it at me. "You might get cold on the ice," he says.

I don't imagine Kyler will mind if I borrow a sweatshirt of his. I slip it on, and his scent wafts over me. It's warm and cocoons me as I carefully follow Bristol and Jasper out of the locker room and toward the ice arena.

The discussion about the suspect with Jasper will have to wait.

Jasper grabs my hand, helping keep me steady as

I'm clutching every nearby orifice to hold on to. I don't want to fall on my ass and make an idiot of myself.

"You've got this," Jasper says.

"Do I?" I laugh, not the least bit confident in what we're doing. I should be watching and protecting Bristol, not giving myself a concussion when I fall on the ice, which is inevitable.

"Yes," Bristol says with the widest grin I've ever seen. "Just follow what I do." She glides onto the ice with ease and twirls around before skating backward.

The fuck I can't follow that. It takes concentration to glide with one foot and then the other on the ice.

"Man, if I knew you couldn't skate," Jasper says, "I'd have offered you lessons a lot sooner. We could have surprised my brother with a routine on the ice and really made him jealous." There's a teasing tone in his voice, and while I imagine that he likes to rile up his brother, I don't get the impression that they fight over girls.

"He doesn't know how bad I am on the ice. But he did ask me once if I could skate," I say.

"And you told him the truth?" Jasper asks. He pulls me farther into the center of the rink and works with me to keep my balance and focus on my movements.

"I wasn't about to lie to him."

"Small fibs aren't necessarily lies," Jasper says. "And I'm honestly shocked that he agreed to date you. He swore he'd never lay eyes on a woman who couldn't ice skate and didn't love hockey."

I chuckle. "I know nothing about hockey, and I suck at ice skating. A match made in heaven," I joke.

"Both of those things are fixable." He lets go of my hand but skates alongside me, making sure that I'm steady.

I'm slow, but I haven't fallen on the ice... yet.

Bristol skates up to us and glances me over. "You're slow," she says.

"Thanks, kid," I mutter as she skates away and does more twirls, spinning rapidly. "Has Kyler ever thought about putting her in competitive ice skating?" I ask.

"She hates playing competitive sports. The pressure gets to her, and she goes off and does her own thing. Bristol is a bit of a free spirit."

I watch her on the ice, not seeming to care that we're on the opposite side of the rink. "I've noticed."

There's more commotion and noise as several other teammates head onto the ice with their hockey sticks and a puck, working on practicing for their next game. Jasper should be doing that instead of babysitting me and Bristol on the ice, but I appreciate his patience.

"We should give the boys their space," I say. My ankles hurt, and I don't want to interfere in practice. I wave at Bristol, attempting to gesture for her to come over to me, but she just waves back and dances to the beat in her head.

It's cute and also a bit unnerving when I'm trying to get her attention, and I'm not good enough on ice skates to go chase her down.

"It's all right. We can share the rink for a couple of hours. It'll be good to teach the boys some discipline about not fighting with every player who trips them up and gets in their way."

I narrow my gaze. "It's really no problem. Bristol and I can wait on the bench."

Jasper shakes his head. "You can, but you won't. My niece is happy, and I don't want what's happened today to affect her," he says. "She's bound to overhear the guys talk, or Kyler when he gets done with the league's interview."

We spend another hour on the ice, and my ankles by now are very sore, but I don't want to complain. The guys have slammed each other into the glass at least a dozen times. They're wearing their full gear, but even so, it has to hurt more than my little ankle discomfort.

"Ryan! Jasper!" Kyler shouts for us, and I frown, unsure why he's using my last name. I get the dreaded sense that he's putting distance between us, and we haven't even talked about what happened with the league.

"Looks like your fiancé is done," Jasper says.

"Daddy!" Bristol squeals and skates over to the bench. He opens the door, letting her exit the ice arena.

It takes me a few more minutes to get there, and Jasper is beside me, making sure that at least if I fall, there's someone to help me back onto my feet.

"Learning to ice skate?" Kyler asks as I step off the ice.

"Something like that."

He leads us back to the locker room, and the minute we're inside, I sit on the bench, working the laces free.

"How'd it go?" I ask, trying not to worry Bristol, but I want to know what's going on.

"I've been suspended for the remainder of the season." His jaw is tight, and he helps Bristol out of her skates. "The NHL doesn't want to make public knowledge the reason for my suspension because it could jeopardize the integrity of the game. The team has scheduled a press conference for this afternoon, and I am expected to give a statement to the press and tell them that I'm taking the rest of the season off to focus on my family."

"Wait," Jasper says as he puts his gear on. "You're out the rest of the season?"

Kyler nods. "It's only a few more games. We have zero chance of making the playoffs. I'm going to shower and get cleaned up for the press conference. I'd like you and Bristol to be there," he says, staring at me.

"You want me at your press conference?" I'm surprised, and I'm pretty sure that's evident on my face. I try to keep my cool, because there's no reason I need to be there other than for support.

I change into my sneakers, and Bristol does the same, seated beside me. I glance from her to Kyler.

I have so many questions about the man who was threatening Bristol, but I have to wait until we're alone to ask them.

And more importantly, what happens now that his daughter is no longer in danger?

He'll expect me to pack up my belongings at his house and move out. There's no reason for me to continue living with him under his roof. My responsibility as Bristol's bodyguard is over.

Later that afternoon, I'm standing beside Bristol, her hand in mine. Mitchell picked clothes up for all of us to wear for the press conference. Bristol is in a dress with a gingham print. I'm in a black skirt and a matching blouse. Kyler is wearing a suit.

She clutches my hand and wiggles uncomfortably. "Can we go home?" Bristol whispers, staring up at me.

We're in the background, on the side, for pictures and for the press to make us look like a family during the interview. He's standing at the podium, answering questions rattled off by a number of journalists.

When he walked out, we were beside him, but he's at the podium by himself while we are patiently waiting for him to finish his spiel.

"Thank you all for coming here today," Kyler says into the microphone. "I know this might come as a surprise, but I'll be taking the rest of the season off to focus on my family. As you may hear, there were some recent threats to my family's safety, and while the police have found the suspect, arrested him, and he's being charged with numerous crimes,

I find it in my family's best interest to take some time at home."

There's chatter among the crowd, and then one reporter gets the microphone. "What types of threats were there?" a reporter asks.

Kyler's jaw tightens. "The kind that threaten a child," he says.

Bristol squeezes my hand. "What's Daddy talking about?"

I gesture for her to keep her voice down. Why the hell are Bristol and I here if Kyler is going to talk about the threats? We were trying to shield her from all of it.

More chatter erupts among the journalists.

The microphone is passed to another gentleman. "Are there any other reasons that you've decided to postpone your career right before playoffs?"

Kyler laughs. "I'd love to say that the Ice Dragons will be making the playoffs this season, but we have zero chance, given our record."

A soft rumble of laughter registers through the crowd.

"I can assure you that I will be back next season," Kyler says.

More noise erupts, and he gestures for the audience to settle. Whether he heard the question or he's decided to answer before a reporter specifically asked is hard to tell. There are a lot of voices vying for attention.

"No, I haven't received a contract yet, but I am in negotiations with the current owner of the Ice Dragons."

Is he in negotiations, or is what he's doing a tactic to help push his career for next year? Will he even want to return to the Ice Dragons after what happened with Fitzgerald's brother?

Fitzgerald is a certifiable asshole, pulling out his dick and trying to make me uncomfortable. He did manage to do the latter, but I don't want it to affect Kyler's chances with the team he wants to be on, where his brother plays.

"Any other questions?" Kyler asks.

More chatter erupts, and then he covers the microphone and gestures for Bristol and me to join him. I assume it's for a photo, that he's trying to milk this angle as best he can. The league is giving him the opportunity to protect his career, even if they're looking out for themselves.

"I do have one announcement to make," Kyler says. "As many of you may know, this is my fiancée and my daughter." He introduces us to the press.

Kyler takes a question in the front row from one

of the reporters. "It's common knowledge that you're a wealthy billionaire, and you don't need the NHL's money to play the sport. Have you considered purchasing a team in the league?"

He smiles, and his shoulders seem to relax with her question. "If I do that, it would be against the league's rules for me to play the game."

"So, when you retire?" she asks, probing further.

He leans forward into the microphone. "I have no plans to retire, now or anytime in the near future," he says, making his position absolutely clear. "This is just a short break. A couple of weeks to focus on my growing family."

"Growing family?" the woman asks. "Does that mean that you're expecting another child?"

Bristol's eyes widen, and while sometimes she doesn't pay complete attention to what's going on, this time, she catches every word. "Am I going to be a big sister?" she asks with an excited squeal.

No doubt, every reporter heard her excitement, and a few of them even managed to get it on video.

"No comment," Kyler says, but it's too late. The rumor escaped, and there's no chance of leashing this monstrosity.

TWENTY-THREE
KYLER

I END up paying Lia for the day but letting her go home early. With Bristol safe at the arena and Em keeping an eye on her, there really isn't any reason to have the nanny pick Bristol up. But now, I regret not having Lia home to cook us all a nice dinner or watch Bristol in the evening.

I could use some alone time to talk with Em. I don't want her to think that last night was a one-off incident.

I don't want no-strings-attached sex. With Em, I want the whole package.

I end up ordering dinner, and Mitchell is generous enough to pick it up and bring it back to the house before he takes off for the night.

Bristol helps set the table, and once dinner

arrives, I stalk upstairs to find Em, who seems to have been hiding from me since we got back from the arena.

I give a firm knock on her bedroom door, and it squeaks open. The latch wasn't secure. She's standing beside the bed, her suitcase open and the dresser drawers open as she folds her clothes and packs her belongings.

"Are you planning a trip?" I ask. She hadn't mentioned going anywhere, but she's certainly got the money after the last couple of months that I've been paying her six figures.

She glances up at me, and her gaze flinches. "Not exactly."

"What does that mean?" I ask, stalking into her bedroom. I glance at her bag, curious if she's packing summer clothes for the beach or maybe she's planning on going someplace in the mountains and needs some cooler clothes for the climate.

She's got everything stuffed into one bag, from her bathing suits on top to her sweaters peeking out underneath.

"The contract is over, Kyler. I've finished off my job now that James Fitzgerald has been arrested and is behind bars. You and your daughter are safe."

"That's what this is about? You don't have to leave."

"Don't I?" She laughs nervously and bites down on her bottom lip. "Who are we playing make-believe for now?"

"The team thinks we're engaged."

"And?" She's holding her lacy black bra in her hands, folding it in half, but she doesn't put it into her luggage. She's fiddling with it. "We knew this had an expiration date. Just neither of us knew when it would be."

I wish I could argue with her that she's wrong, but she's not. I didn't ask her to marry me out of love; it was all part of a farce to get Fitzgerald to renew my contract.

Which didn't work.

I'm still waiting on a phone call from him, but what the reporter said has been itching through my head since the moment I left the arena. *Ownership.*

I could own an NHL team.

My body tingles at the thought of being in charge of the team, kicking Fitzgerald out, and hiring a new general manager while I'd be on the board.

I could also just get him fired for harassing Emerson. I'm not sure what he did, she hasn't shown me the photos, but knowing his reputation, it was vulgar, offensive, and unprofessional.

But I love playing on the ice, and I'd have to sit back and watch from behind the glass or on the bench. I'm not ready to hang my skates up just yet. In a couple of years, it might not be such a bad investment. And I've felt like that money was cursed. At least I'd be throwing it into something that I love.

And if I never make another cent from it, I wouldn't care because I love hockey.

"What if I don't want it to have an expiration date, our relationship?" I say, stepping closer to Em.

"Last night was great, but what we have isn't real," she says, reminding me of our agreement. The one where I'm putting boatloads of money into her account.

"My feelings for you are real."

She places the black bra into her luggage and folds her arms across her chest. "You just don't want me to leave because you're going to be off from now until the next season, and you like my company."

I grin. "I do like your company," I say and rest my hands on her hips. "I also like everything about you. From the way you smile and your giddiness lights up your eyes and face to the sassy sway of your hips when you walk. You're the most honest and genuine woman I know. You speak your mind, and you always know what you want."

"I don't—" I kiss her to silence her protest. It's soft and warm, and my fingers stroke her hips as I pull her closer to my body. "You don't want me," she whispers.

"I do. I have," I say. "Last night wasn't just about a good time with the bodyguard."

She glances down, avoids my stare, and smiles sheepishly.

Do I make her nervous?

"I had fun last night," she whispers, and my stomach twists, waiting for her to let me down. Did it mean nothing to her? Maybe she just wanted to have a little fun since it's been a while.

"But?"

She shakes her head. "No, but. Just, I had fun."

"And that's all you want?" I guess.

Her eyes narrow. "I didn't say that. You're putting words into my mouth."

"Because you're not communicating with me," I say. I run my hand through my hair, taking a step back. How is it that this woman who I have such strong feelings for, also irritates me?

"You're a professional hockey player, Greyson. Our relationship is fake."

"The sex last night on the sofa was pretty damn real," I say. "So was the orgasm I gave you."

She blushes, and I know for a fact that she didn't fake a single moan last night. "That's beside the point."

"Is it?" I push harder, not wanting her to walk away from me. I step closer, and this time, she steps backward as I trap her between me and the wall. "I could have told everyone that you're having my baby during the press conference."

Her eyes narrow like two sharp daggers. "You wouldn't have."

"It crossed my mind after Bristol's comment," I say.

"That's evil."

"Or maybe manifesting what I want." I lean closer, and her breath catches in her throat. "You will have my baby, Em. We will get married. And you'll let me worship your body and give me your heart because you love me."

Her eyes are dark. Her lips pucker as she exhales a soft breath. There's a flush that's spread across her cheeks and her chest. Desire is written all over her, and the way she looks at me tells me that she wants me, that she wants this life I've described.

"What else?" Em whispers, and her breath is

warm against my cheek. "What do you see happening for us?"

My gaze tightens, and I see the desire and arousal as she stares at me with such warmth and affection. "You'll have to wait and see, Em."

She leans in and presses her lips softly to mine. The kiss is soft, chaste, questioning what we are, and full of uncertainty. I don't want her to have any doubts about us, about my feelings for her.

I deepen the kiss, pulling her closer, tighter, letting her feel my erection poke her through my trousers. "You're the only woman I want," I whisper against her lips. "And I do think that you should move out," I say.

Her brow pinches, and her bottom lip juts forward. It's the most adorable expression, and I want to kiss the worry right off her lips.

"Out of your own room and into my bedroom."

———

We're officially dating.

Lia has promised to babysit Bristol while I take Em out on a real date.

"I can't promise there won't be paparazzi

following us," I remind her as I poke my head into our bedroom while she's getting ready.

"Out!" she shouts and points at the door. "You're not supposed to see me like this."

"It's not a wedding," I say with a shrug. But damn, does she look good. The black and red dress hugs her body in the best way possible.

I shift uncomfortably when I feel my cock twitch in my pants. *Not now, boy. There's plenty of time for that later.*

I want to wine and dine her. She deserves a real date. One where we're not holding hands and forcing smiles because the guests are trying to decipher our relationship status. This isn't a show that we're putting on to impress anyone else.

Well, there is one person I'd like to impress, and that's Emerson. It's a tall order, considering that I'm a billionaire, but she made me promise nothing extravagant. No flying her to Paris for an early breakfast or Aruba for a midnight stroll on the beach.

Damn. Both of those were on my 'dates with Em' list.

So, I'm trying to do something normal. I'm not the least bit normal when it comes to dating women. I have a kid. And let's face it. Em is living with me.

We've done this dating to get to know each other completely backward. Ass backward if you ask me. But I don't mind it, because I've already sampled the goods and absolutely love them.

I want more of her.

More of this wild romance with Em, so tonight is about two normal people going out in New York City for a typical date. She made me stick to a budget.

One hundred dollars.

I'm tempted to sneak a few extra hundred-dollar bills into my wallet because her budget is unrealistic for me. Let's face it, a bottle of wine is at least twice that cost. Plus appetizers, dinner, and suppose we go anywhere at all that charges admission, like a stroll at the zoo or a walk through the museum, and my budget is already blown.

One hundred dollars will barely cover dinner.

I want to make this night special with Em, and while I wholeheartedly agree to keep things from being extravagant, I also want to wine and dine her.

The girl isn't after my money. I mean, sure, I've paid her six figures a month for her to fake date me, but she's earned every cent. Especially when I proposed to her on the ice, and she had no idea what I was doing.

The media still thinks we're engaged. There are

rumors we're pregnant, but we haven't addressed those with the media. Let them talk. I've avoided their questions, and now that I'm no longer on thin ice with the league, I'm out cold, and the news media isn't interested in pestering me. They got their interview and have moved on.

Their most recent focus has been on James Fitzgerald, who has only delivered one line repeatedly to the press: "No comment." He has since been arrested for threatening my daughter, among a number of other criminal charges.

It turns out that I'm not the only hockey player he blackmailed who has a kid. And the league has quietly suspended those players as well. They've all taken time off to be with their families and support their kids. Especially since we all have one thing in common, we're single fathers.

My phone buzzes in my pocket, and I step into the hallway, letting Em finish getting ready. It's Fitzgerald, the slimy owner who at least did one decent thing with his life—he admitted that his brother was behind the threats.

"Greyson," I say, answering the phone.

"I wasn't sure you'd take my call," Brent says.

"Why? Because you sexually harassed my fiancée, or your brother threatened my daughter?"

There's silence that befalls the line. Seems I've made him speechless. That's a first.

"She showed you the picture on her phone?" Fitzgerald says, and he huffs under his breath. "I'm surprised you haven't taken it to the league."

Em never showed me any photo, but I can bluff like the best of them. "Maybe I should. Seeing as how your brother fucked me over, and you're trying to fuck my—"

"Fine. I'll do it."

"What?" I'm not sure what he's agreeing to.

"You want a contract with the Ice Dragons next year. I'll do it," Fitzgerald says.

I shift the weight on my feet and lean against the wall in the hallway. Not like this. This isn't how I envisioned my new contract negotiations going with Fitzgerald. I'm not about blackmail and seedy deals. That isn't how I play, and it's not what I want to get me onto the Ice Dragons for another year.

"I want you to resign," I say.

"Fat chance, Greyson." He laughs like I've suggested the most ridiculous suggestion in the world.

"Even with the pictures my fiancée has on her phone?"

He clears his throat. "Pictures? She took more than one?"

"Of course," I say, sounding firm and confident in my bluff. "She has several and a video."

"Fuck me," Fitzgerald mutters to himself a little too loudly.

The bedroom door swings open, and Em looks spectacular with the knee-length black and red dress hugging her in all the right places. The red emphasizes her breasts, and I can't stop staring at her, amazed at how good she looks.

"Who is that?" she whispers, pointing at my phone.

"I have to go," I say to Fitzgerald, keeping control of the conversation. "You'll send me the contract and then offer your resignation effective at the end of the season."

"And if I say no?"

Em grabs my phone from my hands with a smirk. "I'll send the press the photos and video of your dick in your hands and yanking off—"

My eyes widen, and she ends the call. I'm not sure if it was intentional or she accidentally hung up, but thank heaven she did, or my bluff would have been ruined.

"He did what?" I'm ready to drive down to the arena and kick the shit out of him.

Em rests a hand on my forearm. "It's fine. I'm over it."

"Well, I'm not!" I shrug out of her touch and stomp down the stairs.

"Kyler, wait up," she calls after me. Em's footsteps are soft and light, padding down the stairs while I'm quickly putting my shoes on and heading for the garage.

I can't stand the thought of what the slimeball did to Em. Maybe I wasn't there for her when Clemens forced himself on her, but I sure as hell am not going to let Fitzgerald get away with sexually harassing Em or anyone else.

Em grabs her purse and her heels, racing me out the door. She jumps into the front seat beside me before I can back out of the driveway.

"You're not about to ruin our date by stopping at the arena," Em says. She slips into her shoes once she's seated in the passenger side of the SUV.

Her words slice through me. I gave Mitchell the night off so that Em and I could have a date night alone. And now, I'm about to ruin our special night by focusing on Fitzgerald.

My hands grip the steering wheel hard as I hit

the button for the garage. The garage door slowly rises.

"What am I supposed to do? Just let him harass other women? Show me the video. The photos. I need to see it, Em."

"I don't think that's a good idea." She clutches her purse to her lap. "Let's go out, have a nice dinner together like we planned, please."

I rub my forehead, my stomach tossing and turning. "You deserve to be cared for, Em. Protected."

"I don't want you fighting Fitzgerald." She is firm in her answer, and her hold doesn't loosen on her purse.

I exhale a heavy sigh. "Maybe I could suggest we play a game on the ice together. I'm sure he has his skates from his younger days."

"Why? So you can beat the crap out of him fairly on the ice?" Em smiles as she stares at me, shaking her head. "No means no. You are not going to fight my battles for me. I can handle his dumb ass. In fact, I did when I was in his office. You have to let it go."

"How am I supposed to let it go? He admitted to masturbating with you in the room!"

"He's a pervert," Em says. "Karma will catch up with him. But he did one thing right."

I refuse to see her point of view. "He's a douche pervert."

"And he admitted to seeing his brother plant the threatening note in your mailbox," Em says, her voice soft and calm. She rests her hand on my arm and slides it down to my fingers, intertwining our hands together.

Her touch is soft and soothing, like a drug that settles my anger and my adrenaline. How the hell does she do that?

"I hate him," I seethe between clenched teeth.

"Don't waste your energy on him. He's not worth it, babe."

"Babe?" I glance at her, surprised by her term of endearment.

Em shrugs. "Just trying it out," she says. She gives my hand a squeeze and releases her fingers from my grasp, her hands protectively clutching her purse. "Now, where are you taking me on this cheap date?"

I chuckle and shake my head. "You'll have to wait and see."

DINNER IS ABSOLUTELY DELICIOUS. Sitting across from Kyler, I can't believe that he found this cute little hole-in-the-wall Italian restaurant.

The prices are affordable, which meets the requirements I set for him to spend no more than one hundred dollars on our date. Which is still a lot of money, but to him, it's nothing. He griped about my budget for several days before our date.

I half-expected him to prepay for dinner or take me someplace fancy and have the restaurant foot the bill because he is friends with the chef. Neither of which he did.

I'm impressed.

I'm also lovestruck, which makes me nervous and giddy around him. I'm trying my damndest to keep my cool. It's Kyler Greyson, the man I used to work for as his daughter's bodyguard and had a fake romance with, but now, it's real.

The pressure is definitely there, at least for me. I want to live up to his expectations. And it's hard when I swear every girl on the street turns her head, or there are whispers inside and glances as people recognize him.

It doesn't seem to faze Kyler in the slightest, or maybe he just doesn't notice it anymore. He's been in the public spotlight for years.

Kyler orders us one dessert to split, and it's divine. I've never tasted chocolate quite so good in my life. Apparently, I've been missing out.

He smirks as he watches me lick the spoon.

Is he seriously getting turned on right now, watching me eat? The tips of his ears are red, and his eyes have darkened as he stares at me.

I glance down at the dessert. "Are you going to have any more of it?"

Kyler shifts in his seat. "I'm thoroughly enjoying watching you lick that spoon," he confesses.

I'm sure I'm blushing from his comment, and I glance down, smiling nervously. Why does he make me feel like I'm a teenager all over again? I don't get nervous around boys or on dates. But with him, he makes my stomach flutter and my heart race.

His stare is intense as he watches me, and I glance away, noticing a woman at another table sitting alone, watching us.

"You've got a secret admirer," I say, nodding toward the brunette alone at the table a few feet away.

"Let her look," he says, his gaze entirely on me. He doesn't so much as glance behind himself. It doesn't bother him in the slightest.

"I recognize her," I whisper, trying for a moment to pinpoint where I've seen her before.

It takes a minute for the cogs to click into place. She was outside Briarwood months ago. I assumed she'd been waiting for her child.

Kyler's brow pinches, and he glances over his shoulder and sucks in a breath.

"Do you know her?" I ask. The slight sound he makes indicates to me that he does. That he's surprised to see her.

"I do," he whispers, and she stands, coming to the table to approach us. "Ashleigh," he says, and the name on his tongue clicks into place.

She's Bristol's biological mother.

My fingers clench onto the spoon as I stare up at

her. She has the bluest eyes, just like Bristol, and a warm smile.

"What are you doing in New York?" Kyler asks.

She stands at the edge of the table. I'm grateful there isn't another chair, or she might invite herself to our table and interrupt our date. However, she's technically interrupting it right now.

What does she want?

Kyler's question is kinder, asking her what she's doing in New York. I'd be asking her what the fuck she wants and why she's bothering us.

I'm a bit moody at the moment, staring up at her. She's got perfect skin, her hair is gorgeous, and her body makes me even more envious.

I take another bite of the chocolate dessert. Not exactly what I need, but I'm stewing in my jealousy. I can admit what I feel, at least to myself.

I keep my lips zipped, letting Kyler and Ashleigh do all the talking.

"I wanted to see Bristol," Ashleigh says, her voice soft and fragile. She doesn't seem threatening, but that doesn't mean anything.

"You made the decision to grant me full custody," Kyler says, his jaw ticking.

Ashleigh raises her hands. "I promise I'm not looking to change that, but sometimes I wonder what she's like. I saw Antonio Moretti at her school. Are you sure she's safe, sending her to Briarwood?"

"I have it handled," Kyler says. "The biggest issue I have with him at the moment is that Bristol and his son, Liam, haven't been getting along in class. Not that it's any of your concern."

"I'm her mother," Ashleigh whispers.

Kyler shakes his head. "No, you were her surrogate."

She winces. "I love Bristol. You know I've always wanted what was best for her."

Kyler stares at Ashleigh, letting her finish speaking.

"I granted you full custody because I thought that was in her best interest. But I'm concerned that she's in the same class, and what if they do a family tree or learn about DNA tests and realize they're related?"

"They're six," Kyler says. "Her family tree won't include your family, and they're not going to learn about DNA until what, high school?"

"It could be middle school," Ashleigh counters.

"Great. Bristol is in elementary school. We have plenty of time, and I don't think the kids are going to compare samples to each other. You're grasping at straws to make this into something it isn't."

"I just worry about her."

"And you think I don't? That we don't?" Kyler says, gesturing toward me. I'm not sure I should be included in this conversation. I remain quiet, letting him deal with Ashleigh. This doesn't quite feel like my place. "Why are you here?" Kyler asks, getting directly to the point.

"I just want to see her."

"Are you going to fight me for custody?" he asks, going right for the tough questions.

Ashleigh shakes her head no. "I wouldn't do that to Bristol or to you. I know you're a good father. I saw on the news that you're engaged." She finally glances at me like I haven't been sitting here for the last five minutes. "Congratulations."

"You didn't come over here to congratulate us," I say, finally having enough. I've tried to keep myself out of the conversation, but it's difficult with the two of them having it right in front of me.

The brunette sighs. "No, I suppose I didn't. I want Bristol pulled out of Briarwood."

"That isn't your choice to make," Kyler says. "She likes her school, and she's doing well. I'm not transferring her."

I can hear the tension seeping out of his voice, and I reach across the table for Kyler's hand, trying to calm him down. "Do you agree with her?" he asks, pulling back when I touch his hand.

"No, I don't. But we also don't know where we'll even be next year. Your contract is up. You could get offered a deal with another team in another state."

"I don't want to play for another team," Kyler says. He takes my hand and squeezes it. "I'm playing for the Ice Dragons, and Bristol will continue to attend Briarwood."

Ashleigh opens and shuts her mouth several times. I'm not sure if she's speechless or just realizes that she can't win an argument with Kyler Greyson.

She turns and heads back to her table, drops a few twenties, and then grabs her coat and heads outside.

"Well, that was something else," I mutter.

Kyler untangles his hand from mine. He takes a sip of his drink and gestures the waitress over. "Can we see your wine list?"

For the rest of the evening, Kyler is much quieter and more reserved than I'm used to witnessing. He has one glass of red wine and offers me the wine list. I turn down the offer, and he doesn't push, which I appreciate.

He settles up with the bill, and then we walk a couple of blocks to Central Park. He still seems lost in his head, probably overanalyzing what happened with Ashleigh earlier.

"Do you want to talk about it?" I ask, nudging him as we walk.

"Fitzgerald offered me a contract for next year," Greyson says, the words thick and heavy, like he's not happy about the news.

"That's what you wanted, isn't it?" I ask, turning to face him. We stop walking, and I reach for his hands, trying to offer a small amount of comfort. This is something he needs to decide on his own, what he wants from his career.

"It was. It is." Kyler sighs. "I don't know anymore. After what happened with Bristol and finding out it was Fitzgerald's brother, I'm torn."

"How so?" I ask, leading him to sit on one of the nearby benches with me.

He plops down, and I sit beside him, our legs brushing together. I rest my hand on his thigh, trying to help ease his mind.

"Fitzgerald would continue to be my general manager if I sign with the Ice Dragons. He's a pig," Kyler says, glancing up at me.

"And karma will give him what he's due in time."

"I keep thinking about getting him fired."

"Do you want me to report him for what he did in his office?" I ask.

Kyler shakes his head. "You don't deserve that type of media attention." He leans forward, folding his hands together. "I'm considering buying the team."

"Is it for sale?" I ask.

"Everyone has a price, babe." He glances at me with a smirk, giving me the same nickname I gave him earlier.

I nudge him playfully. "Babe, huh? Couldn't be more original?" I ask, teasing him.

"Okay, we can go back to M&M." He chuckles and rubs his eyes while laughing.

I pinch his arm. "I'm not a chocolate-coated candy."

"But you could be," he says, glancing me over from head to toe. "I have some chocolate sauce that I could cover your naked body with and lick—"

I lean in, capturing his lips, taking a taste, my fingers tangling through his hair. I'm trying to offer him comfort, warmth, and love because I don't want him to go through all of this alone.

"And what about your hockey career? Can you play and be the owner of a team?"

Kyler sighs. "No, it would be against league rules.

I might be able to appoint a trust as owner and continue to play, but I'd need to consult a lawyer, and I'd have to appoint someone I trust to run the team."

"You can appoint me," I say.

He laughs at my suggestion. "My fiancée, who knows nothing about hockey?"

"I know that you're the best player in the league," I say with a cheeky grin.

He wraps an arm around my shoulders and pulls me closer. "That's sweet, babe. But you really know nothing about hockey. I'm the best player on the Ice Dragons, but there's some other talent out there."

"Not true," I say. "You don't give yourself enough credit."

He pulls me onto his lap, and it's unmistakable, the bump of his cock poking me. He has a wicked gleam in his eyes, and I run my fingers through his hair before leaning in to kiss him. "So, what's it going to be, babe?" I tease.

Kyler groans as our lips pull apart. "I want to take you home," he whispers, crashing his lips on mine again for another searing kiss. The pads of his fingers skim my thighs, grazing bare skin as his fingers play with the hem of my dress.

"You already get to do that," I say, reminding him that we're living together.

He growls as he kisses me more forcefully, pushing his tongue past my lips. His fingers glide under my dress, caressing the elastic of my panties.

"Someone might see us," I whisper.

"Let them." His lips cover mine once again, his fingers sneaking into the side of my panties, and I shift closer, wanting his touch elsewhere. "I want them to know that you're *mine*," he growls.

"Yours?" The air is sucked from my lungs, and my head is cloudy, pulled through the fog of a storm at sea.

His kisses move from my mouth to my jaw as he whispers into my ear, "Spread your legs for me, *babe*."

I inhale sharply and do as he commands.

There's a grin on his face. His eyes are dark, and they match the night sky that affords us the only hint of privacy outside.

He's not the least bit gentle when he yanks my panties to the side and runs his fingers over my slit.

I moan, unable to stop myself, and his lips cover mine, silencing me. "Fuck," he breathes.

Is he surprised by the sounds that he's caused?

My body responds solely to him, and right now, I want him.

"You started this," I whisper, struggling to stare into his heated gaze as his thumb teases around my clit. He knows the right ministrations, two fingers grazing over my labia, riling me up, teasing my folds apart.

My insides shudder for him, aching with an intense need, but he doesn't fill me. "I did start this, Em. And I want to watch you come on my fingers, in my mouth, on my cock every night for the rest of my life."

I gasp, and my breathing catches in my throat at his words.

"You like dirty talk, babe?" A smile grows on his face. "I'm going to fuck your tight little pussy when we get home."

I whimper, and one finger glides through my wetness, offering him my arousal, unable to deny what he does to me. Not that I'd want to deny him anything.

He pulls his finger from my pussy and brings it to my lips. "Open," he commands.

I part my lips, and he pushes his index finger into my mouth. I suck my juices, his eyes on me the entire time. "Fuck, babe. You make me want to have you right here, right now."

"Do it," I say, daring him to fuck me on the bench.

He groans, and I see the inward struggle. "We can't." He stands and lifts me over his shoulder.

"Kyler, what are you doing?" I squeal with laughter.

My pussy throbs, and he spanks my bottom as he carries me back to the car. "Showing you who's in charge."

I swear I hear him growl.

He puts me down, letting me walk as we exit the park. His hand is in mine, keeping a tight grip on me, not letting me out of his sight.

The minute we reach his car, he opens the back door.

"What are you—"

"Climb in," he says, his gaze eating me alive.

I suck in a breath and climb into the backseat. He follows and shuts the door behind himself. He's on me in seconds, his tongue in my mouth, my fingers raking through his hair.

My insides throb, aching to feel his cock, and he's pushing his tongue past my lips, fucking me with his mouth. I need more. Crave more with him.

I push my panties down, lifting my dress and giving him all the access that he needs. "Fuck me," I say, wiggling underneath him. I'm not above begging at this point.

"Gladly," Kyler rasps, staring down at me. He climbs down, guiding my legs apart and pulling them up on his shoulders as he tongue fucks my pussy.

There's not a lot of space, but we make it work, the backseat big enough for our little tryst.

My fingers claw at his hair, his neck, anything I can grip as he shoves two fingers inside my wetness, thrusting and stretching me.

I want him more than I've wanted anything in my life.

"You're such a tease," I grumble as he gets me near the edge and then pulls back, his lips trailing a path up my torso, pushing my dress higher to reveal my breasts.

"Just enjoying sex with my fiancée," Kyler says with a wicked grin.

Except he's not my fiancé. We're—just dating. And that thought is lost on me when his tongue moves back down to my clit. With one hand, he's playing with my nipple, and with the other, he pushes three fingers inside, stretching me.

I groan from the pressure, the build-up, the intensity, and his mouth doing that thing that makes me tremble and gasp for breath.

I feel myself teetering on the edge.

"Come for me, Em," he encourages, and I tug at his pants, my fingers attempting to unzip him and free his cock.

"Not until you fuck me," I mumble. "I want your cock in me."

He groans and pulls back long enough to disrobe, pushing his pants down around his ankles and gripping his cock. He drags out the moment, sliding the crown of his cock across my slit.

"You're such a fucking tease," I grumble. "Are you going to fuck me like a man or a girl?"

He growls and pushes into me, inch by inch.

I grip the handle in the car above my head as he drives deeper inside of me. I gasp from the mixture of pain and pleasure. He's huge, and he fills me as I groan.

"Condom," I say.

He pulls out and grabs his wallet, grumbling when he flips the condom over and examines it. "It's expired."

I curse under my breath and exhale a heavy sigh. I've been regularly tracking my cycle. I shouldn't be in my fertile window, and if I am, I'll deal with it. "Just pull out," I say.

"Are you sure?"

"I was," I say with a nervous laugh, but he doesn't sound confident, which is rattling me.

He presses a soft kiss to my lips and guides my dress back down. "How about we finish at home, in a real bed, and I worship you the way that you deserve?"

I groan, but he's right. We shouldn't be doing this in the back of the car. We're adults, not teenagers trying to hide it from our parents.

The minute we get home, Kyler makes sure that the nanny is asleep in the guest room before he joins me in our bedroom. It feels weird to refer to it as our bedroom, but I like sharing his bed with him.

I find it funny that Lia never asked about us sleeping in different rooms when we pretended that we were together. Maybe she saw through the charade, or she was polite enough not to ask.

I toss my dress and my panties off, climbing onto Kyler's bed.

"Get over here," I say, gesturing for him to join me as he loosens the buttons free on his shirt.

He's methodical and takes his time, watching me

as he undresses. "Touch yourself," he commands. "I want to see what you like."

My nose scrunches up. "Really? I'm lying here naked, waiting for you, and you want me to masturbate?"

"Yes, that's hot," he says, and I swear there's steam emanating from him.

I exhale a nervous breath and let my fingers wander across my stomach, and I tease apart my folds. I'm still achy and wet from our little adventure in the backseat of his vehicle.

"Spread your legs. I want to watch," Kyler says, and he lets his dress shirt hit the floor as he stalks toward the bed.

I inhale sharply, and his gaze is transfixed on my pussy as my fingers trace a path along my lips, teasing myself, going slow.

He unbuttons and unzips his trousers, letting them hit the floor. His cock is standing at attention in his boxers, and he removes the last thread of clothes as he crawls onto the bed.

The mattress dips, and I bend my knees, giving him a view of my pussy lips as I touch myself. My fingers slowly caress my labia, the blood flowing and warming my body from head to toe.

"You're flushed," he says, watching me, a twinkle in his eyes.

"And wet," I say, letting my fingers graze over my pussy, and I slide the tip of one finger inside, coated with juices.

This time, he captures my hand and brings his mouth to my fingers, sucking the liquid and swirling his tongue around my finger.

I whimper, and he straddles me, pushing my arms into the mattress, pinning me down. "I like it when you do what I ask. Watching you touch yourself, it's a huge turn-on."

The room swelters, and he kisses me. "Don't be embarrassed. There's no reason to feel bad about giving yourself pleasure." His lips move down my body, and he's back where he was earlier. This time, he's tongue fucking my pussy.

My breathing is labored, and my fingers tangle in his hair.

The room is warm. My body tingles with pleasure from head to toe as he makes my toes curl.

I swear I can feel the smile on his lips when my hips gyrate and buck off the bed. "Slow down," Kyler says. "We have all night to enjoy this together."

"All night?" I pant, already breathless. I need to feel his cock inside me. Is he going to tease me all night until I'm on my hands and knees begging him to fuck me like a good girl?

"You heard me, babe. All fucking night long." He fingers my pussy, and his tongue teases my clit, making my hips rock back and forth, needing more, desperately craving release.

"Kyler," I moan, his name spilling from my lips.

"Don't come yet. I want you to come with my cock inside you," he says.

I moan, and my pussy walls clench down on his fingers. "I'm close," I rasp, feeling the edge coming for me, and he pulls away, grabbing the condom and sliding it on before gliding into me.

Every sensation inside my body is on overdrive. I tingle all over, like electricity runs through my veins.

My inner walls clench, spasming as I tremble in his arms. My back arches off the mattress, pulling him deeper, tighter, and farther within me. My toes are curling, and I'm unable to hold out any longer.

He grunts and thrusts, trying to keep up my pace, and it's only a matter of seconds before I'm letting go, and he's following close behind with a groan.

"Holy fuck," I mutter, panting for air.

Kyler rolls off me and climbs off the bed to discard the condom. He cleans up before flopping back down beside me, draping an arm across my stomach.

"Good?" he asks with a smirk as if he couldn't tell by the sounds I made and the feeling of my pussy walls squeezing his cock.

I smack his arm. "Do you really have to ask?" I laugh, and he leans in, kissing me.

"We should have been doing this a whole lot sooner." He drops soft kisses from my lips across my jaw. "You've been living under my roof all this time..." he trails off.

"I wanted to," I confess, refusing to look away. "But I'm glad we waited as long as we did. It was worth it."

He pulls me closer. "I'm not. All this time wasted when I could have been doing this," he whispers, brushing his lips over my neck and trailing a path down to my breast. "Or this." His tongue flicks across my nipple, and I shudder.

"Kyler," I moan, unable to suppress the desire burning through me when his mouth teases me.

The smile on his face never wavers. "I love it when I make you do that."

"Make me moan?" I laugh, and my cheeks redden.

"Yes, when you moan my name."

TWENTY-FIVE

KYLER

"I CAN'T BELIEVE they agreed to have dinner with us," I grumble. I honestly thought that the Morettis would cancel, tell us they were sick, or make up some other last-minute excuse to prevent them from showing up at my house.

Em refused to accept us going over to their house for dinner and was concerned that if we went out, it could be an ambush.

"This was the better option," Em whispers, the two of us keeping our voices down while we grab dinner from the kitchen.

Aleksandra and her husband, Antonio, are seated at the dining table with their son Liam and his twin sister, Sophia.

"What are we whispering about?" Bristol asks.

"Grab the bottle of lemonade from the fridge," Em says.

"Can I have wine?" my daughter chirps.

Seriously? The kid is going to send me to an early grave. "No," we both say in unison.

Em and I carry the platters out to the table for dinner, and we finally sit. We haven't spoken too much, excusing ourselves to finish prepping dinner. Lia helped with the recipe, but I let her leave early because there was no sense in getting her mixed up with the Morettis.

And Mitchell is watching the property from the security office, making sure that the Morettis don't bring company.

The night is quiet, almost too quiet, when it's the mafia at your dinner table.

"Please, help yourself," Em says and gestures toward the food, letting the guests serve themselves.

Aleksandra glances at her husband and serves the children and then herself. The kids wait patiently before digging in. I don't think Bristol has the same amount of patience. She's sitting on her knees and reaches for the tongs for the salad the moment Aleksandra relinquishes it to the bowl.

Bristol piles food onto her plate and then starts eating.

Antonio and Aleksandra watch Bristol gobble up her food before they tell their children to eat.

Did they honestly think we might poison them?

The twins grab their forks and dig in, both of them clearly hungry, while the adults wait for us to finish dishing out our food before eating.

"Kyler, we heard you took some time off from hockey," Antonio says.

"Yes, to be with my family." I force a smile. It's hard to feel anything but dread with the Morettis in my home. But this dinner wasn't by choice. The headmaster insisted that we break bread together, or both families risk expulsion from the school.

A bit harsh if you ask me, especially considering our generous contribution, but the kids have been finding it difficult to get along. And maybe there's something to be said for finding common ground.

What could we have in common, other than our children are both the same age and attend the same school?

"That's nice," Aleksandra says. She reaches for her wine glass, swirling the dark liquid around before taking a sip. "I wish you could do that, take time off to spend with me and the kids," she says, glancing at her husband.

"I do that. We went to Cancun in the winter and—"

"Those were work trips, and you know it," she says with a smug grin. She's playing with him, and he shifts, albeit uncomfortable with where this is going.

"What type of work do you do?" Em asks.

"The business kind. It would bore you," Antonio says, staring at Em. "And what about you? Are you a stay-at-home mother, or do you work outside the home?"

Aleksandra elbows her husband. "Being a stay-at-home mom is work."

He glares at her, but she doesn't so much as cower. It's clear they're both strong-headed individuals.

"I'm taking some time off right now," Em says, avoiding the question. I suppose she doesn't want to admit that she was Bristol's bodyguard or that I hired her to be my fake girlfriend. And saying anything about previously working for the FBI or being hired by Eagle Tactical probably isn't wise, either.

"Have you two made any wedding plans yet?" Aleksandra asks. "We saw the proposal on the news.

It was so sweet, asking her to marry you at the Ice Dragons game. Wasn't it sweet, Antonio?"

"It was sweet," he mutters, staring at his food. He's not enjoying the conversation, but he does seem to be enjoying the meal, or at least using it as a distraction.

Em smiles at the twins. "What do you both like to do for fun?" she asks, trying to direct the conversation to the real reason that we're together—finding common ground.

"I love riding my bicycle," Liam says. "I want a dirt bike for my birthday, but Dad says I'm too young." He rolls his eyes, and I smile. I've seen that same look from Bristol.

"You are too young. No ATVs. No dirt bikes. Not until you're at least double digits."

Liam whines, and his nose twitches. "That's forever away."

"Can I have a dirt bike?" Bristol asks, her eyes lighting up. I'm not even sure the kid knows what it is, but because Liam can't have one, she probably wants one to rub in his face.

"No," I say, and Em is trying to hold back her laughter.

"What about you, Sophia?" Em asks. "What do you like to do for fun?"

"I love ice skating and hockey."

"Me too!" Bristol's eyes widen. "Ice skating is my favorite."

"Hockey isn't your favorite?" I ask, my jaw dropping as I tease Bristol.

"I don't like playing hockey. The kids hit hard, and I don't like falling on the ice. It hurts too much."

Sophia grins. "I don't like playing hockey. I like to watch it. Mom took me to a game so we could google the players."

"Ogle the players," Liam says, tattling on his mom and sister.

Em covers her mouth to keep from laughing, and the look on Antonio's face is pure gold. "Is that so?" he asks, staring at his wife.

She gives an innocent shrug. "Like you don't enjoy the cheerleaders at football games?"

"I don't go to football games," he says and straightens his back like he's above sports or some shit.

"No, but you still like cheerleaders," Aleksandra taunts.

I'll bet the guy has his wife don a cheerleader costume for some crazy role-play shit in the sack.

Antonio clears his throat. "It seems our girls both have a common interest, ice skating."

"Can Sophia and I go ice skating together?" Bristol asks.

"Liam, do you like to ice skate?" I ask, hoping we can get all three kids to bond, but I'd at least settle with the two girls being friendly toward one another. Maybe next year, they'll be in the same class, instead of Bristol and Liam.

The little boy shrugs. "It's okay. I prefer playing hockey over ice skating."

Aleksandra smiles. "Did you know that Bristol's father is an NHL player for the Ice Dragons?"

Liam's eyes widen. "What? Really? No way."

I smile. "Yes, I'll bet I have an extra jersey that's in your size."

"Can I have one too?" Sophia asks, her eyes wide. "And could you sign mine with a heart next to your name?"

———

Dinner with the Morettis went better than Em or I could have ever anticipated.

Sophia made it clear that she had a crush on me, which was cute. I can't help but wonder if that stemmed from her mother's interest in the sport. And there was a commonality between the girls.

We have an ice-skating date set up for the three kids, and each of us is to bring at least one parent to attend. I can't imagine Antonio letting Aleksandra go after learning about her interest in hockey.

Although that has less to do with the sport and more to do with the players or, as her daughter later put it, eye candy.

"Could you imagine having two kids?" Em asks.

She's helping me finish the dishes while Bristol wipes down the dining room table.

"I don't think two is that bad, but twins. Raising two infants and then toddlers at the same time."

"They're both six," Em points out.

"Yes, but imagine two Bristols," I say and nod toward the dining room.

"You got lucky with Bristol. She's a good kid." There's a wide grin spread across Em's face. "But I prefer one at a time. Gives a parent a chance to screw up one kid, not two, before the next is born."

I can't help but laugh. "Are you saying that I've screwed up Bristol?"

She exhales a heavy breath and shakes her head. "No," she says cautiously. "Just that it can't be easy raising a daughter on your own. First-time parents are bound to make mistakes somewhere along the way."

I turn to face her, pinning her with my stare. "What mistakes do you think I've made?" I ask.

Em sucks in a sharp breath. "None! I'm not saying you've made any, just that the firstborns always get in trouble and never get away with anything. Parents are stricter on the first kid than the second."

"And you know this from experience?"

"I have a younger sister, Amber. Our parents were a lot stricter on me than they were with her."

"So, you're saying that when we have another kid, we'll be less strict on our little boy or girl because we've already done this once before?" I step closer, and she pulls her teeth between her bottom lip.

"Maybe?" Her voice squeaks.

"I thought you were pretty confident in your answer."

"I am, but I'm less confident in us giving Bristol a sibling," she says. Her cheeks redden, and she leans on her tiptoes to kiss my lips.

"Why is that?"

Whatever hesitancy I sense vanishes from her features. "It's hard to get pregnant when we're always using a condom." She chuckles, and I sense there's more to it than her little joke.

"Are you telling me that you want us to try for a baby?" I grab her hands, intertwining our fingers together. "Because I'd love that."

She exhales nervously. "But what about your team? The game? You won't be around much if you sign the new contract for the Ice Dragons, and I am terrified to do it alone."

Fitzgerald sent over a generous three-year contract, but I've been stalling on signing. It's everything that I want and more, but he is still the general manager. And I want him gone.

"We still have plenty of time," I assure her. She's twenty-four. We don't have to rush into expanding our family yet.

"Daddy, your team is on television," Bristol chimes from the other room.

I thought she was cleaning up the table in the dining room, but it seems that she abandoned her post for a little more entertainment.

I turn the small television on in the kitchen and watch as the headline announces that four women have come forward, accusing Brent Fitzgerald, the general manager, of sexual harassment and sexual assault.

"What does that mean?" Bristol asks, coming into the kitchen.

"You shouldn't be watching the news," I tell my daughter. "Go turn on cartoons." I'd rather her not ask a million questions about Brent Fitzgerald.

She scampers off to the living room, and I turn up the television, trying to get as much of the story as possible.

The news further elaborates that criminal charges are being pursued and that Brent Fitzgerald has resigned from the Ice Dragons, effective immediately.

"What does this mean for your contract?" Em asks.

"I have no idea. I can renegotiate for more money, or I could just buy the team."

EPILOGUE

EMERSON

THERE WAS zero chance of Kyler turning down the opportunity to play for the Ice Dragons, and when the new general manager offered him a three-year deal with the same terms, he jumped at it.

It's never been about the money for Kyler. He has plenty of it. And while he still believes it's cursed, he's put it into a trust that will make an offer on the team the moment he's out of the game.

His lawyers insist that he can't play for the NHL and be the owner of an NHL team simultaneously. And he loves being on the ice too much to hang up his skates. But he will.

He talks about it with me and his brother, Jasper, all the time.

It's our little secret.

And I like that Kyler trusts me like family. We are practically family—we're still fake engaged, and since we're dating, we've just kept the fake relationship news a secret a little longer.

No one needs to know the truth. It's no one's business.

And I honestly don't mind hockey, especially watching him play. It's been nice meeting the hockey wives and their kids. Bristol has made a ton of new friends since the first day I was invited to the wives' room. And I've made a lot of new friends myself.

None of them know that what Kyler and I had wasn't real in the beginning. But it's real now. One hundred percent genuine.

Bristol and Sophia have become best friends ever since the dinner. Once a week, we take the girls ice skating, and Liam tags along.

Bristol and Liam seem to be warming up to each other. At least they don't fight in school anymore, and while they're not best friends, they're getting along. I'll consider it a win.

"Jasper's coming by," Kyler says. "He met a girl and wants us to meet her."

My eyes light up. "Oh, is he asking us for our approval?" I can't help but feel a little bit giddy that

Jasper has found a girlfriend. He's Kyler's brother and is like family to me. He deserves to be happy.

"Something like that. Do you want to put on dessert—on second thought, how about I do the food prep, and you pull out the dishes."

"Are you saying that I can't make dessert? It just has to go in the oven," I say.

Lia made several peach pies from scratch during the summer. We froze a few of them.

"Yes, and I'm not taking a chance that you'll burn it, M&M. I love you, but your cooking leaves much to be desired."

I grab the dish towel and smack him on the ass with it.

He yanks the towel, pulling me toward him as he spins around to face me. "Are you seriously trying to spank me?"

My lips part, and I laugh nervously. "What are you going to do about it?" I taunt.

Kyler drops down on one knee and pulls a ring box out of his left pocket.

I clasp my hands over my mouth as I stare down at him. "Kyler?"

"We didn't do this the right way last time. When I asked you to be my wife, it was entirely for selfish reasons. I had feelings for you, but they weren't anything close to what they are now, M&M."

"No."

"What?"

"You are not proposing and calling me M&M." I grin. "Continue, but with my real name."

He snorts. "Emerson Ryan, will you do me the honor of being my wife?" Kyler flips open the blue Tiffany's box and shows me the diamond engagement band.

My knees wobble, and the air suddenly leaves my lungs. It takes too much energy to stand, and my legs give way. I drop down to my knees, shocked. His arms reach out, catching me, pulling me onto his lap. "You're not supposed to be down on your knees too, babe," he says and kisses me.

"You're going to give me a heart attack." I laugh, resting my hand on his chest.

"Me? You're the one telling me no mid-proposal." The smile never leaves his face.

I lean in and brush my lips over his. "I'd never tell you no. Just don't call me M&M, babe."

"But it's a term of endearment," Kyler says. With one hand around my hips, he nestles me on his knee. He shows me the ring. "Will you be my wife?"

"Yes." I give him my hand, and he slides the engagement ring on my finger. It's a perfect fit.

The front door swings open, and my lips are locked on Kyler's, not paying the least bit of attention to the arrival of our guests. I know they're here, but I honestly don't care.

Jasper clears his throat.

"Maybe we should come back," a female's voice chimes, and I recognize that voice. I'd recognize it anywhere.

"Amber?" My eyes widen, and I nearly tumble off Kyler's lap as he pulls me to my feet to stand.

I'm trying to comprehend how this happened. When did they meet? How?

My mouth must be hanging open because Kyler glances at me and smiles before reaching a hand out to introduce himself to Amber. At least, that's what I think he's about to do.

"It's good to see you again," he says.

Kyler knows my sister. Since when? My head spins, trying to comprehend what the hell is going on.

I glance from Amber to Jasper, awaiting an explanation. "You're dating my sister?"

Jasper grins and shakes his head. "We're just

friends. Your brother introduced us when he needed help picking out the ring at Tiffany's."

"You're just friends?" I glance at my sister and then at Jasper.

Jasper nods, and my sister forces a smile. "That's right, just friends." Something tells me that she wants more from him, but it's Jasper. He's focused on his career, not dating women.

I spin around in Kyler's arms. "Why did you tell me Jasper was bringing his girlfriend?"

"Girlfriend?" Amber coughs on the words, and I glance at her over my shoulder. Her cheeks are reddening.

"I wanted to surprise you with the proposal. And if I told you my brother and your sister were coming over, you'd be suspicious."

He's right. I would have asked a dozen questions and known he was up to something. "Well, you did a good job with the surprise," I say, placing a kiss on Kyler's lips. I turn around in his arms, facing Jasper and Amber.

"Well, did you say yes?" Amber asks and glances at my hand.

I show her the ring on my finger. "I'm engaged!"

———

Thank you for reading Faking it with the Billionaire. I hope that you enjoyed Kyler and Emerson's story. Continue the romance with Jasper and Amber in *Daring the Hockey Player.*

I didn't plan on dating a hockey player. It just kind of happened.

At least, that's what I'm telling everyone. Except maybe I did plan it. Maybe it wasn't a coincidence at all...

Jasper Greyson is hot, flirty, and the epitome of trouble.

But he's off-limits. He's my sister's brother-in-law, or at least he's about to be, which kind of makes us family.

I should be staying as far from him as possible, except I like hanging out with him, watching him on the ice, and grabbing drinks with him and the guys.

Yes, I intentionally showed up when I knew he'd be at the bar because he posted it on social media. I've been stalking him.

I keep telling myself it's a harmless crush. Feelings don't have to be acted on.

We're friends. I'm not sure he'll ever see me as anything else. That's problem number one. I've been friend-zoned.

Problem number two. My apartment complex caught fire, and I don't have insurance. I have nowhere else to go. I don't want to burden my sister with the news.

When Jasper finds out, he insists that I stay at his place, in his guest room. Stalking my crush online is one thing. Living with him is entirely something else.

Subscribe to my newsletter to be notified when *Daring the Hockey Player* is available.

GIVEAWAYS, FREE BOOKS, AND MORE GOODIES

I hope you enjoyed Faking it with the Billionaire and loved Kyler and Emerson's story.

Sign up for my Willow Fox newsletter for new release information.

Want to read my books first? Gain early access, vote for your favorite characters to get their own book, ARCs, discounts on audiobooks, and more! Find out more on my website under membership.

If you enjoyed Faking it with the Billionaire, please take a moment to leave a review. Reviews help other readers discover my books.

Not sure what to write? That's okay. It doesn't have to be long. You can share how you discovered my book; was it a recommendation by a friend or a book club? Let readers know who your favorite character is or what you'd like to see happen next.

ABOUT THE AUTHOR

Willow Fox has loved writing since she was in high school (many ages ago). Her small town romances are reflective of living in a small town in rural America.

Whether she's writing romance or sitting outside by the bonfire reading a good book, Willow loves the magic of the written word.

Visit her website at:

https://authorwillowfox.com

Dangerous Boss

Bossy Single Dad Series

Billionaire Grump

Mountain Grump

Bachelor Grump

Ice Dragons Hockey Romance

Faking it with the Billionaire

Daring the Hockey Player

Looking for kinkier books? Try these spicy stories written under the name Allison West.

Boxsets

Academy of Littles

Western Daddies Collection

Obey Daddy Collection

The Alpha Collection

Western Daddies

Her Billionaire Daddy

Her Cowboy Daddy

Her Outlaw Daddy

Her Forbidden Daddy

Standalone Romances

The Victorian Shift

Jailed Little Jade

Prefer a sweeter romance with action and adventure?
Check out these titles under the name Ruth Silver.

Aberrant Series

Love Forbidden

Secrets Forbidden

Magic Forbidden

Escape Forbidden

Refuge Forbidden

Boxsets

Gem Apocalypse

Nightblood

Royal Reaper

Royal Deception

Standalones

Stolen Art

Printed in Great Britain
by Amazon